The Next Day

Foothills #2

Carrie Thorne

Published by Thorny Books

Carrie Thorne

https://carriethorne.com/

Also by Carrie Thorne

A Demon Hunter Romance

Six
Wildest
Changed
Echo
Fury (TBD)

Foothills

All the Days After
The Next Day
A Day Late
A New Day
About Yesterday
280 Days (2025)
Day Dreaming (2026)
Again Tomorrow (TBD)
Days of Summer (TBD)

A Beachside Romance Series

Chasing Forever
Running Home
Hiding Away

Standalones

The Christmas Bet: A Double Feature Christmas Standalone.

Enjoy free books, first looks,
review team access,
and occasional hellos from Carrie?

Let's do this: carriethorne.com/newsletter

For my family. All of them.
Pacific Northwesterners to the core.
Characters who will appreciate the loving references dabbled
throughout, like the note on the door about the key under the
mat. Yeah, that happened.

1

The Key is Under the Mat

"Supposedly there are mountains around here." Shifting his weight with the truck as he rounded yet another bend in an endless series of S-curves, Zane remarked on the thick trunks that lined the narrow road. Pressure built in his ears as the altitude climbed, forcing him to swallow to equalize.

After another few miles of rapidly alternating light and shadow, flipping his sunglasses up and down as he was either blinded by burning sun or dense shade, the forest opened beyond. An unfamiliar pang clenched and loosened in his chest as the vast valley beyond glowed under supernaturally blue skies, feathery green trees coated the jagged slopes, and diamonds glinted off the anastomosing river beyond. As the wind kicked up, no longer diffused by the trees, the tarp over his possessions in the back of the truck flapped against the tie-downs.

"What do you think, Jack? Hell and gone from San Diego or New York." He glanced to the simple steel box buckled into the passenger seat at his side. The urn didn't respond. Rubbing his eyes, he chuckled at himself. "No offense pal, but it's time to scatter you somewhere around this absurdly beautiful place. If I keep this up, people are going to think I've lost my fucking mind."

In her digitally smooth voice, his phone advised him to turn right in two miles. "About time," he muttered. He eased up on the brakes, delicately balancing burning out versus losing control at ninety miles an hour, thanks to the heavy load down the steep decline.

A few more miles, and he reached a carved wooden sign reading, *Welcome to Foothills. Population 8,698.* There had been a three at the end, but it had been painted over with an eight in its place. Another sign behind it congratulated its football team on winning state last year, then another advertising local trails and campgrounds.

Foothills proper was excessively charming. Colorful buildings dotted Main Street, and the sidewalks were packed with a whole lot of hiking boots. In under sixty seconds, he'd reached the opposite end of town. The sultry voice interrupted his music again, urgently demanding he take the next right. *Keep your panties on.*

More windy roads. More trees with the occasional gorgeous view that flashed by in a blink. Shit, this place was isolated.

From nowhere, a deer leaped out in front of him like a damn suicide bomber. Slamming on the brakes, he cringed as he waited to hear the crash of his stuff breaking free from the tie-downs and shattering the rear window. Holding his breath, he looked back and confirmed the load was still secure. *Phew.*

Pleasantly ignorant, his GPS informed him that his destination was on the left.

The narrow drive was canopied with more green; maple and cedar that had been there since early last century. The house was a faded-brown craftsman style home sat at the top of a sprawling park-style front yard. Some of the shutters were at odd angles, the paint chipped, but it was sturdy. Nice place to call home.

Asher was a lucky guy.

Zane pulled into the carport off the detached garage. Tucking his phone into his back pocket, he hopped out. His joints crunched as he stretched his arms and rolled his shoulders. Just under thirty-six hours on the road. Not bad considering he hadn't cared to make a road trip out of it. He'd been lucky it hadn't rained; his tarped load might have done the job, but it would have been dicey.

He dashed up the garage stairs to his new apartment. A bristly welcome mat informed him to 'fuck-off' unless he'd 'brought beer'. The corner of his mouth quirked up. Classy. Asher's touch, no doubt.

Pulling a red envelope off the front door, he read the message. *Guess you found the place. Give me a call when you get in. Key is under the mat. –Asher.*

As promised, he found the key under the mat. He rolled his eyes as he slid the key into the lock. Crime rate must be pretty nonexistent around here.

Not bad. The windows were all wide open, but a lingering smell of wet dog was unmistakable. Prior tenant must have been a dog person. He didn't mind, he'd always wanted a dog. Maybe now that he lived in the fucking sticks...

Otherwise, the place was spotless. Faux-wood flooring spanned the main room, an L-shaped plush couch faced an electric fireplace. On the tag was a sticky note that read, *Happy Housewarming*, in elegant handwriting. Not Asher's. Who the hell would have bought him a couch?

The breeze from outside gusted in through the open windows, the warmed cedar tickling his nose before spiraling up to the exposed-beam ceiling. Open and airy, the place had just been updated. The kitchen had shiny black granite countertops, stainless steel sink and faucet, with matching appliances. Shit, nice digs.

Zane couldn't say what he'd been expecting, but this wasn't it. Probably something more like the tired shoebox he'd had in San Diego. He'd moved into the place when he'd joined the SEALs, a cheap place for a couple just starting out; he hadn't felt like getting a new place even when he'd paid off his student debt with the GI Bill and his combat pay.

He fired off a quick text to Asher, *Here. The place is great.*

His phone buzzed a few seconds later. *I'll let you get settled. See you tomorrow?*

Bring breakfast.

He dashed down the stairs to start unloading. What he was going to do after that, he didn't have a fucking clue.

Freya chugged her water. The cool flow soothed her scratchy throat but failed to lighten the lead coating her eyelids. Jetlag was a bitch. She would kill for a caffè, but as she'd have to attempt sleep again in another few hours, she didn't dare.

She glared at her suitcases. It hadn't been worth the money to ship her few belongings from Florence, so she'd just kept her clothes, a few favorite trinkets, and then shipped her art supplies and the completed paintings she hadn't been ready to give up just yet. Flying back for a showing and to pack up her things had been a headache and a half. Double jetlag was like a monster of a hangover, and she hadn't felt one of those since her foolish early twenties. At least Sophie had enough basics to stock the house for now, and Freya would only be here for a few months while she looked for something more permanent anyway.

Permanent. That would be nice. The last few years had been a whirlwind, couch surfing when things were tight, living in closet-sized studio apartments with roommates or boyfriends when she had the cash. Art school, internships, waiting tables. None paid well.

Until the last year. Things seemed to be taking off. Not like a jet leaving the runway, more like a rusty sedan in need of an oil change, but she'd established enough of a foothold in the art world that she might be able to continue the momentum from home. A few big galleries had even expressed interest in carrying her work on an ongoing basis. Her income was meager but steady... otherwise she would still be over there.

An engine rumbling down the driveway pricked her attention. Too big for Sophie's new RAV4 that she'd paid cash for with her inheritance. Freya had thought herself frugal, but Sophie spent so much of her childhood rationing every penny that she rarely splurged.

Foothills was too spread out to function without a car, unless she wanted to move closer to downtown, but she had craved the wide-open spaces of rural Foothills. While she needed a car, the expense was daunting. By the time she made it to the window to see who was here, she saw the rear of a truck loaded with tarped boxes in the carport next to the garage.

Hmm. This must be Asher's SEAL buddy, Zane. He'd mentioned that Zane would be arriving soon, and to give him some space. Her cousin had been hurting when he'd gotten home from the Navy a few months ago, and apparently Zane was worse off, as he didn't even have a supportive family to get him through.

Uncle Paul and Asher had moved fast to get the apartment fixed up before Zane arrived. Her aunt and uncle had practically adopted Sophie the first time their daughter had brought her home, and brought her further into the fold each time. It looked like they were on track to take Zane right under their wing as well. No wonder they were her favorite aunt and uncle. Their children have been her best friends since childhood, and Paul and Denise were honest people that cared about their home and family, blood related or not.

While the dust still settled in the driveway, Sophie pulled up in her new SUV. Freya would say *shiny* and new, but the driveway was a dustbowl, so nothing was shiny around here for long. Uncle Paul, officially still the owner, had promised to have it graveled before fall, or it would be a mudhole. Parking in the empty two-car garage, Sophie appeared with a pair of grocery bags and sneakily eyed Zane's truck, but resisted the urge to go pry.

As soon as Sophie made it inside, she dumped the groceries on the kitchen island and joined Freya by the window. With her heels, Sophie just topped Freya in height. "Did you see him?" Sophie asked.

Still holding her water close to her lips, wishing it were caffeinated, Freya shook her head. "No, I just missed him. He's been here," she glanced at her slim black watch, "three minutes."

"Should we introduce ourselves?"

"Asher said to give him space."

"Dang it." Sophie pulled off her cotton cardigan and tossed it onto the entry hook. Freya had known Sophie for just over a month, and already found her to be eternally put together, aside from her fingernails that were typically chewed to nubs. Not a huge wardrobe, but precise and stunning. Shrugging, Freya decided she'd just have to help herself to her friend's closet now and again.

Not that they were built anything alike. Where Sophie was slim and athletic, Freya was height and boobs and butt. As a teen, she'd hated her figure. In her early twenties, she'd risked basic nutrition in an effort to trim down.

Something about turning thirty had changed everything. She no longer hated her dark, frizzy curls, and loved that she had a curvy figure like the classic paintings and sculptures. And she no longer gave a damn that she was taller than most of the guys she dated, something she knew Sophie could relate to, as both were taller than average.

When Sophie had called to see if she wanted to be roomies while they both got settled, Freya had jumped at the opportunity. The pair had hit it off in the weeks before Pippa's wedding. And, according to Sophie's pleas, Sophie needed a buffer so she and Asher would take things slow, a roommate to keep her within her meticulous budget, and, offered a generous discount for Freya's artistic eye in fixing the place up. Freya had done a happy dance and a half. She loved her parents but couldn't imagine bunking with them again, and she didn't want to blow her budget on a place of her own yet.

As they stood staring like a couple of drooling puppies waiting for a treat, Zane came dashing down the steps.

Oh. She tightened her grip on her water, nearly dropping the cobalt glass as her attention locked on. Naturally, she'd expected the SEAL to be built. She hadn't expected... yeah, *that.*

Suppressing the sigh before she proved to her new roommate that she was the sex-deprived horndog she felt like, she bit her lips together. Solid muscle, his black t-shirt clung to some ripped shoulders, hugging some spectacular abs she wanted to lick, and she hadn't even seen his skin yet. Spiked up after a long day on the road, his walnut hair was just a little wild, an inch past a military fade.

Loosening the tie-downs on the back of his truck, he wound them back up and set them in the backseat of the truck, then did the same with the blue tarp. *Damn*, he moved like a confident man on a mission, but with a leisure that said he didn't give a fuck how long it took. A horny sigh passed her lips without her awareness, followed by a whimper.

Grinning at her side, Sophie teased, "Enjoying the view?"

Freya nodded. "He is a work of art. Look at the way he moves. That is pure power." He hoisted a huge box and carried it up the steps like it didn't weigh a thing.

"Think we should offer to help?"

"Maybe. Or you can pour us some wine and we'll just watch the show."

"I like you," Sophie teased. "But I do feel bad, just standing here while he carries all that by himself."

Freya glanced down at the strappy camisole and leggings she'd tossed on. Her dark waves were unrulier than usual, despite the shower. Wiggling her toes, she glared at her chipped blue nail polish. Sighing, she nodded. "I'll get some shoes."

"I'm going to go get changed first. I know I don't need to dress in slacks and heels for accounting work in Foothills, but I can't get used to not dressing up for work."

Smiling as she tossed on her canvas shoes, Freya shook her head, "Wear what makes you happy. Can I borrow a hair thing? Mine are lost somewhere in my luggage."

Sophie pulled out her ponytail and handed over the hair tie. Freya pulled her damp hair back into a messy bun and dashed out the door.

Sliding the cardboard across the slick floor to tuck another load under the kitchen bar, Zane spun on his heel and headed for the next box. His footsteps reverberated on the wooden steps as he thundered down. Slamming on the breaks, he skidded to a stop in the dirt before he crashed into a box with legs.

Behind the box, a muffled voice said, "Hi. I'm Freya." A pinky lifted off the box; was she trying to shake hands?

He grinned at the odd gesture, his eyebrows scrunched in curiosity. With a gentle pinky shake, he tried to see the bearer of the box. "Zane. Thanks for the help."

A lyrical quality to her voice, that flat west coast accent had a hint of something else he couldn't place, danced behind her as she headed up the stairs, "Anytime, neighbor." As she strolled up the steps, her hips swayed, her strong arms held steady around the box. Dumbfounded, his feet rooted to the ground until she disappeared into the apartment.

Shaking his head at the odd meeting, he grabbed another box. Nearly dropping the damn thing, he boosted it higher, his forearms already burning to keep the thing from crashing to the ground and crushing his toes. He chuckled when he read the Sharpie label in front of his nose, *Kitchen, HEAVY*. At least he'd tried to warn himself.

Freya's feet tapped in a cheery rhythm as she dashed down the steps. He stood to the side as she brushed past. Carting the box up the steps, he had to lean forward so he didn't fall backward, his hands near shaking as he gripped the thing. Yep, he'd packed his entire kitchen in one massive box. Dumbass. Maybe cast iron hadn't been so brilliant after all.

He carted this one straight into the kitchen and turned to get the next. Another walking box appeared in the doorway. Dashing back down the stairs, he tried to keep up with her pace. Didn't want his volunteer to carry in more of his stuff than he did.

When he reached the bottom, a gorgeous woman with a slim runner's body came jogging out of the house. Recognizing her from the photo Asher had shown him, he didn't need the introduction. She smiled as she approached, "Glad you made it okay. I'm Sophie."

"Hi, glad to finally meet you. Where's that deadbeat boyfriend of yours?"

Rolling her eyes, she grinned, "Claims you could use some time to get settled. I think he just hates moving."

Tilting his head to the side, he teased, "Always the lazy one."

Glancing up, he saw Freya's fine ass swinging up the stairs as she carted up a pair of lamps. Suppressing a groan before he let on how long it had been since he'd even noticed a woman, the last few years in the Navy having crushed his sex drive to a flaccid pulp, he felt an almost foreign, but miraculously welcome twitch in his pants. Didn't matter what the woman's face looked like, he was absolutely interested. Closing his eyes, he kicked his mental ass for being such a shallow dickwad, while cheering that things were still functional down there.

Turning, he checked the boxes and grabbed another that said *HEAVY* on it. Not that he doubted his new neighbors couldn't handle it; hell, Freya's bare shoulders said she was fit as fuck, but it was his shitty packing job, he'd take the crap loads.

A few more times up and down the stairs, and they were already done. Trekking down the stairs for the last item, he watched as Freya's curvy backside strutted out of sight.

Sophie waited at the bottom. "See you around. Don't be a stranger. You need anything, directions, food, whatever, just come on over, okay?"

His breath came easy as he reached the ground. "I really appreciate the help. Thanks. Know any good pizza delivery around here?"

Shaking her head, Sophie grinned. "My first time living in rurality too. Say goodbye to conveniences like delivery. Anonymity. Variety. Walking anywhere useful."

Chuckling, he shook his head. "You know, my sister said I could stay in her apartment in Denver while she's deployed. Should have taken her up on it."

"Give it a few weeks and then let me know how you feel." She backed up a few steps. "Check your fridge. Paul and Denise stocked it for you, among other updates."

"Asher's parents did all this? I got to know them a bit on their trips to visit Asher. They'd take the three of us to dinner every time."

"They're good people. Be careful, they take in strays."

There was that damn pang again. Like the one he'd felt on the drive in. "The couch?"

She nodded. "And the bed. See you around, Zane."

Shit, he hadn't even been in the bedroom yet. He'd been planning to sleep on the floor the first night or two until he picked up a mattress. The truck gate vibrated his palms as he slammed it shut.

Crunching the dirt under his feet, he halted. Heaviness in his gut weighed him down as he remembered he had one more load. He opened the passenger door and unhooked Jack. Carting the cool metal under his arm, he trudged up the stairs for the last time that night.

His eyes blurred as he looked around the room. Where the hell did one store their dead friend? Shaking his head, he blinked away the weird question. "Not like you're going to care, you're just a tin can of dust." He tucked Jack's urn into the back of the coat closet.

2

Good Morning, Sunshine

Thundering louder than the caffeine headache he was brewing, Zane awoke to a fist pounding on his door. Fucking shit, Asher. It was seven in the damn morning, and he hadn't slept more than a quick nap at a rest stop on the drive up. Grumbling, he pulled on a pair of black sweats.

Swinging open the door, he snagged the coffee straight from Asher's hand. "Hey," he muttered.

"Good morning, Sunshine," Asher grinned back. As he stepped into the apartment, his feet echoing on the floor as it was still essentially empty aside from the couch and stack of boxes, he whistled. "You've got some unpacking to do."

Zane flipped him off as he wandered to his new couch, plopped down, and popped the cap off his coffee.

Asher explored, ducking his head into the bedroom before scoping out the rest. Zane still couldn't believe Asher's parents had done all this for him. His own parents hadn't even returned his call yet so he could let them know he was out of the Navy. As soon as his moving team had left last night, he'd crashed face down on the pristinely made bed.

Asher dumped his bag of savory-scented something in the kitchen and crashed on the other side of the L couch. "I think my mother likes you better than me. I got dishes as a housewarming present."

Zane flashed him a sleepy wink. "It's mutual. Mind sending me her number, your dad's too, so I can thank them for setting this place up so nice? You made it sound like I was moving into some tired old dump, the apartment over your grandfather's garage."

"You were. Then they took one look and decided to do the remodel they'd been planning. You owe me too, by the way. Paul decided this would be a perfect father-son project—which he knows I hate. I had to rip out dog-piss carpet for you. Fourteen-hour days getting this place cleaned up so it would be done before you got here. And I'm stuck bunking with a snooty attorney that already divided up our cooking nights."

"Why didn't you nab this place for yourself?" He glanced around. "Don't your folks own this and the house?"

"Yeah. I'm buying the house in a few months, but for the first time in my life I'm trying to *not* rush into a situation. Sophie says I'm not allowed to propose until we've been together at least six months, I can do my own laundry without turning my whites pink again, and can cook a decent dinner that doesn't involve open flames or peanut butter. Living next door sounded like a little too easy of access."

"Smart woman. I should have done that same fucking thing." Zane took a pull on the dark brew, wishing he'd left the lid on longer as it was already lukewarm.

"I can't say I regret never meeting your ex-wife. Sounded like a real peach."

"She's half the reason I joined the damn Navy, after she'd dug us irretrievably into debt." Zane had joined a few years before Asher, and they'd hit it off immediately, then Jack joined up, and the rest was history. Blaire hadn't even made it through his first op before the screaming matches and guilt trips began. That had been a hell of a homecoming. *I need someone who will be here for me. To not be called away at a moment's notice while I'm trying to build my career.* She'd claimed she couldn't handle worrying over him like that, not even knowing where he was, yet in the same sentence she blamed him for making her miss a critical conference call.

Asher winced.

Zane hauled his ass off the couch and scowled out the window. "How the hell did we get on that stupid fucking topic?"

"Sorry. My fault."

Across the field, the lawn made way to a wide patio that created a perfect lookout, right down to the rustic log fence before dropping off to the valley beyond, the view like something out of an REI ad. Right in the center, that crazy woman with the perfect ass was upside-down in a yoga pose, her leg pointed straight up to the sky, and her wild black hair was free, skimming the mat at her feet.

Gently swaying with the breeze, the trees at the edges of the yard seemed to welcome the morning right along with her. Moving gracefully into the next pose, she stood and raised her arms above her head like the mountain in the distance.

Asher cleared his throat, "Hungry?"

Nodding, Zane swallowed the desperate whimper that nearly gave him away. His voice came out croaky. "Starving."

Tearing into the English muffin that sandwiched the melty sharp cheddar over fried egg and seasoned sausage, he asked through his full bite. "How'd you end up living with a snooty lawyer?"

Grinning, Asher ripped off a bite of his own breakfast. "I just needed a place to crash for the next few months, and I get to annoy the hell out of Grady while I'm at it."

"Nice arrangement."

"I thought so. Honestly, he's a good guy, *he* just needs to realize it instead of defaulting to prick. So, I help him get his head out of his ass, he teaches me how to cook and clean and all that bullshit I managed to dodge the first thirty years of my life."

Zane took another gulp of coffee, downing the last of it as his headache retreated to the periphery. They ate in silence for a bit. After enough years of ops together, they had no problems not filling the silence in with small talk.

Clearing their trash from breakfast, Zane stuffed everything in the paper bag and tucked it under the sink, adding kitchen garbage can to his shopping list. Bathroom too, he supposed.

Asher hopped to his feet and eyed the boxes. "Need a hand unpacking?"

Shaking his head, Zane's vision blurred as he took in all the work ahead of him. "Nope, thanks though. As I have zero plans for the next... eternity, I may as well take my time."

"It'll come to you."

"I guess. First time in my life I don't have a single thing on the calendar."

"Why don't you make use of that degree of yours?"

"Did I mention I only studied architecture because my parents are architects and Blaire wanted to be an architect and how romantic to be partners in life and in business? Turns out, not so romantic when one of us has no interest in designing shit for other people to criticize. Married, divorced, and broke before my twenty-fourth birthday." He ripped open the kitchen box and pulled out his coffee pot, unwinding the kitchen towel he'd wrapped around the fragile glass carafe.

"Well, now you're thirty-four, frugal as an old man, have absolutely no responsibilities, and are already making eyes at my cousin."

"Your cousin? Shit man, I'm sorry. Was I that obvious?"

"You've still got a stream of drool running down your chin. Have at her; she'll have no qualms about telling you off if she's not interested." Asher winked and headed for the door. With his hand on the knob, he shrugged, "I'll be back tomorrow and we can head into town, pick up anything you need. Careful, if we spend too long at the hardware store, my dad may try to rope you into working for him."

Zane snorted, "We'll see. I think I'll take the rest of the summer off."

❧

Prickles sprouted from her skin as the breeze cooled her sweat-soaked body. Freya ended her morning routine and rested her hands on her hips, taking in the ridiculously epic view. In all her travels, she'd never found any place that quite matched the Pacific Northwest.

Scooping up her mat, she headed back toward the house. The old craftsman structure had certainly seen better days, but Uncle Paul kept it in good repair. She could still picture her grandfather teetering on the ladder, cleaning out the gutters and having her run the bucket across the yard to dump the leaves over the embankment, then bring it back again. Between loads, she'd grab a handful of blackberries, plus a few extra for Grandpa.

Okay, so a niggling part of her was jealous that Asher and Sophie were buying the place, but more, she was glad it was staying in the family. After a decade of roaming around Europe, she was still wondering how she felt about the idea of settling down at all. Buying a house was a long way off.

Asher had been by, but didn't stay long. Sophie's car was gone for the workday, but Zane looked to be home. Biting her lip, she paused, then kept walking toward the main house. As much as she wanted to see that face close up, she'd give him space.

For now. One little pinky-shake, and the pheromones had pinged back and forth between them. And he'd totally checked out her butt.

Sauntering inside, she set her mat under the entry table. To the left, the open kitchen was sparse, with a few small boxes of Sophie's on the far counter that hadn't been unpacked yet. There were four stools, but still no table. To the right, a stone fireplace took up half the main wall, with built-in shelving on either side. A couch and TV were in place, although not hooked up yet, but otherwise the room was pretty empty.

After a quick shower, she hopped on her phone to order a Nespresso machine and some pods. For now, she grimaced as she caffeinated with bland drip coffee. There was really no going back once becoming hooked on viscous Italian brews. She dragged one of the stools to the window.

Resting her feet on the windowsill, she pulled up her banking app. Sneering, she didn't care for the checking account balance. The move over had pretty well emptied it, and her primary gallery in Florence only deposited every ninety days.

Rolling up the cuff of her jeans so the distressed fray at the ends would stop tickling her ankles, she moved on to read the news. At least the jetlag was easing a bit.

Gravel crunching under tires caught her attention. Checking out the window, she saw the dust cloud trailing behind her mother's F-150. Setting down her coffee, she strolled barefoot onto the covered porch and leaned against the pillar. The worn wooden planks cool against her feet, her toes curled around a loose nail. She'd have to swing by Sutherland's to pick up some basic tools.

The truck door wobbling behind her as she rushed down the path to the house, Tammy giggled out loud. Freya dashed down the few steps and flung her arms around her tiny mom, both rocking on their feet and grinning like a couple of fools. "My baby's home at last. I'm so happy," her mom said, wrapping her arms around Freya's side as they walked into the house together.

That last little bit of wondering why she'd come home melted away as she remembered exactly why. "I was just here two weeks ago for Pippa's wedding," she teased.

"You know what I mean. Now it's permanent." Tammy helped herself to a cup of coffee. "Sophie at work?"

Nodding, Freya held out her mug for a warm-up. "Monday through Friday, nine to five."

"And when will you be looking for something similar?"

Oh boy. Already? Letting air flow in and cool her lungs before she huffed, she exhaled and said, "My easels and supplies should be arriving in a few weeks, and once I'm settled, I'll head into Seattle to buy what I couldn't ship."

"Yes, but are you sure you can make a living at that? I mean, I know you have been, but long term? Do you want to couch surf for the rest of your life?" Tammy led the way back out to the porch and parked on the shade of the front step, continuing once Freya sat beside her.

Dig that hot poker a little deeper. Freya was worried enough about losing her in-person presence to build her brand. "I'm scared but I'll figure it out. Mom, that vineyard painting I sent you the pic of is being featured at an auction in Rome next weekend. I've been making a name for myself and some pieces have become investment pieces for big spenders; this auction and the additional pieces this new gallery picked up should set me up for months."

Crickets creaked in the distance, a cheerful bird squawked a redundant tune as she waited for her mother to either argue or pander. Could go either way, really.

"I'm sorry. It was one thing, getting to see you in action in places where art matters. But here? Making a living at art seems so beyond Foothills. I still have that sweet little painting from your first day of kindergarten on the mantle."

She leaned into her mother as they sat side by side on the porch steps. "I know, Mom. I'm not that little girl anymore. I wouldn't have come home yet if I didn't think I could continue to make a consistent living at this."

"I know, just let me adjust. But if anyone can make it happen, you can. You have always been a force of nature."

Freya took a long sip and feigned a smile. That force of nature spirit usually resulted in her spinning her wheels or bowling right past anything useful.

Jerking upright, her mother chirped, "Speaking of little girls. Your cousin Lulu is getting married on the tenth."

"Little Lulu? What is she, nineteen? Twenty?"

"Twenty-one and madly in love with a boy she met at college. They've planned the ceremony at this fancy hotel at Lake Tahoe."

"Why not at Uncle Joe's place? Doesn't he still have the cabin there?"

"He does, but they're planning a huge reception. I was actually hoping you'd agree to go." Her mother smiled winningly, showing every pearly tooth in her mouth.

Groaning, Freya set her coffee on the step between her feet and scrunched her fingers in her hair, the curls still damp and tangled. "I've reached that age, haven't I? Everyone's getting married. I see no point in flying out to a cousin's wedding I haven't seen in ten years."

"That whole side of the family came to your wedding."

"And I still wish they hadn't." She cringed.

"Just because you didn't show up doesn't mean they weren't at least there to support you."

"I didn't not show up… I just… I'd changed my mind."

"And hopped on the first flight out of the country." Tammy's voice oozed with disappointment, the regret still palpable.

"Can we not go over this again? Randy wasn't the one—and no one hates this more than I do—that I didn't figure it out until an hour before the ceremony. And he's happily married and living in Bellingham now."

Tammy wrapped her arm around Freya's shoulder and hugged her tight. "I know, Sweetie. I'm sorry, I shouldn't have brought it up. It might feel good to see everyone again, flaunt your success a bit. Now if only you had that sexy Italian fiancé to show off, that would help."

Snorting, Freya's abdomen bubbled with laughter. Only her mother would suggest braggery to fix hard feelings. "If it means that much to you, I'll go. Giovanni was pretty, but he was an egotistical ass, and we had nothing but pheromones to keep us afloat."

"You and your pheromones," her mother rolled her eyes, the corners of her mouth turned up in a soft smile. "He was tasty eye candy."

Freya giggled, "Wow, Mom. Eye candy?"

"You're a beautiful woman, and you two looked awfully nice together."

"You and Dad look nice together." Freya rose to her feet and reached out her hands, hoisting her mother up. "I'll go to the wedding."

"Maybe give them a painting for a gift? And see if you can find a date?"

Like a fishhook snagged in her cheek, she relented to the ironic smile. Freya often wondered where she had come from. She was the spitting image of her father, but being the only artist of her thirty-nine cousins and seventeen aunts and uncles, an only child of very traditional parents, she was accustomed to being the odd-woman out.

"I'll throw together a quick something. Send me a picture of them and I'll do charcoal since my other supplies are probably still somewhere over the Atlantic?"

Tammy beamed, "That would be such a nice gift."

"*That* will be fun. The date thing? That might be a bit of a stretch."

Feet pounding down the garage apartment stairs interrupted the silence as Tammy wracked her brain to answer that one. Freya watched as Zane left his apartment with little more than a glance in her direction, her pulse fluttering out of her skin that screamed of pheromones shooting her direction, but then he hopped in his truck and drove away.

Oblivious, her mother didn't notice Freya's cheeks heat red as she wondered if the face and the personality were as tempting as the rest of him.

"Seth Lawless just moved home after finishing his medical residency. His mother is in my Zumba class."

Closing her eyes, Freya shook her head in a valiant last effort to prevent another of her mother's fixups. "No, please, just don't."

"You remember Seth. Wasn't he a handsome one?"

"Yes. Which is why I lost my virginity to him at my sweet sixteen party."

Tammy looked like she'd swallowed a bird, her voice even chirping like it. "You never told me that."

"Love you, Mom, but there are a lot of things I've never told you."

Scowling, her mother rested her hand on Freya's arm, running her thumb over the oleander bloom tattoo she'd traded a portrait for a few years back. "I guess that's motherhood. When you have children one day, you'll understand."

Freya shrugged, not wanting to answer.

Typical, her mother didn't miss it. "I know you're jaded right now. Two broken engagements would do that to anyone. But you'll find the right someone, I know it."

Biting her lips together, Freya nodded. Her voice coming out a hoarse rasp, she muttered, "Three."

"Three?"

"I never even told you about Vince."

"The boy you were dating from Florida?"

She nodded, biting her lips together again.

"Oh honey, I'm sorry. I knew you really liked him."

Liked was an understatement. Once she'd recovered from the guilt over leaving Randy at the altar, she'd felt *alive*. And more recently, after Giovanni, she felt a strange optimism, like she wasn't getting roped in for a lifetime of living someone else's dream. But Vince... that had been awful. She'd drowned in his pheromones, which he'd shared with half of their class. Apparently, he lacked the objective eye their instructor had pushed, and enjoyed having their classmates model nude for him... but felt they were much more relaxed if they'd slept with him first.

Nausea rolled in her stomach, remembering his flippant expression when she found out, claiming she'd never be the artist he was if she couldn't loosen up about that sort of thing. She hadn't worked up the nerve to tell her mother about the embarrassingly brief engagement.

"It's okay. We'd only been engaged for about twelve hours before I ended things."

Her mom yanked her close and wrapped her arms around her. "Okay. No date."

Inhaling her mother's familiar lilac scent, she felt her muscles untense, the threatening tears fade away. "I still date. Regularly and enjoyably. Just no visions of wedding bells. Please. I'm done. If the third time is the charm, what is the fourth? I call it stupidity."

Tammy nodded against Freya's collarbone. "Lots of people find happiness without needing to get married to find it."

"Thanks, Mom."

She backed up a few steps, ready to finish unpacking so she could get started on that wedding gift. "Invite me to breakfast Saturday?"

"Will do." She hugged her mother again and waved from the porch as Tammy strolled down the path, then halted. "By the way. I already gave Seth's mother your number."

Shaking her head, she laughed. "*If* he calls, and *if* he seems likeable still, I'll see if he's up to attending a wedding with me. Have a good day at work."

3

Which is More Dangerous?

Freya sat bolt upright in bed. A loud crack shattered the quiet of the night. Taking up half the volume of her chest, her pounding heart was about to bust through her ribs.

What the hell was that?

Scanning the back field, she climbed out of bed, staying in the shadows and peering outside. The half-moon was high in the sky, its glow illuminating only the most reflective leaves and rocks. Hearing nothing more, she sat on the foot of her bed and watched the darkness through the French doors that led to the back field.

Okay. It was nothing. Just her imagination, right? Her pulse was still ticking at twice the speed of the hall clock, but it was probably just a weird dream.

She was about to lie back down, when she caught a glimpse of a figure rustling the shrubs across the yard. Blinking, she rubbed her eyes and looked again.

Nothing. It's fine.

No, that was *something*. And it wasn't a deer. Nor was it hunting season.

Tiptoeing out of her room, she went to wake Sophie. Bedroom door wide open, bed made... Shit. Her pulse kicked up a notch as she remembered Sophie was crashing at Asher's tonight. Great. What was the point of having a roommate when there was a potentially violent, armed creep in the backyard, and she wasn't home to tell you it was just your imagination?

Keeping to the shadows, she snuck back into her room and grabbed her phone. She leaned against the headboard, scanning the field through her window as she called her cousin.

Asher answered on the second ring. "Freya? It's after midnight. You okay?"

Whispering for a number of foolish reasons, she said, "I'm fine. I just... I think I heard a gunshot, and I think I saw someone outside."

She heard the sheets moving as he sat up. "Are you sure? Call 911."

"I'm not sure. It could totally have been my imagination, then I'll feel stupid for having called."

"Call anyway. No one would fault you for being cautious."

"But why would anyone be shooting guns and sneaking around in the middle of the night?"

"Just call the police."

"No. I'll feel stupid." She felt stupid for even worrying about feeling stupid. "They won't find anything, and I'll feel like an idiot for calling."

Grumbling on the other end, he said, "You have a Navy SEAL living above your garage. Call Zane."

"No. He'll think I'm crazy, and I don't have his number anyway. You're my cousin, a SEAL, *and* are about to be a police officer. And you're sleeping with my roommate, and she'd want to know what's going on. Can you see why I called *you*?"

"I'll take care of it," his gravelly voice relented as he clicked off.

Feeling even sillier as each passing second raised more doubt that the entire thing had been her imagination, she was at least going to be smart in case she wasn't hallucinating. She snuck from room to room, checking that all the doors and windows were locked tight.

Tapping her fingernails on her teeth, she stood in the hallway, unsure if she should just go back to bed, or wait to hear back from Asher.

Another minute went by, according to the sixty ticks of the hall clock.

The doorbell chimed chipperly, echoing from wall to empty wall before buzzing her eardrums. Wow, that was fast. Leaping up, she rapidly tiptoed to the front door and whispered through the dense wood, "Asher?"

A growl on the other side said, "It's Zane."

Great. Asher's genius plan was to call Zane. Huffing an exhale big enough to shift her hair out of her face, Freya accepted that her new neighbor was going to think she was a fraidy cat.

Unlocking the deadbolt, she opened the door just enough for him to slide inside.

Knocking her on her metaphorical ass like a meteor plummeting into her chest, a wallop of blazing-hot pheromones rocketed at her. Like a photon blast or superhero serum, the effects of it fueled her veins. He was...

Tall. Built. Ripped. Okay, so maybe she was being dramatic, but holy shit, she'd seen attractive men before, but Zane emitted one hundred percent Freya-altering pheromones.

Midnight forest eyes held dark secrets. Those lips were somewhere between pouty and stern, yet hinted at a wicked sense of humor... and could kiss all night without coming up for air. Big hands that would fit perfectly over her...

She nearly choked on her own saliva as she tried to remember how to breathe. How to stand. How to use her useless brain that would be irreparably rewired.

Okay, Freya, stop staring at the Norse god standing in front of you. Holding back the blushing giggle she hadn't heard herself make in a damn long time, she bit her lips together and tried not to pant. "Hi."

Middle of the fucking night, and his new neighbor, great ass that she may have, got spooked and needed someone to come scare away the big bad wolf. He tossed his phone back on the bed and contemplated the many ways he was going to kick Asher's ass for this later.

And he'd just fallen asleep. Dammit, Asher knew what it was like those first few weeks out. Between the nightmares of the day Jack got hurt, among many messed-up-as-fuck ops they'd been on, he still jerked out of bed every few hours, thinking the rest of the team had been called out on a mission, and he'd slept through it.

Tossing on a pair of jeans, he grabbed a shirt, clicked off the music he had blasting in his headphones to keep the monsters at bay, and paused at the door.

What if she was right? Fuck. He shook his head, hating the damn indecision. If there were really a shooter out there, he'd tell her to lock up and lay low, that neither of them should be going outside right now. Not much chance they were targeting either of them.

But she was probably wrong. This adorable little town probably hadn't had a murder or violent crime in the last half century.

And if she was too chickenshit to call the cops like she should, she might spend the whole night sobbing in the bathtub. Wouldn't be the worst hostage rescue he'd pulled off. Five, maybe ten minutes, and he'd be back in his own bed.

Rubbing the sleep from his bleary eyes one last time, he pulled on his shoes and checked outside through the windows, then slipped out the door. Nothing unnatural about the night; he heard only the wind rustling through the trees in the distance. Sticking to the shadows, he crossed the yard until he reached the front door.

Not wanting to scare her more than she already was, he rang the doorbell to announce his arrival, still scanning the area while he waited. Out in the open like a sitting-fuck-ing-duck. Asher owed him more than a few favors for this one.

Half a second later, he heard a voice ask through the door, "Asher?"

At least she wasn't a complete idiot. "It's Zane," he responded.

The door creaked open, while she hid behind the door. Running a hand through his hair, he geared up and stepped inside, dreading the weepy mess he'd be walking into. A dim light on the ceiling cast an amber light across the entry, the rest of the house otherwise was cloaked in blinding darkness.

Instead, he was knocked on his ass by the fierce woman that greeted him. He swallowed his damn tongue as every logical thought in his brain was pulverized by... everything about her.

Pushing the door closed, he stood and stared like a gawking dumbass. That wild black hair was curled with inherent rebellion, a few strands framing her angular jaw. Piercing blue eyes saw and understood every deep imagining that had passed through his soul from the moment he'd stepped foot on this earth.

Fuck, that wasn't even the half of it. A lacy tank left little to the imagination, and miniscule shorts revealed some perfect, curvy legs that should be wrapped around him *right now*.

Okay, brain out of gutter, he chided himself, clearing his throat and trying to say something before he melted to the floor.

"Hi," she said, as breathless as he felt. At least it was a mutual dumbfounded ogling.

He raised his eyes to her face again, ignoring the spectacular breasts under that top, pretending he hadn't noticed her nipples tighten under the delicate cotton as she responded to him. And hoped to hell she didn't notice his cock salute back.

"Hey," he nodded, burying the overwhelming visions of peeling off those tiny shorts to find out if that ass was as grabbable as he'd dreamed. "So, uh, have you seen any more sign of anything?"

"No. It's probably nothing. I mean, I'm still a little jetlagged, so, I'm sure it was my imagination."

"Well, I'll hang out until we know it was nothing." And absolutely not make a move. Hell, after the divorce, he'd played the field more than he should have. When Asher joined up, the pair had wreaked havoc on the single female population of San Diego. But the last few years, the job getting to him more than it should, he hadn't even pictured a woman naked.

"Thanks. I'm really sorry for waking you. If I thought it was anything serious, I would have called the police."

"So you called Asher instead?"

"I got my driver's license first and hauled his ass all over town for months, so he owes me many a late-night rescue."

Nodding, Zane found an easy smile quirking up the corners if his mouth. "And I owe him a favor or two. Could you tell where the shot came from?"

"I haven't heard a lot of gunfire, and I was asleep, so I couldn't even begin to guess."

"Well, I have. Show me where you saw them."

She crossed her arms over her chest and led the way across the main room and toward the back bedrooms. "It was probably my overactive imagination, but I would swear I saw something move just to the right of that maple."

"Okay." He hung back in the shadows and watched out the door.

Standing next to him, she stared along with him. Wasn't even touching him, but his skin prickled at the heat radiating between them.

She didn't strike him as the sort to make a big something out of nothing. Maybe it was the sharply sketched flower tattoo on her arm or the tree of life over her left upper back. That she'd jumped in to help unload his truck, without even sticking around for a thanks. Or maybe it was simply a vibe; she was solid, not crying or fussing. Instead, her breath came slow and easy, her eyes scanning the darkness, sporting a scowl of frustration that she might be right.

"Seriously, it was probably just my imagination. You should head home." She stepped back and sighed.

"Do you imagine a lot of gunshots? I mean, I do, but that's the PTSD talking," he shrugged, hoping she didn't think he was totally nuts.

"No, that was a first. But I haven't been back in the States long; must be all the talk about everyone having guns around here," she rolled her eyes at herself, her mouth turned up in a soft smile.

"Well, I'm not leaving until we know the coast is clear."

She brushed past him, hopping onto the far side of the bed and propping up her pillow against the headboard. Leaning back, she stretched those long legs and took a deep breath that drew the tank lower. Patting the spot next to her, she waved him over. "You can stand there or get comfy."

Rubbing a hand over his face, he willed away the fucking rock-hard erection at the sight of her inviting him to bed. As she rested another pillow in the spot she'd saved for him, he held his breath, hoping his jeans were snug enough that she wouldn't notice how desperate he was.

"Really, I feel terrible waking you for a figment of my imagination. No qualms about waking my cousin, but you I feel bad about. Besides, if this wasn't my imagination, and you just risked your life for a panicky woman that couldn't just lay low and call the police?"

Shaking his head, he found that rusty smile taking over his face again. He relented to the inevitable and plopped down on the bed next to her and kicked off his shoes. Leaning against the headboard, he glanced at her, then back out the window. Going to be a long fucking night... he suppressed an inappropriate laugh vibrating under his ribs at his poor word choice. No fucking tonight. Sadly. "You mentioned jetlag?"

"I just got home."

"From?"

"Italy."

"Fun trip?"

"I lived there."

His brow furrowed as a distant bell was ringing in the cobwebs of his memory. "Painter. The sunset in Asher's apartment."

Grinning, she pulled her legs up and rested her arms on her knees as she relaxed into the cushy headboard that matched his own, suspecting Paul and Denise had spoiled her return, too. Must get a nice discount through the store. "That's me."

He glanced around the room, noting the lack of other furniture and personal possessions in the room. "I heard you were making a living at it. Are you still? I mean, Foothills doesn't seem like a good spot to be for a professional artist."

"No shit," she muttered, glaring at the window.

And he'd stepped in it, as usual. Biting his lips together, he watched out the window, willing the gunmen to return. At least that was something he knew what to do about. Polite conversation? Not so much.

She sighed, "Sorry. I mean, I know I'm going to need to travel a lot and it's a huge risk, moving home. Marketing and social networking and all the crap I hate about pimping out my passion. But I'd been gone for too long. You ever get the draw to return home? That nowhere else in the world will suffice?"

He snorted, wishing more than ever for that damn shooter to reappear. "Not really."

Exhaling heavily, she rested her chin on her knees.

Goddammit. Half the damn reason he'd joined the military rather than following the path his parents and Blaire had planned for him, was so he wouldn't have to deal with communicating like normal people expected. Clearing his throat, he tried to redeem himself, "I mean, my parents have moved like six times since I left the house, and I hate New York. So not *home*, no, but I get the desire for familiar."

Her satin pink lips drew up in a quiet smile. Watching the dark night, she said, "Asher is familiar."

He nodded, a knot swelling in his throat. "Yep. Dragged my ass up here for good reason. I don't exactly have much going for me these days." Turning his head, he looked over at her.

Voice musically light, she said, "Sometimes you need to start over to find out where you want to be." Her bottom lip pulled into her teeth, breath coming fast as her infinite blues locked on and searched his muddy green.

Like a fucking idiot, he leaned in.

A distant crack struck the air.

Ricocheting around in his skull, bringing him right back to too many firefights, Zane looped his arm around Freya and rolled her off the bed with him.

Knocking the wind out of him, his back hit the ground and he absorbed their combined weight. Without pause, he flipped their positions, so he covered her body with his. Ears tuned in to every noise, unblinking as he watched out the window for the slightest shadow, he stilled. Pulse beating slow and steady under his skin, he listened.

Nothing. Would have to be a pretty unlucky random shot to get them inside the house, with how far away that shot was. But better safe than sorry with all the unknowns. Like why the hell someone was shooting a gun in the middle of the night in nowhereville.

Beneath him, Freya's chest rose and fell as she caught her breath. Alert, panic under control, she watched him rather than peering out the window.

No more gunshots. The night was dead quiet.

He rose to his elbows, looking down to see her expression easing from stunned to amused, her wicked blue eyes flashing with merriment. From somewhere in his brain, his chest, he blushed and grinned and shook his head at the absurdity. "I, uh. Yeah. Sorry. I've been shot at a few times."

"Impressive reaction time." As the moment quieted, her fishhook grin widened. "I was hoping we'd end up in this position eventually."

Chuckling, he parked his tongue between his teeth as he considered what to make of her.

Sighing like she was settling in for the evening, arms resting over her abdomen, she asked, "All okay?"

He nodded, relenting to an ironic laugh under his breath. "I don't think you imagined the gunfire."

She trailed her fingers along his forearm, then tracing up along his triceps, stirring a tingling in her wake. "As you seem awfully calm, it must not have been very close?"

"Nope."

"Should we call the police?"

"Probably." He couldn't make himself move. Her body calm and warm and half naked under his, her fingers teasing his skin under his sleeves, she drove him mad with a desire he hadn't felt in way too long.

While he wracked his brain for a single reason to move off her, she wrapped one hand around his shoulder, and the other gripped the back of his neck and pulled him to her. Leaning up to meet him, she pressed a silken kiss on his upper lip, then another on the corner of his mouth.

Helpless, enchanted, he stilled. Her tongue grazed along the crease of his lips, then she gently nipped at his lower lip.

Groaning at her simple touch that drove him absolutely beyond the tipping point, he took her mouth with his. Exploring, savoring her spiced, feminine scent, heat surged through his limbs, the outside world fading into nothing as she kissed him back, no holds barred, like she was as drunk on the chemistry as he was. Again and again, he tasted, learning the contours of her supple lips, a zing of electricity zapping him back to life with each touch.

Plunging her tongue inside his waiting mouth, she moved deeper, then looped her bare leg around his and clung like a horny Koala.

Lost, found, starving, he massaged velvet against velvet, heat building between them.

Crack.

And again.

More fucking gunshots.

Pulling away, his breath lost, her lips kissably warm and soft from the fucking best kiss he'd had... ever... he sat up and muttered, "Better call the cops."

4

Tasty Lips

Waking from a delicious dream of those tasty lips on hers, Freya grumbled and picked up the damn phone that rattled her eardrum. "Hello?"

"Miss Marks?" A very official sounding voice asked, somewhere in between polite and brisk.

"Yes?"

"It's Darren Miles from the Foothills Police Department. I wanted to follow-up with you regarding your call last night."

She sat up in bed and smoothed her hair out of her face. "Did you find anything?"

"There's only so much I can tell you, of course. That was gunfire, but it appears to have been aimed at a practice target and no violent intent was apparent."

Scowling, she rubbed the sleepiness from her brow. "In the middle of the night? Shots fired nearly an hour apart?"

A heavy sigh. Never a good thing. "That's the official story anyway, and action has been taken to ensure this shouldn't happen again. Honestly, I would appreciate your help. The entire thing screams of domestic violence to me, but we can't prove it. Young couple, they just moved into town a few weeks ago."

"Oh. That's terrible. Are you sure no one was hurt?"

"Not last night, fortunately. But if you wouldn't mind reporting anything you hear coming from the neighbor's property, I would sure appreciate it."

"Absolutely."

An icky feeling stirred in Freya's gut as she thought about the rough night in the property neighboring theirs. When she was a kid, she only knew of it as the place where the weird couple lived that had twenty-three cats and their kids had all grown and moved on. She hadn't realized the owners had passed away, but she supposed they would have been in their nineties or older by now.

Scooching out of bed, she took a quick shower and tossed on a breezy skirt and spaghetti strap top. She poured the pathetically weak coffee in the empty kitchen, popped in a quick piece of toast for breakfast and slipped on her shoes. No yoga this morning; she had more important things to do.

Sweeping her dark hair into a messy bun, she grabbed her coffee and headed across the driveway to the garage. Bouncing up the stairs, she raised her fist to the door, then hesitated. Crap. What if he was still sleeping?

Pressing her ear to the door, she held her breath and strained to hear any sign that he was up and about.

Grunting? Rhythmic thumping?

Had he met some woman *after* he'd left her at two in the morning? He didn't even know anyone in town.

A rumble festered in the depths of her throat like a bad case of acid reflux. And where did the jealousy come from? She didn't care for the odd emotion one bit. One belly-stirring, toe-tingling kiss, and this man was already messing her up.

She began to step back on the landing, when a heavy metal riff blasted from the speakers inside.

Mentally whacking herself on the forehead, she realized her faux pax, breathing out a sigh of relief and self-beratement at the same time. Raising her hand to the door, she waited until the song quieted again, then knocked loud enough so he'd hear.

Seconds later, the door swung open, Zane stood in front of her with an amused twist in his smile. "Morning."

Holding her mug in front of her mouth, she covered her jaw-dropped gawk as she marveled. Bare chested, slick from the vigorous exercise she'd overheard... and those ripped abs she'd anticipated were even better without the shirt. Swallowing a miniscule sip of coffee, lest she choke, she found her smile and hoped her voice came out more than a breathy whimper. "Morning."

He stepped back and welcomed her in, then dashed over and quieted the blasting metal. "You're up early after a late night."

"You too. The police department called me back."

Snagging a shirt off the back of the couch, he slipped it over his head. As quickly as her brow scrunched in disappointment, she masked the expression. She was such a sucker for good abs, and his were... really nice. She sighed and brought her coffee to her lips again to hide her pining.

"Did they figure out what was going on?" He rolled up the exercise mat and tucked it into the corner. His expression was neutral; damn he was hard to read.

"Domestic violence was as much as they could say, and even that's no more than a suspicion."

Resting his hands on his hips, he stilled. "Shit."

"Right? I was thinking of heading over, you know, introduce myself to the neighbors."

"Don't get involved with that. I'll grab Asher and we'll go later."

She set her coffee on the kitchen peninsula before she chucked it at his head. Any more acid in her system, and she might boil over anyway. While distracted by great abs and dreamy lips, she was almost fooled into thinking he wouldn't be like so many of the other misogynistic assholes she tended to fall for. "I'm sorry. I stopped by to see if you wanted to come with me."

"What?" His brow scrunched, looking at her like she was a moron. Yep. Sexist jackass.

"I may have been spooked and grateful you came over last night, but I guess I should have realized you'd go all badass soldier on me and not let the woman-folk anywhere near the potentially dangerous situation. Did you ever stop to think about the victim involved? Do you think two menacing, pissed-off soldier guys strolling up to her front door was going to make her feel safer?" Huffing, she bit her cheek before she got too fired up and blasted insults.

"Whoa, wait a minute." His hands hadn't moved from his hips, his feet still planted on the ground. "Don't put words in my mouth. If people are shooting guns next door, and the police only 'suspect' domestic violence, I'm sorry, but I think I'm a little better trained to walk into something like that."

"Right. Sure. Whatever. I'm going to go pick up a pie or something to take over." Her arms flailed as she paced across the room, loosely in the direction of the door, waiting to hear what pathetic defense he'd come up with.

Gritting his teeth, he closed his eyes and held his position to the silent count of five.

"What?" She fired at him, hand on the doorknob.

"Nothing. Can I go with you?"

"Fine."

"Can I shower first?" he asked, picking up her forgotten coffee cup and walking it across the apartment to her.

"Yes." She snatched her coffee, sloshing a few drops onto the floor. Too pissed to clean it up, she growled under her breath and stormed out.

Z ane tossed on jeans and running shoes, still pulling his shirt over his head as he dashed out the door in five minutes flat. If she'd left without him, hopefully he'd catch her before she got there. What the hell was she thinking, walking into a hot situation without backup?

Calming the fury pumping through his skull, he breathed it out and slowed his pace down the stairs. She'd come to get him, hadn't she? Like she'd called for backup last night. She wasn't stupid.

When he reached the bottom step, he found her waiting with a travel mug for him. "Sorry," she smiled softly, something in her eyes telling him she had no problem apologizing when appropriate. Hell, he doubted she had any hesitations in speaking her mind one way or the other.

"No, I'm sorry. Not to make excuses, but this PTSD shit, well, it sucks. I go from zero to pissed off in half a second." He accepted the coffee, keeping his body calm and neutral rather than punching the wall like he wanted.

A sympathetic smile softened her apology further, a hint of a dimple making an appearance on her cheek. "Wow, I wish I could do angry like you do. As you saw, I tend to yell and stomp my feet and throw things. You turn into a poker-faced statue. I wouldn't know you were mad except for that ticking in your jaw."

He took a testing sip of his coffee. "Pick up a pie?"

Those lush lips turned up in a fricking gorgeous smile, pure ornery mixed with something else he hadn't figured out yet. She went from pissed off to zero faster than he went the other way. "I don't bake."

"Not even cookies? I mean, if you enjoy taking baked goods to new neighbors, I'm fond of chocolate chip."

Throwing her head back, she laughed and somehow moved closer as she smoothed her reaction. Looking up at him, not quite as far as most women as she was pretty tall, she bit her lip in a sexy-as-fuck grin. Like a damn magnet, he started to lean in, compelled to finish what they'd started last night.

Catching himself before he got too close, he stepped back.

A spark of confusion flashed in her electric blue eyes. Or was it disappointment? Something... something that knocked him back like a sucker punch in the gut.

He needed to make it very, very clear that he wasn't looking for anything. Ever. Not even more kissing.

Fuck, had he ever been kissed like that?

When he and Blaire had gotten together in college, he'd been inexperienced and a terrible kisser and, well, they'd figured out the sex thing quick enough, so the make-out stage hadn't lasted more than a few dates. And he hadn't bothered spending more than a night or two with the same woman since, and often skipped the kissing part entirely. Not that he was an asshole or anything, but... no, shit, he totally was. But at no point since his divorce had he even hinted to a woman that he was game for more than a casual thing.

Okay, maybe he would consider indulging in some basic fooling around like last night. *Nope, **not happening**.* With his only friend's cousin? Yeah, let's not cross that line. Not even for rosy lips that would haunt his dreams for the next few decades. Or for those perfectly round... *Nope. Stop it.*

"And how were you planning on getting to the bakery?" He backed toward his truck, dangling his keys.

"I was going to ask you for a ride." She grinned, a wiggle to her hips as she taunted him. Was she doing it on purpose? "I'm hoping to buy a car with my next paycheck. Depending on how well my paintings sell at this auction coming up soon, and as long as my regular sales stay steady." Without waiting for the invitation, she hopped in the passenger seat of his truck.

"Have you eaten?" He asked as he climbed in the driver's seat and clicked his seatbelt into place.

"I was hoping to buy you breakfast as a thank you for last night."

Teasing a smile at the corners of his lips, he held his thought to himself. That kiss had been more than enough. If anything, the best thank you would be to ditch his ass and stop tormenting him with... making him want more. "Great."

She stayed quiet the drive into town. With few words, she directed him toward the bakery. Dammit, he'd pissed her off again, and he didn't have a fucking clue what he'd done now. He preferred her angry tirade to the silent treatment. But at least he knew where he stood with her, not a trace of phony politeness.

Inside, he snuck ahead and paid for the breakfast and pie while she chatted with the woman behind them in line, as a pathetic attempt at an apology.

"Hey, I'm treating," she scowled when she realized what he'd done.

"I know."

"Then why did you pay?" She snatched the bag from the counter and pushed out the door first.

Once they'd hopped back in the truck, he let out a heavy exhale. "Why don't you treat after that auction?"

"I can't afford a car, but I can swing breakfast now and again." She tore into her savory pastry, sausage and cheesy steam wafting from the top that would have made his stomach growl, but his appetite was squashed flat. This is exactly why he didn't have friends. Probably why his family never called, either. Fucking incompetent at basic human communication.

He left his breakfast in the bag, the idea of eating making him nauseous. "That's not what I was getting at."

As he was quickly learning to expect, her eyes flashed with ferocity. "Well, it kinda came across that way." Her tone was moving from defensive to flippant. And he thought he downshifted fast.

Knowing he'd stepped in it and there was no recovering, well, knowing him, he'd make it worse if he tried, he shut the hell up and drove them back out of town. She downed the rest of her breakfast in silence; somehow, even her chewing seemed irate.

When the neighbor's house came into view, he lowered his voice, "Will you please let me get out first?"

"Only if you let me do the talking."

"Fine."

The house was even worse than he'd expected. The front gutter was bent down where a branch had fallen on it and never been removed, now decaying and a gust away from disintegrating. What had likely started as sunny yellow siding was now a dirt-caked mustard. Older than he was and twice as beat-up, a Subaru was parked in the dilapidated carport, filthy with out-of-state tabs that had expired a few years back. In front of the house, a shiny new full-sized truck sat in the middle of a sudsy puddle where it had just been washed.

As they stopped, a woman stepped out onto the creaky porch. Shit, she was too young to be going through this. Too slim, dressed in skinny jeans and a flannel top tied at the waist, her hair was damp from the shower and braided neatly down her back.

Her bright smile almost made the whole scene less depressing, but was so out of place, it really made it worse. Completely ignoring his request, Freya hopped out first.

She had a point. If he and Asher had come out alone, they would probably have intimidated the hell out of the woman.

"Hi, I'm Freya. This is Zane. We're your new neighbors."

The woman's voice was just above a whisper, "I'm Sienna. It's great to meet you."

Standing back, Zane kept his distance. No bruising, and she seemed to be walking okay, but she held her left arm against her chest, her right arm bracing it at the elbow.

Freya softened her voice to match the neighbor's volume. "I am a terrible baker, but I feel like you're supposed to bring pie or casserole or something to the neighbors to introduce yourself, so, here you go." She offered the pie. Damn, she was disarming. Her body language almost meek, Freya silently offered support. "We just moved in."

"Thank you, that's so sweet." The woman accepted the pie with her right hand, using her left only for balance.

Zane's fists balled at his sides as he imagined all the awful reasons why she wouldn't use her arm. Her range of motion was limited, but she seemed to move it adequately when necessary. He doubted anything was broken, but with the way she was babying that arm, it looked to hurt like hell.

He stepped closer and added softly, so his voice wouldn't carry through the open window, "I, uh, just got back from the Navy. SEAL buddy of mine recommended Foothills; he just got hired on with the police department. So, you know, I've got a lot of time on my hands while I settle in. Like if you need any help fixing the gutter or anything like that."

Sienna bit her lips together and nodded. "That's good to know. Thank you." She backed up a few steps. Whatever she gleaned from the conversation, at least she knew she wasn't alone.

A thundering growl sniped from inside the house. "Sienna? Where the hell you at? Late for work, aren't you?"

She cringed, then pasted on a phony smile. "Our new neighbors brought pie," she said as he slammed the front door open and stepped onto the porch.

Clearly, the guy used to be quite the athlete, with a tall, muscular build that had become soft with beer and inactivity. Nodding, he smirked appreciatively at Zane's truck. "Wasn't that nice of them," he was suddenly all politeness. Passing right by Freya, he extended his hand to Zane, "Toby. Which place is yours?"

Nodding toward the house, Zane didn't bother clarifying he was just renting the place over the garage until he figured out what the hell he wanted, "Zane." He accepted the handshake, resisting the urge to roll the asshole's knuckles, but squeezed just shy of causing injury.

"Whoa, firm shake there," he pulled his hand back and shook his fingers dramatically, a charming smile on his face.

Crossing his arms over his chest, Zane added an extra flex with the movement for a number of reasons, none friendly. Backing up a few steps, he said, "We'll get out of your hair."

Once Freya was in the truck, he climbed in the driver's seat, never turning his back on the neighbors. He flipped on the engine and got the hell out of there. Fists clenched tight on the steering wheel, he forced his breath in and out.

Glancing over, he saw Freya wasn't any calmer. Her eyes were glazed over, cheeks pulled tight. Her dimple no longer the exclamation point to her vivid smile, but instead the hyphen that said she wasn't finished yet. "Thanks for coming with me."

He nodded, "I just hope she gets help before it's too late."

"Me too. You weren't exactly subtle," her lips turned up in a feisty smile. Shit, she was downright bloodthirsty when she wanted to be.

"Can't believe that asshole. The money he spent on that truck could have fixed up the house and bought her a decent car."

Freya raised an eyebrow, "How do you know it's not her truck?"

"Just a guess."

She sighed and leaned her seat back a click. "I've never been able to imagine how a person ends up in such an awful situation."

"You don't always know what you're getting into when you say *I do*."

"That's why a long engagement is a good thing. Gives you plenty of time to back out of it."

"You sound like you speak from experience."

"So do you." She rotated in her seat to face him.

Back on the main road, he took the next turn toward their place. "Married the first girl I slept with."

"High school sweetheart? Sounds romantic."

He snorted, "Late bloomer. College sweetheart. Not as romantic as it sounds. Huge wedding after our second year. We rented this incredible apartment she and my parents had picked out, an architect's dream, so I worked full time and paid on the overpriced high rise with my student loans."

"What about her student loans? Didn't she work?"

"She was trying to pull a double major, so she didn't have time to work. And with my income and loans, she didn't need to borrow more than tuition."

"You're an architect? How did you end up in the Navy?"

"By the time we graduated, I was so deep in debt, realized that I didn't give a shit about architecture, and my marriage was not everything I'd hoped. Blaire was out late partying every night, claiming she was networking and that I should do the same. So, I said fuck it, I was done living somebody else's dream, and decided to do what I always wanted."

"And you wanted to be a Navy SEAL?"

"All my life. Was one of those kids that played too many video games, decided I wanted to be a genuine badass, so I took up swimming and football and track, kept my grades up."

"What happened that you didn't do it right away?"

"I knew I needed a degree anyway, so I played the game and majored in architecture to make my parents happy. Chances were slim of making the cut anyway, so at some point I realized joining the SEALs was probably a pipedream anyway. And then I met Blaire, and she hated anything military. She wasn't thrilled when I came home one day and let her know I'd signed on to join the Navy."

"Without asking?"

"Not going to say I wasn't looking for her to bail, and I didn't have the balls to say it out loud."

"I know this isn't a happy ever after."

"Things were pretty tense, and I'd start looking forward to getting shot at. Safer anyway. About a year in, I was called away on an op. Last minute, deep cover, no contact with home. By the time I got back, she'd already packed. Decided she didn't fit the patiently-waiting-at-home role. Needed a man to have her back, not the other way around, this isn't the 1950s."

"I'm so sorry."

"Yeah, me too. No way some woman's dragging me down another damn aisle for some superficial vows that don't mean shit."

And the sympathy was wiped out by that fury again. She scoffed and sat up in her seat. "*Some woman?* Blaire didn't understand you, that's pretty clear. But because one woman refused to share in your dreams, *all* women are selfish and out to dig their claws into you and not support you?"

Slowing, he pulled into the carport, his jaw clenching tight as he shut off the engine. Holding steady, he climbed out and closed the door with a click so he wouldn't slam it and show just how easy it would be to let his temper take over. "Not what I meant," he muttered through gritted teeth.

"No? What did you mean?"

"Dammit, Freya. I've got two friends in this world. Your cousin, who's seen me at my worst and I've seen him at his worst and we know when to leave well enough alone. And the other is ground to dust in a tin can in my fucking closet. That's it. Because I'm always doing or saying something stupid." He hesitated at the base of the steps to his apartment. "Hell, my foot's in my mouth more often than not. So I try to just keep my damn mouth shut."

She reached into the truck and grabbed the bag with his breakfast that had gone cold long ago. A soft smile on her face, she stopped inches in front of him. Those fierce blue eyes danced with that mystery he just couldn't place.

Stepping close, her hand burned into his chest as she anchored him. Holding his breath, his skin prickled in anticipation. She brushed her lips over his and pulled away before he could kiss her back.

"I'm sorry I got defensive. I've been that *some woman* and latched on to someone that didn't want me. More than once. Asher was right to bring you here. Give it another month, then tell me how many friends you have, and how many people have your back."

She flashed him a sultry smile, handed him his food, then turned away. An extra swing in her hips, her skirt swaying with each confident step, she seemed intent on tormenting him. What was that kiss all about?

Unsatisfied, craving more, he resisted the urge to run over and drag her back against him and taste her again. Yep, that had been her precise intent. His temper dissolved and nothing but lust was left buzzing in his veins.

The corners of his mouth turning up, he didn't fight the smile.

5

Virgin Alarm

Freya chucked the charcoal over the hillside, the stubby thing disappearing into the shrubs like a frightened bunny. She'd just managed to whip together a moody sketch for the damn wedding, but had spent the rest of the day madly sketching and resketching until she was satisfied.

Growling under her breath, she glared at the easel in front of her. Coming up from behind her, an unmarked beer bottle covered her vision. Sophie laughed, "Getting frustrated?" Settling onto the bench next to Freya, Sophie nodded to the sketch.

Taking a swig, Freya scowled. "Yes."

"I think it's a great portrait. What don't you like about it?"

Gesturing to the sketch that didn't quite capture the restrained fury that Zane worked so hard to keep in check, Freya bitched, "Look at him. He's all rugged SEAL meets Norse god meets Italian model."

Sophie leaned back and took a sip of her own unmarked brew. "He is a looker, I'll give you that. But he seems really nice. Quiet, but decent."

Snorting, Freya leaned back, keeping her eyes on her sketch. Why couldn't she get that face out of her brain? Those earthy green eyes were so haunted, lips so freaking savory and generous. And that jawline. "I have to go to my cousin's wedding."

"Which one? Asher didn't mention anything about a wedding."

"My dad's side of the family. At Lake Tahoe."

"Is it Zane or the wedding eating at you?"

Taking another gulp of the hoppy brew, she looked into the glass, trying to figure out what the spicy undertone was. "Both. My mom thinks I should bring a date, since I haven't seen Dad's family since I left Randy at the altar when I was my cousin Lulu's age. You know, make it look like I'm not lonely and desperate."

"Are you lonely and desperate?"

"No, but I would really like to make my parents proud. In a massive family of strait-laced normal people, I am too often the oddball that everyone gossips about."

"I would never have pegged you as an outsider when I saw you with your parents and your extended family at Pippa's wedding."

"That's the good side of the family; we're all oddballs."

"And a date would make you look normal?"

"Sort of. I just want to give my parents some bragging rights. Instead of, *Freya broke off another engagement and got homesick so she's renting out a bedroom in her cousin's girlfriend's house and hoping her career doesn't tank*, I'm going for, *Freya's art is being sold all over the world, and she's happy and successful.*"

"You know? I've never had to worry about that."

Freya's heart stumbled as she realized she'd been ranting about the woes of pleasing parents and impressing a huge extended family, when Sophie only had one horrible aunt and had lost her parents and grandparents as a kid. "I'm such a bitch. I'm sorry, Sophie."

Sophie leaned into Freya. "It's okay. I now have Asher, and soon, my best friend for a sister, fierce parents in Denise and Paul, and," she tipped her head against Freya's, "you for a cousin."

"Damn right. I'll just be me at this stupid wedding. They can see the Freya that will tell them to fuck off if they don't approve."

Laughing, Sophie took a drink of her beer and nodded to the picture, "And what about Zane?"

Stepping back a few paces, Freya slumped onto the bench and took a long, long pull on the beer, letting the bubbles ping and pop in her mouth before speaking. "I like him."

"And the problem is?" Sophie joined her and leaned back.

The sun was beginning to lower in the sky, and Freya's stomach rumbled, reminding her she'd skipped lunch and was well on her way to missing dinner. Nearly done with the beer, she was already feeling the buzz on her empty stomach. "I don't want to like him *that* way. I'd love to fool around with him, as, well, he's gorgeous and is comprised completely of Freya-friendly pheromones. But, well, I've been there, done that, bought the freaking t-shirt, and I'm not going down that road again."

Sophie laughed under her breath. "I guess you'll need to catch me up a bit."

Sometimes Freya forgot she'd only known Sophie a few weeks. They'd instantly hit it off in the weeks before Pippa's wedding, and Freya had been grateful when Sophie had asked her to be her roommate while Freya settled back in the States and Sophie tried to not jump headfirst into things with Asher.

"I've been engaged three times."

Sophie winced. "Oh my."

"You know I'm a sucker for good chemistry. So much so, that, well, I get caught up in the romance of it all. And then

I realize there's nothing more than good sex and end up disappointed when the rest doesn't follow and he wasn't what I thought he was and I've lost a little more of myself."

"I see. So you're looking for someone you don't have good chemistry with?"

"Exactly. Like a long-term friend with benefits that I can settle down with and we can have babies together and joint checking accounts... but without that intensity that is too easy to lose yourself in."

"But you just met Zane, what, a week ago?"

"We're beyond the met stage already. Once when we helped him with his boxes. Then Asher sent him to save me from the scary gunshots and, well, within twenty minutes of seeing him up close for the first time, I was already making out with him. We've had our first fight, and our second, and kissed and made up."

"Wow, you do move fast."

"Only when the chemistry is so freaking overwhelming. Whenever I'm within a ten-foot radius of that man, I can't keep my mouth off him."

"Dinner tonight should be interesting then," Sophie snickered, sporting a wicked grin.

"You didn't."

"You'll have chaperones. Asher and I will be there." Before Freya could whimper and whine, Sophie changed the subject.

Freya filled her in about the neighbors. Sophie seethed like she did, throwing out suggestions on how they could smuggle the woman out of there. Shaking her head, Freya said, "She has to figure it out on her own. Zane pretty much offered to kick his ass whenever she is ready, and I let her know I'm a nice person that would be happy to help." She drained the last of the beer. "I've never been in anything even close to what our neighbor woman is going through, but I understand getting lost in someone, and no one can tell you what a mistake you're making."

Rising from the bench, Sophie turned and pulled Freya up. "So you are preemptively avoiding Zane because you are too attracted to him."

"Yes. He's even got that brooding thing down, and I've always wanted to explore the tortured hero type." She found herself grinning at the absurdity of it. Sophie took her empty bottle while Freya gathered her completed work and the easel.

As they wandered back into the house, Freya was welcomed by the scent of roasted vegetables and sausage keeping warm in the oven. She nearly drooled at the scent. "Remind me again how I got so lucky as to live here with you?"

Sophie grinned as she pulled a serving dish from the cupboard. "Because if you didn't live here, Asher would, and we're not ready for that."

She quickly stashed her art supplies in her bedroom, then hopped on a stool and considered that one for a moment. "We can be mutual buffers then. You keep me from sleeping with our garage neighbor, and I'll keep you from moving too fast with Asher?"

"Like a virgin alarm from *Spaceballs*? Or you could get a chastity belt. That Mel Brooks was on to something," Sophie chuckled as she got another round of beers out of the fridge.

"I'd use the words virgin or chaste lightly." Just as the words were out of her mouth, the front door swung open and Asher and Zane strolled in. Zane faltered as he saw her, his gaze darkening, but the corner of his lips turned up somewhere between a dare and smug satisfaction.

A foolish flutter zinged through her, vibrating until the rush of warmth flooded *everywhere*, including her cheeks. Hopping up, she grabbed another pair of beers and glasses from the cupboard.

Asher didn't pause, heading straight for Sophie and pinning her against the cabinets, lips locked before they even said a word to each other.

Turning away, Freya tried to give them a little privacy. After all, they hadn't seen each other in at least twelve hours. She grinned at their joy, indulging in the niggling jealousy that teased in her belly.

Moving to her side, Zane popped the tops of the beers and started pouring. As Freya took the first sip, already buzzed from the beer she'd downed a little too quickly on a pouty and empty stomach, she let out a soft moan as the suds coated her throat.

Zane took a testing sip from his glass, watching her reaction over the rim. "Good?"

She nodded. "Really good. I'm trying to figure out where Sophie got these."

While Zane seemed to ignore her, that mysterious smile resting on his face as he wandered to look out the window, Asher reached around her and snagged the beer she'd poured for him. He took a big sip and raved, "Damn, Zane. This might be my new favorite."

Freya watched Zane's reaction. "You made this?"

He nodded. She wanted to flick him on the forehead to get him to use his words.

Asher answered for him, "We got really bored one weekend a few years ago, so the three of us decided to see who could brew the best beer."

"Zane won?" Sophie asked as she set dinner on the table. Freya grabbed a stack of plates to pitch in.

Zane shrugged, "We messed up the first batch and were all too chickenshit to try it, convinced we'd poison ourselves. The other two slackers were too lazy to try again, but we had so much material left over, plus we'd spent a fortune on supplies, so, well, I made use of it."

Despite the lightness of the conversation, the easy friendship between Asher and Zane, Freya felt the missing part of their trio tugging at her, her breath a little heavy as she resisted the urge to wrap her arms around Zane and ask if he was okay.

S hoveling in the last bite of rosemary roasted veggies, Zane popped up and cleared his plate. Having spent the last half hour sitting inches away from Freya, he needed space. His leg still burned from the moments he'd accidentally relax and bump into her. An odd aching sensation filled his fingers as he'd spent the whole damn dinner resisting the strangest urge to hold hands with her. What the hell was wrong with him? Since when did the idea of holding a woman's hand turn him on?

Didn't help she was a little tipsy from downing the two beers after skipping lunch; he ought to have warned her how strong this batch was. Normally, drunk people annoyed the shit out of him. Not Freya; she was hilarious. Clearly not used to it, she giggled now and again, let something slip she probably hadn't intended.

Except when she'd trailed her fingers along the edge of his shorts, seemingly a mindless gesture for her, but it had raised the room temperature to beyond sweltering. *Combining sharper hops, maybe an apricot concentrate, something to lighten the brew...* he'd planned alterations to his latest recipe in his head before he embarrassed himself and let a little tenting action show.

He went in to start on dishes, but Asher stopped him. Whispering, Asher nodded to Freya, "Take this lightweight for a walk to sober her up before she tries to go to bed and ends up with a nasty hangover tomorrow."

Glaring, Zane nudged him aside, "No."

"Why not? I mean, no, don't sleep with her when she's drunk, but may as well lay down some groundwork."

Shaking his head, Zane muttered, "Groundwork? Shit, man, that's cold."

"Okay. I tried. What I mean is, I'm leaving for training in three days. I'd rather spend a nice night with Sophie rather than worrying about my cousin. Come on. Wingman? I know it's been a while."

Zane shut off the water and dried his hands. "You owe me."

"I thought you liked her?"

"I do. Which is why I'm *not* planning to lay any ground-work."

"You're not making any sense."

Backing away, Zane shook his head. "Not everyone wants what you have."

He found Freya back in her bedroom, folding a load of laundry on the neatly made bed. "Hey," he said.

Flipping around, she caught the edge of the bed to steady herself. "Hi," she grinned.

"Sorry, I, uh, should have warned you, that beer was about eight percent."

Nodding, she grinned even bigger. "A bit late, thanks though. My head is officially swimming. I'm a total light-weight."

He stuffed his hands in his pockets and nodded toward the exit. "Come on, let's go for a walk."

She strolled close and caught him by the waistband before he could back into the hall. Staring down, as if distracted by what she'd found, she lifted the edge of his shirt and traced her fingers over his abs. Holy shit, this was so not helpful. *If he added caryophellene, that might add an earthy, citrus undertone.* He breathed slowly in and out, taming things while he convinced them both this was a terrible idea.

Stilling her hands, he backed away. "Fresh air," he muttered.

Nodding, she closed her eyes. "Worthless virgin alarm," she muttered.

"What? Freya, are you a virgin?"

She giggled. "You're cute." Strolling ahead, she reached the front door and nodded for him to follow. He was in way over his head.

The evening breeze washed over his skin as he stepped outside, the lingering scents from the heat of the day fresh on the air. Swaying with the wind, her blue skirt shifted over her curves with each step. She walked to the middle of the front field and turned toward him. "Well? Are you coming?"

Shit, he shook his head and caught up to her. She held her hand out, and he stupidly took it, walking side by side across the field. As they neared the bench that overlooked the mountains beyond, no more than dark blue paper cutout silhouettes against the sunset purple glow, Freya spun in his arms, nearly knocking herself over with her momentum.

Steadying them both, he held onto her waist.

Eyes searching his, her lips parted, and he was lost. Leaning down, he took her mouth, exploring the soft velvet of her tongue, the spicy-sweet of her breath mixing with his.

A soft whimper passed her lips.

Her hands gripped his shoulders and she arched against him.

Whoa, shit. He pulled back, stunned at himself. At his recklessness. "Sorry," he whispered on a breathless exhale.

Her mouth opened and closed, then she surprised the hell out of him again, muttering, "My baby cousin is getting married." Dropping his hand, she crossed to the bench, sat, and leaned forward to rest her elbows on her knees.

"I'm sorry," he winced as he sat down next to her.

"I have to fly down to the wedding and prove that I'm not avoiding them. That I didn't leave the country because I was embarrassed."

"Why would you be embarrassed?"

"Last time they saw me, I was pulling a *Runaway Bride*." Grimacing, he felt the regret radiating off her.

"Mom thinks if I give them a piece of my work as a wedding gift and bring a date, I'll show them I made the right choice and demonstrate how amazing my life is."

"Why does it matter what they think?"

"I don't know. It's stupid. It *doesn't* matter. But it does. I've been engaged three times. On that side of the family, they're all married and having kids and are doing what they're supposed to do. But Freya's the oddball as usual. Can't seem to get her act together."

"Seriously? From what it sounds like, you've been brave enough to live the adventure most people only dream about. You wanted to paint, so you made it happen, and you're making a career out of it. Yeah, you've been engaged, but you didn't settle when it wasn't right. You're what, thirty? There's no rush to have kids, if you decide you want them. If you don't want all that, there's nothing wrong with choosing the path that appeals, even if it's not white picket fences and two-point-five children."

"You sound like an inveterate singleton," she nudged him, raising an eyebrow in challenge.

"Maybe."

A wicked grin blossoming on her lips, she shifted onto his lap and pressed against him, her hand cradling the back of his neck. "I'm not opposed to all that, but not with someone like you." Pressing her lips to his, she sighed against his mouth. "I don't have the capacity for guys like you anymore."

Scowling, pulled back. "Guys like me?"

Nodding, she tugged him closer and kissed him again. He shouldn't have kissed her back, but he did. Hell, before Freya, he hadn't indulged in so long, and he was rapidly losing the will to resist.

Between teasing kisses, she whispered against his mouth, "Full of pheromones and muscles and broodiness and..." Despite the mere inches between them, she moved closer until her breasts were tight against him. Nipping his lip, she pressed her mouth against his, parting and tracing her tongue over his in a delicious torment.

Sliding his hand up her thigh, he groaned against her mouth, indulging, deepening the kiss. Breathless as he managed to pull away to form a coherent thought, he said, "I don't have a fucking clue what I want. But I know taking this any further won't help either of us."

Her lips downright succulent after kissing his brains out, yet again, she tugged her lower lip between her teeth and looked at him like she was ready to have her way with him until he couldn't remember his own name.

Foolishly, in complete contrast to his words, he kissed her again. When she whimpered a sweet moan, his hand glided up her skin under her shirt, migrating toward those spectacular breasts.

Growling against his mouth, she pulled his lower lip between her teeth, then sucked his tongue in a devastating fore-shadowing of everything else that mouth could do.

Gripping her breast in his hand, his other followed until he cupped both under the thin layer of cotton, teasing his thumbs over her taut nipples. Moaning as if halfway to the moon in response, she tightened her legs around him and leaned into his touch. Leaving her lips for the first time since they'd landed on the bench, he trailed kisses along the sharp line of her jaw, gliding his tongue over her neck.

Freya's phone buzzed from her pocket, a bucket of ice crashing over them.

What the fuck was he doing? Pulling his hands free, he cleared his throat and detached.

"Hello?" she asked as she slipped off of him, puzzled at the unknown number, but equally grateful for the distraction. He glared at his watch. It was nearly nine o'clock, who would be calling at this hour?

Zane didn't bother not eavesdropping.

"Hi, Freya?"

"Yes?"

"It's Seth. Seth Lawless. Sorry to be calling so late, I guess I didn't realize what time it is. Anyway, I uh, oddly enough, your mother gave my mother your number and apparently they are conspiring to hook us up."

Zane heard the amused chuckle on the other end mirroring Freya's. Hook up? Jackass. Not that Zane was one to talk. He'd been a few thin layers of cotton away from turning his only friend's drunk cousin into a thirty second hook-up, if he lasted *that* long.

Rubbing his eyes, he leaned back against the bench and kicked his own mental ass. He'd been the jackass, all over the tipsy siren without any meaningful intention of stopping.

She didn't seem to notice his internal beratement. "It's been a long time. I've been home for a week, and my mother is already trying to set me up."

More friendly laughing. Zane wanted to rip the phone away and chuck it over the hillside. Gritting his teeth together, he reminded himself this was a good thing.

"Oh my god, me too. I've been back a month, and my mother has my whole future plotted out."

Grinning wide, Freya relaxed against his side. Whole new level of weird; Zane's brain was going to fissure in half, undecided if he was going to stake his claim or dodge the bullet, neither side seeming to convince the other.

Freya continued her conversation with the creep that was clearly looking for a way into her pants, "My mother both jumped for joy and plugged her ears when I told her we'd already been down that road."

"You never told her we had a thing? Hell, I was grinning like an idiot for the next week after we lost our virginity together. My parents finally pinned me down and I had to confess I'd made it with a woman."

Freya's laugh sparkled as she continued to lean against Zane. Okay, he needed to get the hell out of here. He was relieved she wasn't a virgin, but really didn't want details.

Closing his eyes, he let himself pretend for precisely five seconds that he was the one making her laugh so lightheartedly. And three, two, one. He jumped to his feet and mouthed, "Goodnight." Their make-out had sobered her up enough; she'd be okay.

Biting her lip, she nodded. "That sounds great," she answered Seth. "I can do Friday night."

Rip off the damn band-aid now. Two fucking years since he'd been with anyone. Hell, he was going on three. This was exactly why. Sappy-ass romantic no matter how hard he tried.

The lights dimmed in the corner bedroom overlooking the front yard. Nothing frantic or urgent or rushed, he caught the outline of Asher and Sophie undressing each other, savoring each touch, each kiss.

Giving them their privacy, he headed straight home, checking from the window that Freya made it back home okay. Maybe he'd give his sister a call after all, take her up on the offer to sublet her apartment.

6

Drunken Burpees

He couldn't make himself pack again. Couldn't drive across the damn country again, and no way in hell he was going back to the east coast. Even drunk Zane knew better.

Checking his email, Zane shook his head. Fuck. He didn't know why he even bothered. For all his parents knew, he was getting shot at again. Or was dead already. Would the government have tracked them down until they could deliver the information firsthand, or would they give up after multiple failed contact attempts?

Why did he even bother trying to reach out? How many school functions had he been the kid to hitch a ride home with the neighbors? To take the subway home from football practice? They'd helped with enough of his first year of college to get him into the exclusive program but then he saddled the debt he thought they'd planned to share. They'd been heavily involved in his wedding, but hadn't offered more than a quick condolence at his divorce.

Just often enough to keep him coming back, they would pretend to be parents of the year. His first major deployment, they'd mailed regularly, thrilled when he'd gotten home safely. Each deployment, they seemed less interested, apparently not realizing his survivability didn't increase with experience.

Unkillable, he dodged every damn bullet. He'd sprained his ankle once, but that had been his own stupidity in a training exercise, showing off, jumping out of the chopper when it was too high off the ground.

Sitting on the top step outside his apartment, overlooking the driveway and the moonlit front yard, he didn't have the guts to sit on the bench he knew Freya favored. Hell, he'd hardly slept the last few nights, imagining what might have happened if she hadn't been drunk. If that prick hadn't called to ask her out.

If she hadn't been wearing panties. If he'd had the guts to pull her onto his lap, to peel that top off and appreciate those spectacularly rounded breasts without any fabric between them.

Groaning, he closed his eyes and fought the image, yet again. He glared at the empty beer bottle, and the two behind him. Shit, wait, it was three behind him. Four. And another that had rolled down the steps, miraculously unshattered. When had he downed so many?

No longer on active duty. Not beholden to anyone, why the hell not? He hadn't touched a drop the night Jack died.

His eyes welled at the awful memory. The call that his friend was septic in the ICU not two days after Zane was out of the Navy. That Jack had been fucking with heroin.

He'd been dodging Zane's calls, usually responding with a quick text that he was fine, that they'd get together and celebrate Zane's honorable discharge next weekend. The back of his throat burned with stupid fucking mucus, salty tears coating his cheeks. How many surgeries had Jack had to go alone while Zane was too busy, waiting on the damn discharge to go through so he could take care of his friend? If he'd just held on a few more days.

Looking over Jack's pasty corpse in the ICU, his ribs crushed from failed attempts to revive him, the machines dark now that he'd gone, Asher hadn't let Zane stew. Said he had two weeks to get his ass to Foothills.

Head swimming, throbbing from the fucking cryfest, Zane tugged his shirt over his head and cleaned the soaked mess of his cheeks. Leaning to round up a few bottles, his head spun from the awkward movement and he nearly upchucked his lack of dinner.

At long fucking last, he heard Seth's practical sedan coming down the drive. No dust kicked up, he drove politely over the freshly filled potholes that Zane had courteously taken care of that morning.

Coming to a stop, perfectly calm, good-natured Seth leaned across the center console. Freya met him halfway. Too pansy-assed to kiss her properly, Zane watched through the windshield as they exchanged a polite peck on the cheek.

Grinning as she climbed out of the car, Freya waved at her boytoy.

She headed toward the house, then paused when she caught sight of Zane. He drained the last of his beer and air toasted. Fuck, she looked so damn good. The black dress draped low in front with a taunting cowl, a crisscross laced back let him know she'd ditched the bra. Those long, shapely legs were on full display, the dress ending just below her mid-thigh, her heels defining those fucking spectacular calves. A few weeks ago, he would have claimed he was a boob guy through and through. Might be a leg guy now. But damn, even braless, that was a perfect—

Freya shook her head, turning and walking toward him. He bit his lip as she strolled up the stairs, tilting his head in the foolish hope she wasn't wearing any panties. The movement nearly knocked him over, his head swimming from too much to drink.

"Alright, Sailor. Let's get you to bed," she grinned, reaching forward to give him a hand up.

"Yes, ma'am," he winked, waggling his eyebrows up and down to let her know he was fully on board.

Eyeing the empty bottles behind him, she tucked her wild hair behind her ears and set his empty bottle with the rest, and then gave him a hand up. "Oh boy, and here I felt silly for drinking too much. I was tipsy. You're hammered." While he stumbled along in front, she leaned around him to open his front door.

"Hey, I haven't been drunk since..." he closed his eyes, trying to remember. The ground rose to meet him as he crashed onto the doormat, his palms stinging as the rough fibers dug into his skin.

"I see that. You're a bit heavy, so I'm not going to even try to catch you if you fall again."

Moving his hands in for a push-up, he found his body completely uncooperative and couldn't manage the simple exercise he'd done a few dozen of this morning. "You may be right. I'm slashed," he slurred.

She laughed, "Slashed?"

Gritting his teeth, he forced a few quick push-ups, bounced up from the ground, then steadied himself against the doorjamb before his nose touched the doormat again. Calculating, he nodded, "Yeah. Somewhere between smashed and sloshed and... trashed."

Gripping her hands on his hips, she pushed him gently forward like the sexiest damn train he'd ever been a part of. Fuck, he zinged at the sensation. Couldn't get it up right now if he tried, but might be worth the effort. "In you go," she urged. "To bed."

He grinned. "You going to tuck me in?"

Driving him toward the bedroom, she chuckled as they reached the threshold. She steadied him when his head started swimming again, "Maybe you should drink some water first," she winced.

"Good idea." Without waiting, he crashed face down on the bed. A few moments later, a water glass appeared in front of his face. Dopey grin tugging at his cheeks, he dragged his ass up and sat on the side of the bed. "Thanks," he said breathlessly after gulping down the entire contents of the glass.

"Alright. Sleep it off sailor. I'll be back to check on you in the morning."

Chortling, he reached for her hand. "You'd better sleep here to make sure I'm safe all night."

"Charming," she backed away and took the empty glass from him, refilled it, and left it on the nightstand. "I'm not taking advantage of an intoxicated man."

"Come on, a few more minutes the other night and I would have taken advantage of you," he slurred.

"But you didn't. Nor will I. And I was warm and fuzzy, you're going to be lucky if you remember any of this tomorrow."

"How was your date with Dr. Practical? Was he as good of a kisser as me?"

"What was that you were saying about always putting your foot in your mouth? It might be a good time to extricate that foot and go to bed."

His stomach rolled as he let his imagination run wild; maybe that goodnight kiss had been the G-rated version compared to what they might have been up to earlier. "Didn't feel like making a night of it?"

"No."

"Did he agree to go with you to the wedding?"

"I didn't ask him."

His eyes fought to shutter closed, but he couldn't seem to stop himself from chewing on his own bullshit. "You're pretty. He's an idiot."

She stared, hesitating in his bedroom doorway with her arms crossed.

Fuck no, not sympathy. He really couldn't take it from her. Furious Freya was so much safer. "I've got nothing, Freya. No future. No dreams. And I sure as hell don't know what to do with a woman as interesting as you. You'd be bored with me in a day."

"Goodnight, Zane," she whispered, closing his bedroom door, her heels clicking across the wood floors.

Closing his eyes, he crashed and slept hard.

Tapping her foot on the floor, Freya debated. He was so trashed. Heading outside, she crossed over to the main house and eased in the front door, collapsing against it as it clicked closed.

"You okay?" Asher was dressed in nothing but jeans, filling two glasses of water in the kitchen.

"Yeah."

"Have fun on your date?"

"I did. It was nice to see Seth."

"What's bugging you?" he set the glasses down, rested his palms on the island and waited.

Exhaling every last molecule of air before speaking, she shrugged. "Zane's drunk."

"Drunk? Stoic Zane?" His brow scrunched together.

She nodded. "You should go check on him."

He stood tall, looking toward the bedroom, then to Zane.

Her face fell, "You're leaving tomorrow, aren't you?"

He nodded.

"I'll go get changed and crash on his couch."

"No, I should go. That's the whole reason I dragged him up here. Guy hasn't let himself feel a damn thing since that op."

"What happened?"

"It was right before I got out. Zane and I crossed the street to check out a stupid hunch. Jack and the other guys waited behind. Their building got hit. A lot of them didn't make it. Jack did, but he didn't walk again, then, well, you know, he passed a few weeks ago. Zane and I... not more than a scratch between us." Asher's teeth gritted together, a darkness heavy over his expression.

"And Zane just got out, right?"

"Wasn't even out two days when he got the call about Jack."

Freya stepped close and hugged her cousin. Even overseas, she'd tracked his whereabouts, not sleeping while she knew he was deployed, celebrating every return. As had his sister and his parents and aunts and uncles. Zane didn't have any of that. "You go crawl back in bed with Sophie. I'll get changed and crash on Zane's couch. Sort of my fault that he's drunk anyway." She backed away to head toward her bedroom to change.

Feet locking in place, Asher asked, "Your fault?"

"Yeah. I, well, I sort of kissed him. And he kissed me. A lot. And then we keep agreeing on how that's a dumb idea."

"What? When?"

"Um, pretty much every time we've said so much as, 'hello' to each other." She felt her cheeks go red as she recalled every touch. His hands on her, his mouth. Damn, he was a really, really good kisser.

"Okay, so he implied something about he liked you, therefore he wasn't going to do anything about it. Now you're saying the same stupid thing. What is wrong with you people?"

"From what it sounds like, he fell in love once and it was awful and he's not risking it again. I, on the other hand, have been in love many times, and always manage to get my heart broken because I'm too caught up to see the forest for the trees. I'm not getting engaged again. Fool me once, you know. Fool me three times, and I fold."

Asher winced, letting out a less-than-sympathetic laugh. "I'm sorry. But... can I be there to watch when you two get your heads out of your asses and realize that's a load of bull-shit?"

"I'm not risking getting tied up again."

Asher grinned wickedly. "You might like it."

She rolled her eyes. "Shut up. You know what I mean. You and Sophie have found this great balance. Not everyone has that ability."

"You're scared. And that's not like you."

"I am scared. Of getting my heart broken. Again. I'm tapped out."

"Just keep telling yourself that. Randy was convenient, that wasn't love. I didn't get to meet Vince or Giovanni, but trust me, Zane is twice the man they are."

"He is a good guy, I can feel that. But–"

Asher shook his head. "Nope. Stop arguing with yourself. You do what you need to do to protect yourself, and Zane will do the same. Do me a favor? Don't fight it, and see what it can be like with a good guy."

She smiled, "You're a good guy, too. Sophie's lucky."

"I know," he winked. "Goodnight."

Freya tugged off her heels and carried them back to her bedroom. She slipped off the pretty black dress she'd stolen from Sophie's closet, quite a bite shorter and fitted on her than it was on Sophie, but she didn't mind showing a little leg. Pulling on yoga pants and an old t-shirt, she slid her feet into an easy pair of sandals and packed a bag with a change of clothes, toothbrush, hairbrush, and grabbed a pil-low and blanket, unsure if he had the basics yet. Not exactly the overnight she'd been picturing with him; with how drunk he was, she might be there half of tomorrow too, if he hadn't sobered up yet or slept with his head over the toilet bowl.

Crossing through the blue glow over the driveway, she quietly entered his apartment and set her bag by the couch, quickly throwing together a makeshift bed. Before crawling into the blankets, she checked on Zane, finding him out cold, mouth open.

Watching him sleep on top of the blankets, his long limbs sprawled and making the queen-sized mattress look like a toddler bed, she resisted to the nagging hollow in the pit of her stomach, aching to get crawl in with him and make everything okay. To make sure he knew that he was a good guy. One of the best, she suspected.

Scowling, she kicked herself, dragging herself back to the couch. Dropping onto the cushion, she punched her pillow fluffy and threw the blanket over her legs. Fuck. Fuck fuck fuck. She was doing it again. What was wrong with her? A few good kisses with a gorgeous man, and she was flashing forward to snuggling and white picket fences, not giving a damn what it did to her.

How was that going to work when she went on gallery tours? When he was no longer a muse, but a brick that smashed her creativity? Or when he realized she wasn't what he'd wanted after all? That she was needy and moody and opinionated? Getting caught up in the fireworks was blinding; and she'd been burned so bad by the blasts of her past.

She sealed her eyes shut and tried fruitlessly to not imagine indulging, just to experience what she knew they would be capable of together. She was great at casual dating, sex, enjoying the company of a decent man. But there were those few she had met, like Zane, that set her heart on fire.

By late morning, Zane stumbled out of the bedroom, head in his hands to block the chipper birds and bright sun. She'd showered, brushed, changed, and curled up with a book. Cozy in the corner of the couch, Freya adjusted her coffee and set her book down.

He scowled when he saw her, "You didn't have to crash here."

"Yes, I did. You looked like hell."

While he stopped in the bathroom, she poured him a cup of coffee and a glass of orange juice. Pulling out a frying pan, she got started on a big greasy breakfast to absorb some of that liquor.

Feet shuffling across the floor, he looked like a beat-up sexy teddy bear, all drippy from the shower, rumpled and ripped. He parked at the stool where she'd set out his hangover coffee and juice. After a testing sip of coffee, he looked up at her, "You don't have to make me breakfast, too. Bad enough I acted like an ass last night."

"The worst you did was call me pretty and compliment your own kissing skills."

"I remember. It takes a hell of a lot more than that to make me forget a gorgeous woman in a little black dress," he grinned, his smile crinkling the corners of his eyes.

She cracked the eggs and added some milk and cheese, fluffing them up, enjoying the sizzle as she poured the savory mixture into the pan. "I suspect you needed to let go a bit. When's the last time you did something reckless? Alcohol-related or otherwise?"

He snorted, then gulped down the juice until only the lingering pulp coated the side of the glass. "Long time."

"You were due. Sometimes it's good to make stupid mistakes. Reset the bar a little." She'd made more than her fair share of mistakes; not learning from them would be downright moronic.

"Maybe."

"No offense Zane, but you're less of a mess than you think."

She scooped a heap of scrambled eggs into a bowl and slid it toward him, dishing up another for herself.

Inhaling, he closed his eyes before digging in. "We'll see. I've got a hell of a lot of memories from a great military career, both good and horrible. Sometimes I think I should have stayed until retirement like I'd originally planned, but I was so fucking done. And now? Now I'm a thirty-four-year old unemployed, divorced, socially-awkward nobody crashing at his only friend's parents' apartment while I come up with something to do with the rest of my life."

"So, you don't have a dream right now. That's okay. You could use a break, some time to find yourself again. You'll figure out what you want."

"Easy for you to say. You're living your dream."

"I am. And now I'm home again, another dream that doesn't jive well with my career. As glad as I am to be home, I've got so much work ahead of me, to keep this going. It wouldn't be hard to lose everything I've accomplished."

"But you know what you want."

"Mostly." She held her bowl in one hand, her fork in the other, and leaned against the opposite counter. Stuffing her mouth full with a huge bite, she shrugged, unsure what to say. That she felt lost and found all at once? Being home was amazing, but selling her work was going to be so much harder.

"Do you still need a date to the wedding?" He didn't look up, but ate another bite. Why was he so hard to read? Did he want to go? Or was he just feeling guilty?

"I think I'll go alone. Let them know I don't give a shit what they think."

He swallowed another bite and chased it with a gulp of coffee. "Whatever you think. But it's not like I've got anything else going on right now."

"Are you sure? I mean, it won't be fun. It will be a gigantic party filled with family I haven't seen in years."

"Lake Tahoe you said? I've never been, but I've heard it's beautiful. We can go as friends, maybe make out a little, nothing major, then we can go hiking, swimming, whatever."

She grinned and rinsed her bowl out before adding it to the empty dishwasher. "Make out?"

"I'm not saying it's why I'm offering to go with you, but let's face it, it's going to happen."

"The hotel is all booked up. Think we can bunk together and not go beyond making out?"

"I'll do my best, but no promises." He glanced down between his legs and shrugged, "This poor guy hasn't seen much action in the last... way too fucking long."

Shaking her head, she couldn't help the corners of her mouth that turned up, the humming between her own legs as she debated if this was the dumbest decision she'd made in her entire life. And she'd done some stupid things. But, as she'd said, sometimes you have to make a few mistakes to reset the bar. "Alright. I'll call the airline and see if there are any seats left. If we do end up having sex, remember, what happens in Tahoe stays in Tahoe."

Shaking his head, full grin spread across his cheeks, he cleared his dish, came around behind her and pressed against her backside, one hand splayed across her abdomen while the other reached around her to put his bowl in the sink. "Then we'd better make the most of it," his gruff voice whispered.

Pinning her against the counter, her back still toward him, he brushed his lips along her bare shoulder. Trailing delicate kisses on her skin, the tip of his tongue tracing the contour of her neck, he tormented her. Her legs trembled beneath her until she wanted to start their weekend early. The heat of his mouth on her, the subtle seduction proving exactly why she couldn't keep him. Already, he was so much more than Vince and Giovanni and Randy all combined; if he asked, she'd strip down right here and give herself body and soul.

Turning in his arms, her gaze brushed over his perfect lips, swept over his chiseled jaw, and locked onto those storybook eyes. No wonder she was a goner. Her pathetic brain turned her right into some princess in a remote tower, pining away for the prince that would inevitably let her down. "One weekend. That's it."

No hesitation, he meant it when he agreed. "One weekend."

7

Room Service, Please

S hifting in his seat, Zane stretched his legs out front and wished she'd let him upgrade their seats to first class. *Her cousin, her family*, she'd said, so she insisted on paying.

His fucking knees. Now that the seatbelt sign was on, he moved his foot to the aisle in a bleak effort to get comfortable.

As he closed his eyes, Freya chuckled at his side, "I'm sorry."

"For what?"

"You look like a salmon in a sardine can," she laughed again.

Turning his head, he opened his eyes and let the corner of his mouth quirk up. "Can I please upgrade us to first class on the way back?"

She nodded, still grinning at him, those devilish blues taunting him.

Closing the narrow distance between them, he brushed his lips over hers long enough to absorb the zing he'd come to crave, then settled back and shut his eyes again to relive her taste, the exquisite spice of those lips.

"My parents are only three rows back," she hissed.

The plane jerked forward and back, then rolled away from the gate, the miniscule vent above his head blasting a weak stream of cool air over his eyelids.

"So?" he grinned to himself.

"So?" Her whisper turned to a shrill mumbling, "I told them you agreed to come as a pity date. That you're Asher's friend and you had nothing else to do this weekend and I'm paying you back with a painting."

He could picture the frantic look on her face, those fiery blues sparking at him without even looking. Sighing, poorly attempting to hide his smug grin, he said, "Didn't want to admit you're paying me back with a weekend of nonstop sex?"

Her quiet chuckle erased the last shred of doubt he'd had that this was a stupid idea. "Whatever happened to hiking and swimming?"

"That was before you agreed to sex. I see no reason to even leave our room now."

"I believe I acknowledged that sex was going to happen. But you do have a point. Except we'll have to leave for the wedding."

"Yeah, that. Then right back upstairs." He adjusted his pants and was glad he'd worn thick jeans. One weekend to make up for the last two, almost three years of celibacy. Not exactly by choice, more lack of interest. Too much shit on his mind. May as well make the most of it; his interest was definitely stirred.

"Could you at least pretend we're pretending, for my parents? My mom will get all excited if she thinks we're into each other, and my dad will hold a gun to *my* back and force us to the sacrificial altar."

"And I thought Asher was a commitment-phobe."

"Do your parents get you?"

Well that blew his good mood. He opened his eyes and sat up; his hamstrings spasmed from the lack of space. "No."

Freya bit her lip and lowered her eyebrows in a sincere apology.

Exhaling, he sucked it up to get it over with. "They don't even know I'm out."

"I'm sorry," she reached over and traced her thumb along the edge of his jaw.

"Not the first time they've let me down. And I have no doubt I've let them down many times too."

"It must be tempting to give up on them."

"Tempting?" he raised an eyebrow. "Done. I'm not wasting my time on them again."

Her hand stilled, resting against his cheek. Trailing his fingers along the contours of her wrist, he kissed her palm, then laced his fingers with hers and lowered their joined hands to the armrest between them.

As much as his parents were worthless, hers seemed great so far. When they'd met up at the airport, Freya's parents had immediately enveloped her and asked to meet her young man and fussed and fretted as parents are supposed to. Her father had given him the evil eye, until Freya had made it clear he was coming as her plus-one as a favor. Then he'd only given an occasional suspicious sideways glance. Her mother had hugged him as fiercely as she had her daughter, nearly busting his ribs with her enthusiasm. As much as they didn't understand Freya, they loved her.

During takeoff, Freya inhaled slow and easy, watching out the window as the engines roared, the plane steadily gaining altitude. He watched as her eyes danced with merriment as the cars shrunk to ant-size, the highways no more than lines in the sea of green, and they rose above the clouds. Pulling her feet up, she slipped off her shoes and pulled a sketchbook and a tin of pencils from her purse.

He closed his eyes and took advantage of the numbing rumble of the engine, the quiet murmurings of the other passengers. Force of habit, he was out like a light the second they reached the clouds. Never knew when you could rest again; banking sleep was necessary.

Flashing under his lids, strobe-like blasts threatened to nail a hole in the cargo bay. Jerking up and down, the turbulence tugged at the wings. The snapping of tie-downs behind him. One of the crates whipped from its remaining safety strap.

Unbuckling his harness, he braced his gait and moved to lock it down. Busting completely free, the crate surged toward him, on the way to knock him flat and everyone sleeping behind him. Appearing at his side, Jack and Asher shoved forward. As a unit, they slammed the weight of their combined strength and halted the crate before it took anyone out.

Not fucking fast enough.

Dropping hundreds of feet before stabilizing again, the plane shuddered, the crate rose in the air. In slow motion, the massive thing slammed back down.

A dense metal hook smashed back and cracked into Jack's skull, knocking him out cold.

Shouting over the thunder, the engines screaming to stay in the air, Asher snapped his attention back to the danger they could fix.

While Jack lie bleeding on the floor, Asher and Zane heaved and shifted the crate back against the wall, strapping it back down.

"Hey, it's okay." Freya rested her palm on his cheek, repeating her reassurances like a plea.

Sealing his eyes shut, he blocked the memory that wasn't a memory. Where Jack had jumped back up, unphased and larger than life, Zane's twisted subconscious seemed bent on killing his friend every time he closed his eyes.

Like a never-ending punishment for the time Jack hadn't gotten back up again, but Zane had.

Everything blurring around him, nausea wrenching his gut, he found Freya's intense blue eyes and locked on to the anchor, her familiar voice centering him. Blinking, he inhaled slow and steady.

"It's okay," she said again.

He clenched his teeth and gave her a subtle nod, letting her know he was back.

Above, the seatbelt sign flipped on. The pilot's voice came through, letting them know it was ninety degrees without a trace of wind. Fucking Reno. What the hell was he thinking?

⚘

Sharing the rental car with her parents had been stupid. Zane hardly said a word, his poker face out in full force. Her parents made small talk, her mother saying how bummed she was they'd missed the bridal shower, her father wondering out loud if Uncle Joe still had the boat so they could go fishing.

While offering the occasional nod or polite conversation-furthering question for her parents to keep things light, Freya linked hands with Zane. He stared out the window, expressionless as they passed casino after casino. She remembered Tahoe as beautiful, but Reno was not her type of place.

When he finally glanced her way, she raised her eyebrows, silently asking if he was okay. He nodded, then looked back out the window again. The moment they reached the hotel, he grabbed their garment bag and his backpack, linking his hand with hers as they walked inside.

While she checked them in, he walked to the wall of windows overlooking the lake and stared out at the mountains in the distance. Nodding to her dad while her mother asked the concierge about what sort of view they had and what time the restaurant was open for breakfast and was there room service, Freya accepted the pair of room keys from the attendant and joined Zane.

"All good?" she asked.

He nodded again, his jaw still flexing instead of opening to talk.

She slipped her hand back into his and led the way to the elevator. Up to the fourth floor, she held the key in front of the second to last door at the end of the hall, the light blinking green as the lock clicked open. Travel days were the worst, but this was so much better than crossing the Atlantic and the continental US. No jetlag was brilliant.

Zane breathed deeply as he followed her inside, his shoulders relaxing as he hung the garment bag in the closet and stashed his backpack under it. Freya dashed in the bathroom to refresh, unsure what to expect when she returned.

When she came out, he was standing on the deck, looking out at the lake, the mountains, a breeze rustling through his hair, across his travel-wrinkled shirt.

She joined him on the private deck and wrapped her arms around his waist, pressing her face against his back. His hands rested over hers, and they stood unmoving together. Laughter and squeals of delight radiated up from the beach. Boats zipped across the choppy water. The breeze was a cool relief from the summer day.

His fingers laced with hers, shifting his shirt and moving her hand to his skin. Combusting on contact, she traced along the ridges under her fingertips, goosebumps prickling over his skin in her wake.

Tugging at the bottom of his t-shirt, she eased up the cotton fabric.

As he helped her pull it over his head, he turned and pitched the shirt in the room, immediately wrapping his arms around her. Mouth on her neck, her collarbone, her shoulder, he didn't say a word.

His hands slid down her waist and gripped her hips, lifting her off the ground and carrying her into the room, lips still trailing over her skin.

He lowered her to the bed, following close and finally kissing her. Tenderly, decadently, he tasted. Melting, zinging as he caressed her tongue with his, his leisurely exploration, each savoring kiss sending chills over her skin as every nerve in her body heated in response.

When he paused, she opened her eyes. Whatever had haunted him dissipated; nothing but the moment in his gaze, locked on with hers with a hungry curiosity that stopped her pulse, setting off a new rhythm as the intensity in his look jumpstarted it back into beating.

Reaching down, he slid his hand under her shirt, tracing up and moving under her bra, encircling her breasts with his hands. Her breath caught in her throat, words unable to describe the sensation that coursed through her veins.

Needing more, she tugged her top over her head, snapped off her bra and flung it out of the way.

Groaning, he lowered and pressed his open mouth between her breasts. Moving, tantalizing, his tongue grazed across her curves, finally taking a tight bud between his teeth, deep in his mouth until she cried out and begged for more.

Pheromones blazing, Freya was lost in him. Later, she'd remind herself this was going to be a problem. For now? She felt nothing but him, and his devastating effect on her.

He rose to his knees, still straddling her legs. She sat up and looked up at him, unbuttoning his jeans and lowering the zipper, eliciting a rich, rumbling moan. She grasped his cock in her hands. Grinning, loving seeing him nearly naked and flawlessly built and completely under her spell, she shifted and ran her tongue along the length of his shaft.

He groaned again, moving back out of her reach in regretful torture. "Two years," he muttered. "Almost three." He rose from the bed and tugged off his jeans the rest of the way, snagging a condom from the pocket. Finally, the corners of his mouth turned up as he stood at the edge of the bed, "This isn't going to last long as it is."

Taking the condom from his hand, she tore open the wrapper and slid it over him. As his eyes rolled back in his head, she murmured, "I guess I'd better make it worth your while." She nodded toward the bed.

Moving onto his back, he grinned up at her, as relaxed and happy as she'd ever seen. Imprinting the image in her mind, she hoped she could hold onto every detail to paint him when she got home; from the stubble on his jaw to the upturned corners of his mouth, the fascination in his eyes, each precise muscle of his torso.

Lowering herself onto his rock-hard cock, blazing energy coursed through her as they joined. Adjusting to the thick thrill, she let out a gasp. Rocking, heat radiated from her core, irreparably altering every molecule inside her.

As she climbed higher, grinding, pumping, she tightened around him. Grasping her hips, he met her gaze. Moving her faster as he thickened inside her, she soared higher and higher until an enchanted scream rose from her center as orgasm rocketed through her. He eased her pace, letting her slide up and down, riding the wave as the consuming sensation slowed to a vibrating simmer.

They moved fluidly together, building the foundation stronger as she still teetered on the precipice. Riding higher and faster, each thrust sent her a little further down the lane she knew she'd lose herself in as soon as she gave herself to him.

And she was having a bitch of a time regretting it.

Another orgasm rushed through her as they found their rhythm together, wild and fast and free.

Slowing together, spent, alive, she rested her body on his, skin against skin. Pressing his lips to her forehead, he didn't say a word, mindlessly tracing his fingers over her shoulder.

As the intensity faded to a sweet snuggle, coherent thought managed to bubble into her brain. She nearly cussed and argued and ran away... dammit, this was exactly what she feared; addicting, vibrant, extraordinary.

8

Stupid Pheromones

"No, it's the stupid pheromones. I told you they would be the end of me." Freya kicked off her shoes as they reached the beach, looping her fingers through the straps.

Tammy handed Freya back her coffee and gave her that maternal smile that had Freya confessing her predicament as soon as they'd stepped outside. "Honey, I know pheromones are a real thing. But I think you put a bit too much stock into what the rest of us call good chemistry."

"Mom. Good chemistry doesn't turn you into a blubbering mess like this. I mean, the man's unstoppable. We already had to order extra condoms from room service. A toothbrush, now that's an embarrassing thing to admit you forgot. But to call for more condoms?"

"Okay, good sex then. A healthy dose of lust. And maybe, now I know you don't want to think about it, but maybe something more."

"No. No no no. Not going there. That's where my brain fizzles and I get caught up in everything *him* and start turning into one of those idiots that invests everything into the relationship and next thing you know it I'm sitting on the sidewalk with an overstuffed suitcase and mascara caked on my cheeks and about ten bucks in my pocket."

"You'd better not have ended up like that, or I'd be offended you didn't call me to come get you."

"Well, not exactly that theatrical, but that's what it felt like." That wasn't until after she'd thrown stuff at him and kicked him out, and then realized she couldn't afford the place alone.

"It's been one night. That doesn't mean you're giving anything up for this man."

The breeze sent her dark waves in a chaotic spiral so she could hardly appreciate the gorgeous view. "Not yet. But I will. I've done it before, and I'll do it again. I'll get so caught up in the physical side, I won't notice that he's a jerk. We should settle down and have kids right away because that's what he wants. Or I'll let him take the last of my cerulean blue because he has to nail that sunset where my landscape is fine the way it is. Or give up my Christmas because he can't leave *his* family." She hadn't even touched her coffee yet, too wired to risk the caffeine. "What if I do something really stupid and get engaged again?" Her eyes were wide, the scenery completely distorted.

Linking arms and steadying their pace, Tammy sighed, "Freya. Honey. I won't act naïve and pretend you haven't had enough lovers to not be so swayed by good sex." Her mom's cheeks burned red.

Freya stopped and took in extra air, the wind whipping her dress in a tangle around her legs. "I've had enough lovers to know it's not supposed to be *that* good. Mom, I did things with him last night I would never even have thought of. I feel like I should write a book on the subject now to let others know everything they're missing out on."

Keeping her voice calm, Tammy said, "And what does Zane say about all this?"

"That he's had a lot of time alone to develop some rather elaborate fantasies."

Cheeks now as red as the hotel beach chairs, Tammy clarified, "I mean, is he looking for more?"

"No. He had a terrible divorce and never wants to get married again."

"So what are you worried about?"

A nauseating wave rolled over Freya's cheeks, "Even worse. What if I talk him into getting engaged? And then he's resentful and I give up my own interests because I'm so caught up in him and he goes back into the military because I've spent all of our savings on a career that's never going to pay off."

Halting their walk, Tammy yanked back on Freya's quickening pace, her voice sharp, "Freya. I love you girl, but your imagination has always gotten the better of you. Be the artist you are and experience the now. Feel what you need to feel. And when you're satisfied, put down your brush. You can't decide how you feel about the painting when you haven't even finished it."

"Wow, Mom, that was a nice analogy. I mean, I might have picked something a bit more germane, but..." She grinned a tease at her mother.

"Oh hush. I'm not the artist, you are. You figure it out." Tammy bubbled over with self-effacing laughter, Freya's mood lightening right along with her. "You will always be my independent daughter. No relationship is perfect; your father and I have had to compromise for each other, but we also build each other up. Why don't you take things one day at a time? If he doesn't build you up, then you end it."

"Okay," she took a steadying breath. Although she'd visited as often as she could, it had been tough living so far away. "I'm just done with the whole thing. You and Dad are so good together. I'm surrounded by all these people that are able to make it work. After three failed attempts at getting serious, I'm scared."

"Of course you are. Trust me. When it's right? You'll know."

Freya wasn't so sure about that. She'd *known* enough times to get engaged. But her mother was a hopeless romantic. Like Freya used to be. "Have you seen Lulu or Uncle Joe or Aunt Noelle yet?"

She shook her head. "They're still over at the cabin with the rest of the wedding party. But I think most of the guests of the hotel are here for the wedding."

"Really? There are some rowdy folks here. I figured there was some frat reunion or something."

"Yep," Tammy muttered. "Lulu and her fiancé's friends. I talked with your Aunt Gloria after we arrived yesterday; apparently Lulu is a bit of a partier."

Wincing, Freya paused for a sip of coffee to wash down that image. "Well this should be an interesting evening. Six o'clock?"

"Ceremony is at six. Shall we meet you at your room at five thirty? The ceremony will take place on the hotel lawn, then, from what I hear, all of those doors will open up to the dining room for the reception."

As they strolled back toward the hotel, she watched as uniformed hotel employees were already starting to set up a few hundred chairs. It was a nice spot, but holy shit, there had to be three hundred guests coming. And she'd felt like her hundred-guest wedding had been big.

R esting his feet on the deck rail, Zane sipped his coffee and looked out over the lake, already alive with tourists escaping the sweltering cities downriver. Or, hell, these might all be wedding guests. Below, a few hundred chairs were being set up, a portable arbor, flowerpots holding down a red carpet. Fancy. Wonder how much this weekend set them back. Almost as overdone as his own wedding had been.

His phone buzzed on the table. Rising to his feet, he left the crisp morning breeze. The blankets were in a tangle on the floor, too far gone to be remade without starting fresh. Damn, Freya had been insatiable. He didn't know it was possible to do it that much, and still want her again. After their naked room service breakfast, she'd left for a walk with her mom, and he'd wandered down to the giftshop and bought out their stock of condoms.

Remembering what he'd come in for, he picked up his phone before it went to voicemail.

Gritting his teeth, he almost didn't answer. Shouldn't have. And he'd been having such a nice vacation.

"Yeah," he answered. It had either been that, or *about fucking time*.

"Zane, dear. I'm so glad we finally connected."

Connected. Sure. Whatever you want to call it. "Hey, Mom."

"So you're home and safe now?"

What?

"From your deployment?"

"No. I'm out. Done. Civilian. Moved to Washington."

Long pause. "Oh, that's just wonderful. DC is so nice this time of year."

"State."

"Even lovelier. Why don't you come for a visit?"

"Thanks, but I'm really not looking to travel right now." As far as they needed to know anyway.

"So the reason I called today is to let you know that we finally welcomed Blaire as a full partner in the firm."

"What?" He'd known she'd transferred back east after their divorce, but that she'd had the gall to join his parents' firm?

"Yes. She interned with us after leaving San Diego. I thought you knew?"

Uh, no.

"Zane?"

"Yeah. I'm here."

"Well, I was talking with her about you two and how good you two had been together–"

What the fuck? "No. We were awful together."

"And I was thinking you should come home, at least for a visit. I'm sure you've both grown up so much."

"I've got to go."

"Wait, dear. I know you must have hard feelings about the way things ended."

"Yes, I do."

"Come visit and see for yourself. I think you two will get along famously if you give her a chance to show you how much she's changed."

"Fuck no."

"You might change your mind, see what sparks are still be there. Wouldn't that be wonderful, if you two could reunite, the firm will grow and be fully Harris-owned, and we'd get to share more of your life. I'm sure you're rusty, but you could start slow and it will all come back to you."

"I like where I'm at."

"Then we would love to come for a visit. To see what you're up to. I have no doubt Blaire would love to come, too."

"No." He cringed, walking back outside to figure out how to get through to the dense woman that Blaire and he were *never* going to happen again. He looked down and saw Freya strolling down the sidewalk, her wild curls wickedly tossed about from the windy walk, her black cotton dress dancing over her skin with each step, tangling in her legs with each gust. "That might get weird. I, uh... I remarried."

Shit, had he really just said that? He knew his mother wouldn't stop once she'd found something worth hounding him about. Didn't she ever wonder why he never came home to visit? Normally their calls were easier; his parents loved talking about themselves. When he'd called at Christmas, they told him all about their new puppy. The Christmas before, they'd decided he should invest in a bamboo manufacturer with them.

Usually, it was more work-based, like today. The Blaire approach was new. And horrible. Had they been waiting until he was out to pounce, knowing that had been the last straw that had brought on the divorce all those years ago?

"Oh. Of course. When did you get married? I mean–"

Was she offended to not get invited to his fictitious wedding? She'd missed enough damn milestones. Or was it that he hadn't married the woman she'd picked out? Again?

"Well, your father and I will still come. I would love to explore the latest earthquake designs, and we could catch up with you and meet your wife."

Shit. Foot irretrievably in mouth. Again. Maybe Freya would return the favor and be his fake wife for a weekend. He sure as hell didn't want to face them alone anyway.

The lock disengaged, the knob turning. "We'll see. Gotta go." He clicked off, headed back inside and dropped the phone onto the side table before he chucked it out the damn window.

Freya strolled in, an amused smile on her face. "Apparently this wedding will be one big frat party," she laughed, slipping off her flip-flops and tossing them into the closet.

He winced. "Please tell me we don't have to stay for the whole thing."

Tugging her dress over her head as she strolled closer, she rolled her eyes, "I think we should make a brief appearance, then come back up here."

Sauntering toward her, he pitched his shirt.

Their hands were busy the moment they reached each other.

$$9$$

The Aunts Go Marching

Music pumped in through the open deck door. Unraveling himself from Freya's long limbs, her wild hair, Zane dropped his legs over the side of the bed. Grinning in loopy sex delirium like he was, she sat up and wrapped around him.

"We've got at least another hour," she murmured as she trailed kisses along the back of his shoulder, her breath on his skin flooding heat through his veins. Even after an afternoon of sex, shower, a few rounds of SkipBo, then sex again.

"You said that an hour ago. Aren't your parents meeting us here in..." he glanced at the clock, "Oh shit. Fifteen minutes?"

She squealed and threw her legs over. "Shit. We need to get ready."

Chuckling under his breath at her bare ass dashing into the bathroom, he headed to the closet and unzipped the garment bag, pulling out his slacks and button-up shirt. No fucking way on a tie or jacket for a frat wedding.

Clanking around in the bathroom, finally dumping out her make-up bag into the sink, Freya snapped open her eyeliner and leaned into the mirror, not seeming to care in the least that he could see her "process," as his ex had called it. She was about done by the time he was dressed. Standing next to her, he pulled his hair junk out of his bag and tried to smooth the disarray.

He glanced over, catching Freya's hesitant, lip-biting smile in the mirror. "What?" he asked.

She moved closer and ruffled her fingers in his hair. "I like it unruly. Tame doesn't suit you." Slipping past him, she headed into the room and pulled her dress from the garment bag.

Checking his reflection, he didn't mind what he saw. He ought to be offended, but she was right. Accenting the cowlick rather than flattening it looked way better.

Reentering the room, his heart lurched in his chest as he saw Freya teetering on one foot while putting on her heels. Damn, she was a work of art. Her hair was still wild, but whatever she'd done to it, now each curl was bold. Dressed in a sapphire blue slip dress that clung to all the right places with strappy, icepick heels, she strutted toward him with unabashed self-assurance. Stopping inches away, she hooked her hands in his belt and grinned at him, those intense blue eyes seeing more of himself than he did.

Tracing a finger down her silver teardrop necklace, he wanted to say a million things. Tell her how fucking gorgeous she was. How he didn't want the weekend to end. That damn pang gripped in his chest, thundering that he was onto something.

Pulse racing, he worked up the nerve to believe it. As he opened his mouth, unsure of his next words, she placed a finger over his lips and shook her head.

A knock at the door chilled things in an instant. Leaving him high and dry, she headed to let in her parents. Glancing to the bed, he realized it looked like the sex-fest it had been since they'd checked in yesterday. Grabbing the blankets, he tossed them back on the bed, just as the door opened.

Her parents breezed in. Tammy gave Freya a light, no-wrinkle hug, saying, "Honey, you look so beautiful."

Eamon nodded to Zane, speaking softly while Tammy walked out to watch the crowd filtering in below, he said, "Thanks for coming. I know Freya was nervous about facing everyone again."

Thanks? No idea how to respond, he nodded.

Glancing out to ensure they weren't heard, Eamon said, "Can't blame her. Freya's always been sensitive. Feels things more intensely than most."

Okay... He wasn't wrong, but it felt like a strange time to be having this conversation.

Eyes wandering to the single, hastily made bed, Eamon looked back at him, not indicating his judgment on the observation one way or another. "When she left Randy, it was incredibly brave. Can't say many others would have had the nerve to listen to their heart and not go through with it under all that pressure. Broke her heart to do so. Gives her heart so readily, which has made her distrustful of the concept in general."

Had she said her parents didn't get her? No, they understood her remarkably well. May not have a damn thing in common, but they knew their daughter. He muttered, "I know how she feels."

"Whatever's going on between you two, it's a good thing. You're steady. She needs that. Like I suspect you could use some of her passion for everything."

And he thought Freya panicked at the idea? Pulse accelerating, vision darkening, Zane nodded. "Maybe."

Freya and Tammy were rolling their eyes and laughing secretly as they came back in. Linking hands with him, Freya squeezed lightly and said, "I am apologizing in advance. Between the already-drunk college kids and my large extended family, well, it's not going to be relaxing."

Eamon shrugged and moved toward the door. "Once a decade, Freya. That's all I ask." She snorted but followed along.

The moment they stepped off the elevator, they were immediately engulfed by the swarm. It had sounded busy from their room, but in the thick of it, the chaos was deafening.

Sweat beaded on his forehead, his palms, yet he was chilled to the bone.

Fucking shit, he needed to get the hell out of here.

The elevator dinged closed behind them. No exit in sight; the lobby was completely overrun.

His vision tunneled. With each breath, he felt the pungent odor of bloody, sweat-soaked SEALs packed into the back of the Hummer, his ears ringing as each explosion might be the one that ends it.

Locking her hand around his, unbreakable, Freya had him out of there so damn fast. Like a salmon plunging upstream, she powered through. She kept them moving until the crowd thinned, then kept on pushing until they reached the beach.

Inhaling deeply, he blinked away the blinding panic. "Thanks," he nodded.

"Thought you were going to pass out on me."

"Sometimes I can't even guess what's going to trigger it. I'd heard some of the other guys saying they don't do crowds. Generally I keep to myself so I had no idea how bad it would be. Fuck," he exhaled again, pacing and dragging his fingers through his hair.

"We don't have to go back," she stood a few feet back as he walked it off, her expression so soft, empathetic.

"No. I'll be fine, as long as we can stay outside." The music, the shouting, the shoving, the elbow-to-elbow suffocating laughter; it was all too much.

"Okay," she said, not a trace of martyrdom in her tone.

Stepping closer, he took her hand again, resisting the impulse to pull her against him and hold on for dear life. "Really. Thank you."

Strolling down the path, Tammy and Eamon wore equally empathetic expressions. Each carried an extra champagne, passing one to Freya and one to him. Eamon said as he handed him a glass, "How long were you in?"

Downing half the champagne in one gulp, he came up for air and said, "Twelve years."

"That's a long time. Didn't want to finish it out?"

Staring out over the water, he shook his head. "I'd planned on it. Then a good buddy got hurt and Asher bailed. I was done."

"Sounds like you made the decision that was best for you. I know Asher's glad to have you in town. Thanks for serving our country," he nodded.

Zane had heard that more than a few times. Seemed to mean more when genuinely spoken like this. He nodded.

The music in the distance softened, and a garbled voice combated the static of the subwoofer, announcing that guests should find their seats, the ceremony would be starting soon. Still connected, Freya turned into him and squeezed his hand, "Okay?"

"Yeah."

Her parents headed up the steps first. Like an anchor, Freya didn't let go. They sat and watched the long, boring ceremony in which the bride sobbed, the groom high-fived his best man at one point, and they were announced as married with an abrupt transition to a synthesized rave beat.

Between the panic attack and the heat and the champagne, Zane's head was pounding. No sign of water anywhere, he snagged a drink from the nearest server carting a silver tray. His throat was scratchy, his tongue coated in sawdust, he was so damn thirsty. Taking a sip, he cringed and whispered, "What the hell is this?"

Freya took a sip of her own, "Holy smokes that's sweet. I'd heard they were planning to serve a signature cocktail. This must be it. Tastes like strawberry prune juice."

He took another sip, searching around for a bar or any sort of liquid aside from this awful shit. Nothing.

Downing it quickly, Freya coughed, then searched the crowd. "We've lost my parents. I wonder if anyone will notice if we sneak away now? I was going to make some excuse to my folks, but I'll text them."

"I have a raging headache, if that helps."

She turned to him and looked straight past him, a gigantic phony smile taking over her face. "Aunt Bette. It's so wonderful to see you."

Eager arms clutched at Freya, nearly ripping her hand from his. Freya held strong so he didn't lose his lifeline and get washed downstream. He'd faced some terrifying enemies; hell week wasn't close to as overwhelming as this wedding.

"Oh my, Freya dear. How you've grown up," Aunt Bette pulled away and looked her up and down; quite an eye for detail, she genuinely perused. Clearly didn't realize the gesture was intended to be a compliment, not an inspection.

Freya continued her phony smile, really bringing out that dimple.

"Gosh, I think last time I saw you was at your wedding. Well, I guess I didn't actually see you at your wedding, but, well. You know," Bette's mouth soured and eyebrows dropped as if it were some sort of shameful secret.

"Uh-huh," Freya nodded.

Zane pulled her hand and started walking to the far and of the lawn, "I'm so sorry, but I think I see Eamon calling us over."

"Nice to see you Aunt Bette," Freya continued her smile until she could turn her back. She muttered to Zane, "I think I have a headache now too."

As they passed another caterer serving those awful drinks, they each grabbed one and downed it. It seemed to be mostly juice, so there was hope it would help with the headache.

"My dad wasn't really looking for us, right? Because he's the opposite direction."

He smiled sheepishly, "Must have been one of his brothers or something; I could swear it was him."

The music shifted to a mopey, almost elevator rhythm. That damn ear-splitting voice announced it was time for dinner.

Freya shook her head, "We can order room service."

The scent of prime rib wafted toward them, his stomach growling for something greasy to combat the awful cocktail that was tearing up his gut and making his head swim. "Let's grab some of that, then we can go back upstairs."

As they headed for the food line, another aunt found them. "Hi, Aunt Del," Freya's phony grin began anew.

"Freya, I can't believe it's you. I haven't seen you since–"

Zane cleared his throat, "Wow, another aunt. Freya, how many aunts do you have? What a wonderful family." He sucked at this sort of thing, but would figure something out to keep Freya from getting a cheek spasm with her overly cheerful smiles.

Del shifted her gaze toward him, her hair, as black and curly as Freya's, whooshing from the movement. "Hello. You must be Freya's...?"

Nice one. He resisted the urge to roll his eyes. Freya gulped the last of her drink and blurted out, "Friend."

"How nice," Del's smile oozed with saccharine charm. Raising her eyebrows up and down lecherously, she leaned closer to Freya. "He's very handsome. Tall and strapping young man you've got. Bette says she heard rumor he's a Navy SEAL," she whispered to Freya, as if he wouldn't be able to hear if she spoke out of the corner of her mouth. Her eyebrows waggled up and down, "You know they write romance novels about those guys. How close are they to the truth?" Her eyes tactlessly drifted down and wandered over his package.

Holy shit, how much had she had to drink? She giggled, a hiccup following close behind.

Freya nodded, whispering back out of the corner of her mouth, joining her aunt at mentally undressing him.

"They're close, but, really, they underestimate the stamina and dick-size."

Del's eyes widened and she looked constipated as she struggled to come up with a retort.

Zane's breath rushed from his chest as he grasped what Freya had just said; he gulped as he struggled to adapt a poker face. Taking advantage of the pause, Freya smiled to Del, "Let's try to catch up later." She dragged Zane along as he gulped down the last of his odd beverage.

"What was that?" he muttered.

"I'm sorry, I couldn't help it. For my bridal shower, crazy Aunt Del bought me one of those slutty teddy get-ups, all red and lacy, with a book of sex tips."

"What?" his eyes crossed at the odd relationship. His family was crazy, but they *never* talked about things like sex.

"Seriously. She thought it was hilarious, as did half my other aunts, and they spent the rest of the evening acting like I was a virgin bride and telling me all about penises and orgasms and masturbation. I've spent the last decade trying to flush the vivid imagery from my brain."

Appearing like a mirage, Tammy and Eamon appeared carrying two plates each. Tammy smiled softly, "By the time you two made it through all the aunts, the food would have been gone. Will you sit and eat with us?"

His stomach rumbled at the scent of food, fully rebelling at the sugar and bitter of that damn drink. Nodding, he accepted a plate and they found a table at the edge of the lawn overlooking the water. For a while, the four of them were alone, enjoying the momentary quiet, the rest of the crowd clustered around the buffet table.

As he was finishing up his salad, another aunt, Gloria, with her husband, appeared and joined them at their isolated table. This one wasn't as bad. Gloria was Eamon's spitting image, with the dark curly hair and deep blue eyes, the single dimple.

Clearly this is the side Freya got her height and looks from. How many sisters did Eamon have, anyway?

They made small talk for a bit, commenting on the bride's dress, the energy of the wedding party and their friends. They almost seemed normal.

Her aunt looked to Freya and asked, "How long have you two known each other?"

Chewing her salad for an eternity, Freya nodded as if the simple gesture would answer the question. Nope. Now all eyes stared at the two of them.

Zane took this one, his expression deadpan, "Feels like I've known her all my life."

Hand to her heart, her aunt smiled, "That's so sweet. Truly. Sometimes you can tell when things are right." She looked around conspiratorially, "Not to judge, but maybe Lulu should have had the guts to get the hell out before the ceremony like Freya did."

Tammy slapped her knee she laughed so hard. "You said it, not me. But you're absolutely right."

She sipped on a glass of water. Where had she found water? Gloria added to Freya, "I see Del found you. She still talks about how she saved you from a passionless marriage."

Freya cringed, nodding with her lips pursed tight in disgust.

Tammy rolled her eyes, "Oh boy. Did she say anything?"

Letting a giggle out, Freya bit her lip impishly, "She ogled Zane and pretty much asked what he's like in the sack."

Clearing his throat, Eamon looked out on the water. "So, Oliver, you been out fishing yet?"

Oliver winked at his wife before responding. "Not yet. We should buzz over to Joe's and take him out with us. When do you fly out?"

"Not until late tomorrow."

A server came around and set a plate of cupcakes on their table. Zane grabbed one and finished it off in two bites, but wished he hadn't, the aftertaste was ripe with sugar and whatever weird cooking oil they'd used, making his tongue feel like a sweaty block of plywood.

He was about to warn Freya they were awful, but it was too late. Her face scrunched as she finished hers. In the distance, the music changed again and almost sounded appealing for dancing. The bride and her father spun together on an expansive dance floor surrounded by globe lights. The sun set in the distance and the sky began to darken.

Zane stood and held his hand out to ask Freya to join him. She slid her hand into his and rose from the table. Giving a soft wave to the rest of the table, they snuck away.

"One dance before we head up?" He asked as they crossed the lawn.

"Sure," she grinned.

A server handed them each a glass of champagne and continued to pass out drinks. As they reached the dance floor, typical, the music stopped. A hammy-ass toast from the best man, the maid of honor, the father of the bride... until their champagne was gone. Damn, his head was swimming already, his headache dulled thanks to all the liquor, but tomorrow was going to suck.

As the music started back up again, Freya looped her arms around him and swayed with the hokey tune. "Too much champagne," she muttered against his chest, slurring a little.

"Exactly what I was thinking. I think that cocktail was..." he trailed off as he lost his train of thought. His chest rattled as laughter threatened. Why was that so funny?

Freya pinched his side, "Are you laughing?"

A loopy giggle bubbled up in his throat. "Apparently," he slurred. Even his teeth felt numb.

Giggling like the boisterous partiers, she held his hand and spun out for a twirl.

He wound her back in and wrapped his arms around her waist. Her hands laced around the back of his neck, pulling him close and kissing his brains out in the middle of the crowd.

A million tiny lightbulbs flashed on with a thousand ideas all at once as every train of thought that had run through his head over the past month collided in a jumble of contorted metal. Unlocking his lips from Freya's, he caught his breath. "I'm past slashed."

She devoured him again in a ravenous kiss, then pulled away. "Stoned off our asses. The drinks or the cupcakes or both, but," she inhaled slowly and blinked a few times.

"Let's go upstairs and get some water and sober up. I don't trust a damn thing around here."

Glancing around, Freya nodded. "I wondered why there were no kids here. Huh. Yes. Let's get the hell out of here. I'm so hungry. Let's get takeout from that place across the street first."

10

The Next Day

Mouth parched like she'd swallowed a jar of glue then slept with her mouth open, underwire digging into her chest, thong riding up her crack, Freya groaned and raised her sandpaper eyelids. What an awful night. If her cousin hadn't taken off yet, she was going to tear her a new one for lacing something they'd ingested. Wasn't that illegal? And potentially dangerous?

As she shifted to drink a gallon of water then take a long, hot shower, Freya found herself locked in a firm embrace. Zane's arm and leg were wrapped around her like tree roots, the belt on his slacks digging into her backside.

Grabbing his hand to unlock his grip, a metallic clink and tugging sensation on her finger froze her solid. Lowering her gaze, knowing before she saw, her pulse kicked into high gear. Swallowing a whimper before she woke him, not ready to face him, she managed to free herself from his octopus snuggle.

The shiny band on her finger caught at glimmer of sunlight as she sat up in bed. Holy shit. What had she done?

Sitting on the side of the bed, too dizzy to stand up yet, she stared at her finger. A good-sized sapphire was embedded in a delicate, winding river of platinum. Biting her cheek, she refused to let herself cry. Not that any tears would come out, she was so damn dehydrated.

Without her next to him, Zane groaned and pulled a pillow over his face. Did he have any idea that he was wearing a black titanium band on a very important finger? Part of her really hoped he remembered how they'd gotten in this predicament, but most of her hoped he was as shocked as she was.

Easing off the bed, her legs wobbly beneath her, she snuck into the bathroom and drank and drank and drank until her cheeks were no longer adhered to her teeth. Stalling for as long as was practical, she lingered under the cleansing spray of the shower until her fingertips turned to puckered prunes.

When she could hide no longer, she tiptoed out of the bathroom and pulled on her jeans and a cotton t-shirt. She brewed her vile hotel coffee, cringing as it made out a noisy grinding sound. Looking to the bed, Zane was still hidden under the pillow.

Sneaking out onto the deck, she sipped the bitter brew and stared at her finger. If she weren't so freaked at what it meant, she might have found it a pretty piece of jewelry.

The rising sun glinted off the surface of the water, the peaks in the distance standing tall and proud. Not many people out yet, the property was blissfully quiet. Too quiet. Her memory of last night was a gigantic black hole. Last thing she remembered was escaping that awful party.

Grumbling behind her, Zane rolled out of bed. She froze, hoping he wouldn't come out yet. Let her get her head on straight first. Not looking back, she heard the brewer powering away at his coffee, the shower starting moments later.

Cradling the rapidly cooling mug in her hands, she didn't move when he staggered out to join her. Jeans slung carelessly low on his hips, his black t-shirt hugging that flawless body, his bare feet and unruly hair tugged at something deep in her gut. The romantic dreamer that had probably gotten them into this mess to begin with.

They sat in silence for a few minutes, both looking out at the scenery as if nothing was wrong.

Finally, Zane rested his coffee on his knee. "So," he said, glancing her way then back to the water.

"So," she sighed.

"I've got this thing on my finger. You've got one too."

She nodded.

"I don't have a fucking clue why."

Setting down her empty mug on the table between them, she took a long breath. "I don't think 'why' is the issue. It's the what-are-we-going-to-do that's freaking me out. An overabundance of pheromones, add some champagne and cocktails and weed, then an easy-access wedding chapel... well, that's a Freya-disaster waiting to happen."

"I think it's my fault." His gaze was steady, honest. "The last few days, that's the most alive I've felt in years. The idea of leaving all this behind was eating away at me. Then, well, shit, my mom called yesterday."

"She did? How did it go?"

"Again proved why I should stop trying. First, she had no idea that I hadn't even been deployed the last few months. Then when she heard I was out, well, I guess my ex has been working for them for the last few years and just made partner at their architectural firm. Mom thinks it would be so great if I moved home and got back together with Blaire." He shrugged, then downed the last of his coffee before setting it on the table. "She was so set on it, and I knew I wouldn't hear the end of it. Her badgering can last years. So. Shit. Well, I sort of told her I remarried."

For the first time that morning, a laugh bubbled up in Freya's throat.

Glancing over to gauge her reaction, he caught her look and smiled back, shaking his head at himself. "It slipped out. As usual, my own words bit me in the ass as soon as I'd said them. She and my dad are planning to fly out to meet you."

"We could have faked it," she reached her foot over and nudged his, the corner of her mouth quirking up.

His head tilted, a subtle smile lightening his dark mood. "That was my plan. But I'm thinking, once stoned-me got all sentimental last night with ideas of weddings and that chapel next door to the restaurant..."

"Both of our fault then."

"Looks like."

Freya rose to her feet and leaned her elbows on the rail. Looking out over the water, she felt her brain settling. "Let's pack up and see if we can catch an earlier flight. I'd rather not run into anyone right now. Especially my parents. Then, once we get home, we can call Lincoln or Grady and see if one of them can help us with an annulment."

Rubbing a hand over his face, Zane stood and headed inside. Within a few minutes, they were out the door. Freya texted her mom from the lobby while they waited for their cab. *Trying to catch an early flight. See you at home.*

A few seconds later, she got a text back, *Jealous. Your dad's fishing and I'm hungover. What was in those drinks?*

Or those cupcakes?

I'm going to do some detective work and I'll let you know what happened. I haven't been that high since before I met your father.

Zane and the driver loaded their bags into the trunk as she stuffed her phone back in her pocket. He raised an eyebrow, silently inquiring about the messages.

"My mom's going to kick some ass about where that weed came from."

"Good. That was pretty fucked up."

They rode in silence on the way to the airport. Freya's knee was rattling a mile a minute, searching the internet to see how annulments worked. Zane's leg stretched across the midline, his knee pressed against hers as he squished into the cramped electric car. He didn't budge, his eyes dark, but otherwise he was completely unreadable.

As they drove into Reno, he reached over and stilled her vibrating knee with his hand. He let go. Her knee started back up again. Again, he stilled her movement with his hand. This time, he stayed. The burning connection melted away the tension that the vibration had fruitlessly combated.

At the airport, he took their garment bag again, slinging his backpack over his shoulder. Mindlessly, they linked hands and headed inside. Logically, she knew that sort of thing had to stop, but she was so freaked and wanted out of this asap, she paradoxically needed that connection, to know they were in this together.

They'd timed it well, only needing to wait in line a few minutes before the attendant flagged them over. "How can I help you today?" he asked with a chipper smile.

Zane adjusted his backpack and asked, "Our flight home to SeaTac isn't until tonight, but we were hoping you might have openings on an earlier flight."

"Let's see what we have," the attendant scanned the computer. Looking up, the attendant offered an apologetic smile, "I have a flight leaving in forty-five minutes, but the last two seats together are in first class. For the last-minute upgrade, it will be a hundred fifty dollars per ticket and there won't be time to check any luggage."

He flashed Freya an adoring smile; rather than feel adored, she cringed at the uncharacteristic softness, "What do you think, Babe? Won't that be a nice treat for our honeymoon?"

She swallowed the cringe, smiling just as sweetly. "Oh, I suppose we can pull from the credit card to celebrate."

Brightening, the attendant clicked a few keys. "I think we can waive the fee today. Congratulations on your marriage." After a few more clicks and the hum of the printer, she passed across their updated boarding passes.

Zane smiled, "Thanks so much."

"Have a wonderful trip home."

As they left the counter, he took her hand again, leaned over, and landed a zinger on her; one of those kisses that wasn't demanding or lusty, but enduring and savoring. Like newlyweds should do. Heart stumbling a little further, Freya bit her lips together as they pulled away and kept walking toward security. "We won't get an annulment if we go around kissing and telling everyone we're married," she mumbled, unable to make her voice perk up enough to project.

He nodded with that subtle tilt of his head, the corner of his mouth turned up. "That was for the attendant." As they rounded the corner, he dropped her hand and jammed his in his pocket.

Shoving her own lonely hand in her pocket, she ignored the pang. "Nice finagling. I didn't think you were one to manipulate."

He shrugged, "Not usually. But I can when the situation calls for it. Learned something useful from my parents at least."

The plane slammed into the ground and bounced in a rocky landing. Zane gritted his teeth, flashing back to the time the airfield had been roughened from a recent airstrike, the base mid-evacuation. His team was the military's last-ditch effort to recover the area.

As soon as they taxied into the gate and came to a stop, he hopped up from his seat and grabbed their bags. He handed Freya her backpack, hauling his over his shoulder and wrapping the garment bag over his arm. Keeping his hands to himself, they walked spaced apart as they crossed the speckled white tile, up the escalator, and into the concrete parking garage.

At his truck, he dumped their stuff in the backseat and they hopped in. Not a word on the entire drive back. Shellshocked, regretful, who the hell knew what was driving her silence.

How could he have been so fucking stupid? Sure, he was trashed as all hell, but he wasn't some kid that got the dumbass idea to get hitched while his brain was altered. Nor was he the type to get hammered twice in as many weeks.

Back home, he dropped her off, but stayed in the truck. Before closing the door, her eyebrows dropped as she realized he wasn't getting out. "Where are you headed?"

"See if I can catch Grady at home while Asher's gone."

"You don't want Asher to know?"

"I'll tell him, but I need a plan first."

Nodding, her face fell, dejected. She wanted the annulment, right? She'd been the one to bring it up in the first place. And again at the airport.

He'd lived a disaster of a marriage to Blaire, constantly disappointing her while she drained his soul and his bank account. Stupid fucking mistake, and he wasn't doing that to himself again. Or Freya; she wasn't anything like Blaire, but she didn't deserve to get stuck in his directionless, selfish life.

"Okay," she adjusted her bag and closed the door. He watched as she trudged into the house. Sophie sat curled up with a book on a rocker on the porch. Good. She wouldn't be alone if she didn't want to be.

11

Celery

A shiny new Forerunner was parked in the drive. Asher's truck was notably absent. Good.

Zane rang the bell. A few moments later, a pretty-boy sort that looked like he regularly modeled for O'Neill or Volcom opened the door. "Grady?" he asked.

The guy nodded. "Zane?"

"Yep."

"Freya called; said you were on your way over."

"Cool. Um. Yeah. Did she tell you why?"

"Nope. Said she'd leave it to you. And seemed to be laughing and crying and hyperventilating as she said it. What's up?" Stepping inside, Grady motioned for Zane to follow.

Zane's stomach rumbled, reminding him he hadn't eaten breakfast or lunch. A half-eaten ham and cheese sandwich sat on the kitchen island. He tried to not stare.

Grady grinned, "Hungry?"

"Yeah. Long morning."

"Are you useless in the kitchen like Asher?"

"Hell no. That lazy ass bummed a lot of food off me over the years and made up for it by inviting me over for steak or burgers or PB&J, as he couldn't manage much else."

Pulling the ingredients out of the fridge, Grady smiled, "I'm not sure his PB&J is worth bragging about. As Sophie won't let him move in until he learns to cook, I feel like I've turned into a cooking instructor. Honestly, I'm still not sure how he convinced me to let him live here. With Lincoln moving in with Pippa, I thought I was finally in the clear of roommates." Slapping some mayo on the bread, Grady nodded to the island, "Have a seat and fill me in."

Sliding the sandwich across the island, neatly plated with carrots and snap peas, Zane tore into the ham and cheese, muttering a *thanks* through full cheeks. Grady sat down to finish his own lunch.

Keeping his mouth full as a tried-and-true procrastination strategy, Zane looked around. The place was nice. Nothing high-end, more the practical sort of a guy still new to nine-to-five life. In the corner, a bookshelf held five bowed shelves, filled with about everything from law to history to survival skills to classic and contemporary fiction.

Ha, and a few romances. At least Grady was honest about it and didn't hide the guilty pleasure. If any of his SEAL buddies had caught him reading that shit, he'd never have heard the end of it, so he kept his in digital format.

Grady caught him squinting to read some of the titles. "I read a lot."

"So I see," he said as he swallowed. "I donated most of my stuff so I didn't have to rent a moving truck to get up here. Still regretting that I got rid of my books."

Swallowing the last bite, he knew it was inevitable. He cleared both of their plates, rinsed, and checked that the dishwasher was empty and loaded them in.

Grady strolled into the living room. Zane followed, forcing himself to sit on the opposite chair, his knee threatening to vibrate like Freya's had all morning.

Not saying a word, Grady waited.

"So," Zane began. "I, uh, well. I went with Freya to her cousin's wedding at Lake Tahoe this weekend."

Leaning back, Grady crossed his arms and seemed to smile, as if he already guessed it. Jackass, he let Zane try to put the words together all on his own.

"Bunch of college kids, rowdy as hell. Anyway. Short of it is, according to Freya's mom that asked around this morning, they served the wrong cupcakes for dessert and drugged all the guests with weed. Apparently those were for their friends after all we old folks went to bed."

Eyebrows lowering, Grady shifted in his seat.

Controlling his breathing, Zane swallowed a wave of nausea that lingered from those damn drinks. Even more so from what he'd done. "We'd already had a few drinks, so by the time we left, we were trashed. With a serious case of munchies, we went to the restaurant across the street. Then, well, we sort of wandered into a wedding chapel instead of heading back to our room right away. And, well, we, uh, we got married."

He held up his hand, the titanium band still on his ring finger. Should have taken it off, but he didn't want to lose it. He'd already checked his bank account; last night cost a pretty penny. They'd hit the restaurant, the chapel, the jewelry store. Licensing fees, photographer.

Leaning forward, resting his elbows on his knees, Zane cradled his head in his hands. So embarrassing. He was closer to forty than twenty. What the hell?

Grady rested his hands behind his head and grinned. "As you're here instead of at home with your wife, I'm guessing you're looking to find a way out of it?"

He nodded.

"I'm assuming Freya's wanting out, too?"

"Yeah. Shit. I'm divorced. She's been engaged a few times. Neither of us intended to get married. Eloping with a woman I've known less than a month? Dumbass idea. Can we get it annulled?"

Relaxed as if this were no biggie, Grady plopped his feet up on the ottoman. "Not called an annulment in Washington, it's a Determination of Validity, but same thing. As you were both intoxicated, we have a good case for it."

"Okay, good," he nodded, letting out a long breath he hadn't realized he'd been withholding. "Freya will be relieved."

"But..."

"No buts," Zane stiffened.

"But," the corners of his mouth turned up with ironic amusement, "that won't work if you two go around acting married."

"No more sex?"

Grady muffled a laugh. "Not if you want that annulment."

"I really don't want two divorces."

"Then keep your hands to yourself. Did you consummate it?"

Zane concentrated, trying to bring more of it back. "I don't think so."

"You don't think so?"

"Woke up with my pants on," he shrugged, leaning back into the couch.

Grady laughed out loud. "I can't wait to hear Freya's side of things."

"She doesn't remember any of it."

"Do you?"

Zane cringed, "Not enough. I never forget. But I never drink such awful shit or get high, either."

"Sorry man. Think you two will be able to stay friends?"

He nodded. "That was the plan to begin with. Burn out this chemistry we've got, then come home and pretend the weekend never happened."

"Don't think it works that way."

"I know, but it was absolutely worth finding out the hard way. Or it would have been, if we hadn't fucked it up by getting married." He glared at the ring. Visions of another ring bounced around his thick skull. Wide gold band. Engraved inside, some bullshit about true love. Then handing it back to Blaire when she demanded her freedom. Not caring that he hadn't slept in weeks, had been shot at, pushed to his limits while trying to save the world, his marriage, and their finances. "So how do we get the annulment?"

"As I said, keep your dick in your pants. Don't cohabitate. Swing into the office later this week with a retainer fee so I can process everything for you. Well, unless you want to do all of it yourself."

"Hell no. You can have my entire damn savings, just make it all go away."

Grady chuckled, leaning forward in his seat. "Only enough to make it binding; I'm not profiting on your stupidity."

"Gee, thanks."

"I'll have you fill out some paperwork, then we'll see about scheduling a court appearance and you can explain your drunken night to the judge."

Groaning inwardly, he imagined having to retell this again. In a staid courtroom. In front of strangers. "All that damn work to end this charade, when all I had to do before was scrawl an illegible signature?"

"You messed up, you have to pay the consequences."

What a fucking mess. He hopped up and headed for the door. "Thanks," he said, genuinely meaning it this time.

Grady followed him to the door, then swung back to the bookshelf. He studied the diversity of spines, then grabbed out a book with a ripped guy in dog tags and little else, and handed it over.

Zane scowled, his eyes drawing up from the smutty cover to Grady's beachy blues. "What the fuck is this?"

A smug-ass grin, Grady shrugged, "Don't judge a book by its cover. It's about a cranky Navy SEAL that finds happiness with a snarky schoolteacher."

Looking at his new attorney like he was fucking nuts, Zane tilted his head and raised an eyebrow.

Grady shrugged, "Maybe you can explain what the fuss is over Navy SEALs. Asher thinks it's the abs."

"Nah. More the untamable rogue they think they can domesticate."

"Damn, your ex really did a number on you."

"There's a reason I don't date much."

"Well, when you find one about a small-town lawyer that bunks with a man-child and has a psycho overbearing mother and is a moron when it comes to falling for the right woman, let me know."

"Make this annulment happen, and I'll commission one if I have to." Managing to find a lightness in the weird-ass day, Zane ducked out the front door and hopped in his truck, tossing the book onto the passenger seat.

⚘

Freya dumped her backpack on the front porch and dropped onto the rocker next to Sophie. Leaning back and closing her eyes, she brought a full breath in, and slowly let it out. "I like the new chairs."

"You picked them out," Sophie's voice was light and kind and everything Freya needed.

"And they are going to look stunning with the Turkish blue paint, snow white trim, and walnut accents." Easing with the rhythm of the rocker, the rustling of the forest branches in the afternoon breeze, Freya smiled softly, "I changed my mind on the color for the door and shutters. Celery."

"Celery? Are you sure?"

Nodding, Freya painted the image in her mind. "Or grass. Whichever speaks to you more."

"Huh. Celery or grass. I like it." Sophie's voice brightened further, "Oh, I was going to call you, but I didn't want to interrupt your weekend. Your stuff came."

Eyes popping open, Freya felt the thrill wash over her. "What a relief. I love charcoal, but I miss color and the messiness and the rebellion of paint."

"I suspect you'll keep stealing my dresses even though yours have arrived?"

"Hell yes. I look great in them. Help yourself to mine anytime."

They rocked again in silence. For all the weirdness of the day, Freya relaxed. Like the pace since, shit, since even before Pippa's wedding, since the broken engagement with Giovanni, since she had decided to come home... months of frantic chaos had eased to a pleasant rhythm. No tours on the schedule for at least a few months, a roof over her head, no car meant she had an excuse to not go anywhere... first time in years she wasn't beholden to anyone.

"How was your weekend?"

Well that didn't help. "Weird."

"Wedding was that bad?"

"Worse. We had to dodge my aunts all evening; gossip-happy bloodhounds. One even mentally undressed Zane while asking me how he was in the sack. My cousin and her friends were a horde of partiers. Not a drop off potable water. So, we had a bit more alcohol than we should have, but we'd thought we hadn't had so much that we couldn't keep our heads. After all, we'd had one more night of sex ahead of us. But then they served the wrong cupcakes for dessert and we got high as kites on top of the stiff, sugary cocktails they'd served by the bucket."

"What? How does someone accidentally drug their guests?"

"It was that awful of a wedding." Legs too weak to even rock the chair anymore, she tilted to a stop and couldn't move.

"At least you weren't the oddball this time. They don't sound so normal."

"And then I woke up married."

"What?" Sophie choked and coughed and laughed in response.

"Finding the energy to nod, Freya pinched her lips together. "Zane's at Grady's right now asking how we can get an annulment."

"I'm so sorry. You were already worried about falling for him."

Adrenaline pumped into Freya's limp muscles and rocketed her out of her chair. Pacing on the shady porch, she wanted to throw something or break something or... *Dammit.* She tried to at least slow her pace. "I was so terrified of giving all of myself up for a man. One night of inhibitions suppressed, and I did exactly that."

"Marriage doesn't mean giving everything up."

"No? Married people roll with the orange couch they hated in the store. They tolerate mushrooms on their pizza even though it makes them gag. They don't call their mother on Sunday because he is feeling insecure and needs attention. They don't get to decide to fly back to Europe for shows at the drop of a hat."

"Unless they have a husband that supports them, maybe even wants to go with them."

"Ha," she huffed.

"But they do get to have unlimited access to a shoulder to cry on, a brain to bounce ideas off of, someone to tell them their ass looks great in that dress that really makes them look like a peacock." Sophie calmly rocked in her chair, sipping her water and setting it back down on the tiled side table. "Or was the sex not good?"

Shoulders dropping, Freya bit her cheek and leaned against the post. "It was amazing. I've had some good sex in my life and that was…"

"Like your bodies were built only for each other?"

Flaming hot, acidic tears welled in Freya's eyes. Unable to speak, she pinched her lips closed and nodded.

Sophie slowed her rocking. "Go ahead and get the annulment. If you two decide to get involved, you can do so at your own pace down the road."

Letting out a long breath, Freya nodded. "Three broken engagements and now an annulled marriage. What is wrong with me?"

"Nothing."

"Says the woman who has only been in love once. And she's waiting six months before taking things to the next level even though she knows he's the one."

"How about this. You do your thing. Open your box of supplies and paint if and when you feel like it. Go about your day. Then tomorrow. Eat, sleep, live. Go on like you normally would. Zane will do his thing. I will do mine. The world will turn and do what it does."

"You make it sound so easy."

"It's not. But it's either that or lose yourself, as you're so afraid of."

12

Eat, Sleep, Live, Zing

Monday morning. Ha. As a woman that followed a very nontraditional schedule, Freya had never understood the hatred for Mondays. She'd actually enjoyed them. Until today.

Sophie was at work. Pippa hadn't started the schoolyear yet, but she was setting up her classroom and making lesson plans. Asher was still at training. Her parents were both at work. Grady and Lincoln were at work. Everyone was busy.

Except for Zane. He was right next door. Nothing more pressing on his plate than their annulment.

She was too cranky to paint. So many artists fueled their negative energy into their work. That really wasn't her style. She liked to pull the beauty of the world around her into her art, to convey its power.

Forcing herself outside, she headed to her favorite look-out point and did her yoga. A cool breeze, the sun rising overhead, the scent of summer wafting across the field. It wasn't enough. By the time she finished, her muscles burned and protested at how she'd pushed the limit, but her brain wasn't any calmer.

Stalking back into the house, she refused to look up at Zane's apartment. What if he was watching? Would he wave? If he did, should she come up to visit? Were they still friends or should they avoid each other?

She showered and threw on a lazy pair of jeans and an old cotton t-shirt that had seen better days, updated to match her painting needs with the sleeves and collar cut off, a knot in the back to keep the extra fabric out of her way. Leaving her feet bare, noting at least her toenails still had a fresh coat of peppermint green, she knew what she had to do. Swinging open the front door, she stormed out before she changed her mind.

Not watching where she was going, she slammed right into the brick wall of Zane. Groaning at the impact, he steadied her against him. "Hey," he said as she clung to him, even though the risk of falling had ceased.

"Hi. I was just heading up to see how your conversation with Grady went." Her breath rushed in and out, her pulse kicking up as she tried to control her reaction to him. Every kiss, every touch flashed through her mind, his hands on her sides bringing it all back so vividly.

"That's what I was coming over for."

Hands clutching his t-shirt, she opened her grip and smoothed where she'd wrinkled, the movement quickly turning into an excuse to hold on longer. She tried to gather her bearings, taking a full reset breath.

Turning, she opened the door and waved him in after. Moving into the kitchen, she was about to pour a cup of coffee, but next to the old-fashioned drip, was her espresso-on-demand. A genuine sigh of relief passed her lips as she grabbed a pair of the smaller mugs from the cupboard and turned on the brewer.

Handing Zane the first cup, she waited for hers and joined him a moment later. "Let's go outside," she nodded back toward the front door.

He took a sip and followed. Cowlick unruly, his jaw rough with stubble, his forest eyes even darker than usual, he looked to have slept as terribly as she had.

In the side-by-side rockers, she closed her eyes and found the rhythm of the morning. "Can he fix it?"

Zane nodded. "He's getting the paperwork ready for us today. Then I'm to bring him lunch tomorrow and he'll help me wade through the documents while he eats."

An odd combination of relief and constriction wreaked havoc on her stomach. "That's a relief."

"Sort of. Apparently it's tough to get an annulment, well, have the marriage declared 'invalid,' but we've got a good case. We've got to act the opposite of married while this processes, and we'll have to provide proof that we were incompetent to get married that night."

"Proof? Should we be getting drug tested?"

He chuckled, his head tilting to the side in an amused nod. "I found receipts and temporary copy of the license in my suitcase, and I do have a charge for photography on my credit card. I googled the place, and apparently, they promise that you will receive the photos in the mail in about three weeks. Let's be sure to schedule the hearing when we can bring pictures of us trashed while we got hitched."

"Oh, I didn't even think of that. This can't have been cheap. I'll reimburse you for my half."

"Don't worry about it."

Scowling, she pulled her phone out of her pocket and pulled up her bank account. Scrolling, she found what she was looking for. "I have a two-hundred-dollar charge for a jewelry store." She glanced at his hand and the band he still wore.

"Not even a fraction of what I spent on yours."

She still wore the intricate band, afraid to lose it with how expensive it looked. Apparently, she was right. "Think we can return them?" Bile rose in her throat. Three broken engagements, and now an invalid marriage. And this was her favorite ring yet. The gem matched her eyes, the band told secret stories of its own.

What would her family think if they found out? Last time they'd seen her, she was leaving one fiancé at the altar. This time, she'd irresponsibly let herself get intoxicated and gotten married, annulling it as soon as possible. Her father was always supportive, but he had to be embarrassed.

"Doesn't look like it. I googled that, too. Sounds like a shady set-up to me, late night weddings and attached jewelry store, not caring that the bride and groom slurred through their *I dos*. They look legit on their website, but with the late hours and lack of waiting period? They provide everything you need right there onsite like a mini wedding shopping mall."

They sat and rocked for a bit. Among the many muddled questions in her mind, she replayed the conversation over again. "Define 'act the opposite of married.'"

"No more sex."

"I figure that part. If the judge doesn't buy the drunk thing, maybe they'll care that we didn't consummate it." She winked at him.

"Not sure how we'd prove that, but yeah, that's pretty much what Grady said. No sleepovers, no sex."

"What about coffee on the front porch?"

"As we are friends, not a couple looking to get married, I think that should be fine."

"What if we hold hands?"

"Do you always try to push the boundaries?" he turned to her, his rich eyes sparking with an unexpected charm.

She grinned, "Only when I find them annoying."

"We weren't planning on anything after the weekend anyway. Not exactly how I'd envisioned the weekend going, but this will ensure that we don't reverse on the original plan."

"I suppose. Annoying all the same." More than annoying, but he was probably right. Already, she wanted to curl up in his lap and tug that shirt off, now that she knew how nice things were underneath.

Draining the last of her coffee, she rose from her seat and offered to take Zane's empty cup. Needlessly grazing her fingers over his as she took the mug, she let the zing wash over her before heading inside.

T wo days. They'd made it two days without speaking to each other. And without kissing each other; that was a first.

This would be no problem. Grady would fix it. Some paperwork, a court appearance, and the whole thing will be erased. Hell, the night was already gone from her memory, now to erase it from the court's memory.

Pleased with their progress, ignoring the hollow in her gut, she stared at her checking account balance. At this rate, if she continued to sell at her current trajectory, minus anticipated expenses, she'd be broke within the year. To make it, she needed an upsloping income, not just steady.

Time to take it to the next level. She hated marketing. Advertising. Building that brand. Why couldn't art involve nothing more than painting and sketching and making an occasional appearance in person?

Over the last forty-eight hours, she'd called and emailed three galleries that she had worked with before, and reached an agreement for each to carry two more of her paintings that she had waiting on her porch for the shipper to pick up. She'd dropped in a bonus charcoal for each to consider, a little teaser to demonstrate her range that they may not have been aware of.

She'd taken a few online classes on the business end of things. It wasn't that she didn't know what to do. It wasn't as fun as the actual painting part. But with her brain such a cluster, she wasn't feeling capable of creativity. Soon, she'd need to, as her stock was waning as fast as her checking account.

Grabbing her iPad from her bedside table, she fired it up, then shut it back off. Not going to be enough. Pulling out her phone, she called Sophie.

She answered on the second ring, "I'm not bringing home pizza again."

Rolling her eyes, she shook her head, "I didn't ask. Besides, if I'm going to fit into that slinky dress of yours again, I've got to lay off the comfort carbs."

"I still don't see how you fit your boobs into any of my tops."

"Should I be offended here?" Looking down, she rolled her eyes. She loved stealing Sophie's clothes, and they were definitely a bit snugger in the bust, but, well, play up your assets. Sophie played up those mile-long legs and athletic figure. Freya accented the curves.

"No. I'm jealous. I've got nothing, but you're built. Don't lose those curves. They're too pretty. Besides, I catch Zane checking them out often."

"Not helpful. I'm trying to repel Zane right now."

"I know you want the annulment, but really? Not even a someday when all this is over, even just for fun?"

"No. My judgment, apparently, is shit around that man. All I can think about is getting him naked, which is why I'm calling."

"Pretty sure you can walk next door and ask. My assistance is not required."

She threw her head back and laughed out loud. "No. I mean, I've had enough distractions since getting home. And my finances are at risk because of it."

"I'll be happy to help; sort of what I do for a living."

"I know. And I will probably beg to take advantage of you later. But, I actually have a very simple request. Do you have a computer around here somewhere that I can borrow?"

"Sorry. My laptop broke in the move. Never transport it with the charger attached. And never let Pippa carry anything fragile."

Snorting, Freya pulled a protein bar out of the cupboard and tore into it. See? The man was even distracting her stomach. She'd missed breakfast by a few hours. Swallowing a sticky bite before she'd ground up all the crunchy bits, she choked down a few sharp pieces before responding, "I'd forgotten that tidbit about my endearing cousin. Crap. I think I need to invest in a computer."

"You could go ask our neighbor. Asher and Zane play online games together sometimes."

Her throat now hurt from the chunk that may or may not still be wedged back there. "Not as fun as asking him to get naked. But as it's down to risking my annulment, my career, or my pathetic savings, well, it's no contest. I'll head over and beg." Down on her knees if she had to. Closing her eyes and shaking her head at herself, a wicked grin on her face, Freya indulged in the visual. Imagine how much fun this situation could be if she hadn't messed it up by marrying the best sex she'd ever had?

Crossing the driveway, she hesitated with each step, hating that she was already breaking their pact to keep their distance, but this was business, not pleasure... sadly. Raising her hand to the door, she went for it.

The door eased open, and Zane wordlessly leaned against the door. The corner of his mouth quirked up in a smile that made her want to strip down on the spot and wrap her body around his. Were those biceps so... *edible* last time she'd seen him? She stood and blushed, her train of thought having set sail the moment those forest green eyes landed on her.

Finally, he said, "Hi."

"Hi," she said, practically swaying her hips and blushing like a virgin bride at the sight of him. Catching herself, she cleared her throat and focused. "Hi. I was wondering if you had a laptop I could borrow."

"Sorry, no laptop. I've got a desktop that you're free to come over and use whenever you want."

"You wouldn't mind? I have a lot of work to do, and I need to get my own computer, but I want to wait until I get paid again."

"I don't mind. I mean, you'll have to deal with me puttering around while you work, but have at it."

When did the word puttering become sexy? When Zane said it, maybe it was that deep resonance in his voice, but it sounded like an inuendo. Or maybe that was because her imagination spent all day, every day reliving their weekend. The good parts, anyway.

Waving her in, he sat down at the desk he'd set up in the corner since she'd been here last. He'd really fixed the place up nicely. A few new throw pillows were on the couch that now faced the picture window and a TV. A leather ottoman with a tray on it took the place of a traditional coffee table. The kitchen was tidy without being sparse. Stainless steel containers of differing sizes were nestled in the corner, and matching white ceramic olive oil and vinegar, together with a few jars of spices, were nestled on a tray next to the stove.

While she unsubtly perused the apartment, he booted up the computer. The corner desk could have looked intrusive in the clean space, but the rustic walnut wood with steel pipes holding it together gave it an industrial look. Rather than a typical ergonomic desk chair on wheels, he used one of the dining chairs with a tan cushion.

At the unlock screen, he turned to her. "You said you get paid quarterly, right? Like you might need to use this for a few months?"

She nodded, feeling insecure as she confessed her finances were tighter than she cared to admit.

"Don't get me wrong, you can come over whenever you'd like. If it were only for a day or two, I'd sign you on to my profile. Since you may need full access, I'll set up your own so you don't have to wade through all my stuff."

"I didn't know you knew anything about computers."

"Not by choice. In college, a lot of the designs were digital, then getting back from a mission, when my brain and body were toast, gaming was a nice way to unwind. More recently, I've started keeping track of recipes, ideas for new brews."

With a few quick keystrokes, he had her all set and hopped out of the seat. She brushed past, a little closer than necessary, but she was undoubtedly the moth to his flame. Fisting her hand at the last second, she resisted grazing her hand over his.

She hated computers, but had known this was coming. Although she'd counted the tiresome hours of her digital design course until she could pick up a brush again in art school, she was glad she'd wouldn't have to learn quite so much on the fly.

"You good?" he asked.

She nodded.

He headed to the kitchen and started pulling out some odd-looking contraptions, a few more canisters from the shelf in the dining room, plus a huge stockpot. Organizing his gear, his brow furrowed as he focused on each step, jotting down a few notes as he worked, he looked like quite the chemist. Smiling softly, she turned back to her own work.

Where did she even start? Well, she needed a home base. She'd already done most of the research, now it was a matter of making it happen. Pulling out her credit card, she bit the bullet and bought a memorable domain name. Then a fancy email. A newsletter service. Ugh. This added up quickly.

She hadn't even started to build her portfolio when the shadows stretched long across the apartment. Her brain throbbed as she imagined her next steps, and the utter insanity of attempting to set up a retail page, wondering if it were possible to link to some of the major galleries and online sellers. Checking the time, she realized she'd completely missed lunch and dinner was about to be a lost cause. As her belly grumbled at her, she caught the scent of garlic sautéing.

Turning around in the chair, she saw Zane had long since packed up his beer making supplies, a few dozen bottles capped and tucked into the corner. On the stove, he was stirring something yummy. His hair was long past the tight military fade he'd had when they first met and was now downright scruffy. Nor had he shaved since Tahoe. His cargo shorts rode low on his hips, his white t-shirt teasing at giving her a glimpse of skin.

Shoes already on the floor under the desk, as she'd slipped them off long ago, she walked barefoot into the kitchen and wrapped her arms around his waist while he tended to the stove. Unsurprised, or at least, not breaking stride, he rested his hand over hers and kept stirring.

His voice rumbled through her like a full body massage, "Get a good start?"

She nodded, her hair brushing against the cotton of his shirt. "I officially have an online presence. Not that there's anything to see yet, besides an under-construction memo. The content will have to wait for another day."

"Come back as often as you need. Otherwise that thing's a giant dust collector."

"Thanks." She ought to move. "Smells good in here." And not just the garlic. Breathing him in, like his voice, his scent affected her, a breeze through the forest on a midsummer day.

"Want some?"

"Yes please," she smiled against him.

Still holding her against him, he added chopped butternut squash and walnuts to the pan. On the counter, a wooden bowl was filled with mixed salad greens, two plates already waiting next to it.

Detaching herself, she opened the cabinet next to him and pulled out a pair of glasses, filling both with water. At the square wooden dining table, rustic-meets-industrial like the computer desk, she pulled two circular placements from the center, cloth napkins from the basket and set the table. A few moments later, he scooped the savory mixture over the salad. Like a seasoned chef, he sprinkled goat cheese over the top and drizzled olive oil and balsamic, then a few grinds of cracked pepper.

With a fork and spoon, he tossed the mixture, then loaded up both of their plates. Her stomach growled as he carried the plates to the table.

"You always eat like this?" she asked.

"Like what?"

"This is really good," she said as she scooped in her second bite.

"You watched. It took a grand total of ten minutes. I'm lazy. This is one of my go-tos, or some variation of it, whatever I've got on hand." He tilted his head with an easy smile as he took another bite. "If you had been home all day, what would you be eating right now?"

"Similar, actually. I assumed you were another steak and potatoes guy like Asher." She took a sip of her water, then gestured with her fork, "I've never understood the appeal. Standing in front of a blazing hot open flame on a hot day so I can eat a hot meal? No thank you."

"And there are very few forms of potato worth eating."

"Be careful, or I may come over to mooch dinner more often."

He chuckled, leaning back in his chair. "As long as it's not considered cohabitating."

She grimaced. "Oh yeah. I forgot about that." Looking down at her ring, she bit her lips together and pulled the pretty thing off, holding out for him to take. Without it, her finger looked drab now.

His expression fell, probably from the reminder that they had been so stupid. After a pause, he took it and stuffed it in his pocket. He went to pull off his ring, but she stopped him. "No, keep it. See what you can get for it. I owe you a lot more than that for footing the rest of the bill."

"You don't owe me anything. Really, I think it was my idea."

"Oh, I can easily imagine my drunken-self thinking what a brilliant plan it was."

13

Outside the Little Sailor's Room

Flicking the water out of his hair, Zane cringed as he realized how scruffy he'd gotten. He reached out of the shower and grabbed his towel, drying loosely and lumbering into his bedroom. Still on the charger, his phone flashed blue.

Tapping the screen, he saw he'd missed a call from his father, a voicemail waiting. Nope. Probably asking when they can come visit. Not ready for that.

Grumbling to himself, he finished drying and pulled on cargo shorts and a t-shirt, stuffing the phone into his pocket. In the kitchen, he glared at his coffeepot, wanting one of Freya's fancy instant espressos. Probably shouldn't.

They'd agreed they were friends. Friends bummed coffee off each other. Didn't mean they were cohabitating.

Over the dining table, one of Freya's paintings really dressed the place up. Felt like he was overlooking a flourishing vineyard in the Loire valley. The corner of his mouth quirked up as he recalled Freya stopping by last night, right as he'd been getting ready for bed.

She'd stuttered over her words, suddenly shy. *A thank you gift*, she'd said.

For what? He'd asked.

Well, lots of things. Let's just say it's for letting me use your computer, as I'm going be using it a lot over the next few weeks until I get my own. And for dinner. And as payment for our wedding. Passing it across, she'd left as quickly as she'd come.

Pulling on his shoes, he strolled down the stairs and crossed over to Freya's place. Sophie's car was gone, reminding him it was still the work week. Damn, he didn't even know what day it was anymore. Not that he was complaining, but it was weird.

An alpine breeze had circled around the mountains, bringing cool air to the valley. The lawn was getting long. It was sort of his too, so he'd make a point to mow it this afternoon.

Not that he'd ever mowed a lawn. Freya mowed last, but it had taken all day with the massive park-like front and back lawns, and she had so much else on her plate right now. If it were his place, he'd wipe out most of the lawn with hardscaping and low maintenance gardens, maybe a water feature with natural boulders, intricately branched evergreens, and colorful trailing florals...

Shit. He shook his head. He'd taken a few landscaping classes, as the building can be stunning, but without a coordinating surround, it didn't matter how good your design. May as well use what he knew; he'd draw up some schematics for Asher and Sophie and see what they thought. Hell, he may as well do some mock-ups for the house while he was at it. They had a contractor coming out soon anyway. They may not own it yet, but they were already making it their own.

He might as well accept that growing up with obsessive architects and studying it himself for four years shaped how his brain worked. Not that he wanted anything in common with his parents, and not that he would *ever* let them know it, but he did have a knack for design. Didn't mean he wanted to do it for a living; hearing his parents' monotonous lectures had been even more boring than his college courses on flying buttresses and curved versus angled arches, ancient quarries and brick making. It had sounded cool on the course description, but he still recited some of those slideshows when he couldn't sleep.

Hopping up the steps to the front porch, he raised his hand to knock, then backed up a step. Dammit, he was going to blow this annulment if he kept nosing around. Bad enough they'd had dinner together. A standing coffee date was pushing it.

The door swung open. Freya leaned against the open door, smiling with that confidence that couldn't be tamed... and he'd throttle anyone that tried, fuming at the thought of those asshole fiancés that had come close. Pushing down the temper boiling in his gut, he let his gaze fall on her irresistible blue eyes.

His breath caught in his throat, the air around him spinning as he tried to keep his feet anchored to the ground beneath him. Her amused grin taunted him, lighting her up even brighter, her curls sleek like how she'd worn them at the wedding, and she was dressed in the hottest sundress that begged for a picnic under a shady oak tree... the kind where he'd get to untie those shoulder straps and...

Blinking, he stopped the thought in its tracks. Annulment. No sex. Not even fooling around, even if no one else would know. "Hey, sorry to bug you. You on your way somewhere?"

She shook her head. "Sometimes I need to feel pretty."

"I know what you mean," he teased. Folding his arms over his chest, he restrained himself from closing the distance between them and tugging her against him, seeing if she smelled as refreshing as she looked.

"I saw you wavering outside, deciding whether or not to knock."

He tilted his head with a lazy shrug.

"How about this? No knocking, just come on in. You are my husband, after all, so there should be some perks until we get this marriage erased, like getting to lay eyes on a handsome man first thing in the morning," she grinned and raised an eyebrow in jest, biting the corner of her mouth with something much more sultry.

The corner of his mouth quirked up of its own accord, his imagination running wild, wondering just how much they could stretch things and still get that annulment. They'd agreed handholding was likely acceptable. What about kissing? They were damn good at that. What might the judge ask; have you had sex since you've been married, have you cohabitated? Unlikely to ask if they'd rounded the bases a bit, staying shy of home plate...

Shaking his head, he closed his eyes and swallowed the wicked wanderings of his awakened libido. Coming over on a regular basis was a terrible idea; easy access without even needing to work up the nerve to knock? Self-inflicted torture really wasn't his thing.

"What brings you here this morning?" She stepped back to let him in.

Keeping his arms crossed, he wandered in. "Coffee. I like yours better than mine."

She grinned. "Have a seat."

While he waited at the island, she practically danced as she moved. Had she always seemed so vibrant? "Thanks for that painting. It looks amazing in my apartment, like it should be in a high-end gallery or something. Why don't you sell it?"

She scowled, her posture stiffening and blue eyes boiling. Shit. He'd pissed her off again. At least she didn't pace or shout this time. Instead, she kept her tone measured, as if teaching a foolish student. "I should make this clear right now. Yes, I paint to make a living. But more, I'm happiest when I can give a piece away to someone that I know will appreciate it. I keep a record of everything I've done, well, that's worth keeping anyway, and list it in my portfolio. So even if I won't make money on that one, once I get my website up and going and can promote my portfolio, it will show potential buyers my range."

"Okay," he nodded, a smile tugging at the corner of his mouth. Even with her eyes sparking, she was a siren.

Mirroring his amusement as she finished her diatribe, she smiled and shook her head. His coffee sputtered complete, and she slid it across the island, then nodded to sit outside. They sat on the rockers and gazed out at the morning. This... this he could do every day.

His phone buzzed in his pocket. Shifting his coffee to his left hand, he pulled out his phone and saw Asher's name. "Hey," he answered.

"Hey, man. Tell me, how goes married life?" Cringing, he took a slow exhale, reminding himself of the number of times Asher had saved his ass, and decided to let him get away with the smartass remark.

"Shove it." At his side, Freya smiled, listening in. He rolled his eyes at her and smiled.

"Seriously, sucks to have it go down that way. Freya holding up okay?"

Watching her reactions, the laughter in her ocean blues. "You know Freya. I can't picture anything that would bring her down." Piss her off, yes, but ruin her buoyant humor? Not a chance.

"Got that right. I'm leaving Burien as we speak; I get the weekend off. Want to grab a drink at Ahab's when I get back?"

Zane tried to picture the place, having only seen it on various errands into town. Quirky bar, very touristy, lots of energy. "Yeah, let's do that."

Raising her hand, Freya motioned that she wanted an invitation.

"Freya wants to come. That cool?"

"Totally. I'll call Sophie and we'll make it a thing. I mean, not a double date thing, but, you know."

"Cool. Hey, is there a barbershop nearby?"

"Yeah, drop into Sal's anytime. He'll fix your ugly mop."

When they ended the call, Freya was still watching him, her face adorably contorted in smile-meets-grimace. "We're never going to live this down."

"Nope. May as well make the most of it," he shrugged. "Shit, that reminds me. My dad left me a message while I was in the shower. I think he's trying to schedule something."

She laughed out loud. "At least I don't have to *pretend* to be your wife."

Shaking his head, he cringed. "Hopefully they'll stay in Seattle and we can have one dinner with them and that's it."

A few hours later, perfect time for a late lunch and to dodge the crowds, they pulled into Ahab's. "What is this place again?" he asked. Shit, the parking lot was packed. Did this town ever slow down?

Freya slipped her hand into his. He ought to argue, but he couldn't. Friends held hands. Of course, they probably didn't get off on the electricity of the simple gesture, but the judge didn't need to know that. Halting in front of him, she reached up and ruffled her other hand in his hair and grinned, "I'm glad he left the cowlick. Good cut."

He smiled stupidly, like a pup that had pleased its person.

"Ahab's is a classic. Whaler themed and hokey and re-laxed."

"I'm not having more than one beer."

She exhaled and nodded dramatically, "I think I learned my lesson. Which I have learned many times in my life, but every so often, you have to mess up again. But this one should cure me for a long, long time."

As they walked inside, he was immediately struck by the absurd character of the place. Fishing nets, detailed murals of epic whaling scenes, boats hanging from the ceilings. The server twirled to them, "Two?"

He nodded toward Grady and another guy—must be Lin-coln—at the far end of the room. He'd seen him in a few photos of Asher's family back in San Diego, including the very traditionally staged engagement photos of Pippa and Lincoln. Asher had only mentioned the four of them; wonder what happened. A bubbling bundle of energy came up behind them, tearing Freya away.

Jumping up and down, Pippa squealed in one rapid breath, "Congratulations I'm so excited."

Freya's eyes went wide, looking at Pippa as if she were nuts. "About?"

Flaring her arms out wide, Pippa cheered, "You got married."

In a sarcastic sing-song tone, Freya shook her head, "And I'm getting an annulment."

Scowling, Pippa snorted. "I know. I'm going to keep hoping you change your mind."

Turning, she nearly bumped into Zane, having already knocked into him in her enthusiasm. "Sorry, Zane. How are you? It's been so long since I've seen you. I happened to have called Asher on his way here to see how training went, and, well, the rest of us jumped on board for a much-needed relaxing afternoon."

He nodded, dumbfounded and speechless at the peppiness of Asher's sister.

They pushed through the crowd and settled at the high-top table in the corner. Pippa slid in next to Lincoln and he pulled her close, whispering something in her ear. Zane snagged one of the seats in the corner, Freya joining him. A moment later, Asher and Sophie came in and took the other seats on the wall-side.

A pitcher of beer appeared on the middle of the table, the server returning with a plate of sliders and another of quesadillas.

Grady started pouring, his face dark like he was debating saying something.

Zane nudged him, "What's up?"

"Didn't know if you wanted any updates in public."

"If you have an update, I want it."

"Right before I left the office, I confirmed your court date. Not bad, it's in three weeks."

Nodding, Zane exhaled with a sigh of... relief. It was definitely relief. Regret wouldn't make any sense. "Great. We can handle that." He slid his hand under the table and laced his fingers with Freya.

Her head bobbed with enthusiastic agreement. "That's not bad." Beer untouched, no food on her plate, she scooted back in her stool. "I'm going to go wash up. Back in a sec."

That brightness from this morning had faded. She must be relieved, right? The crowd engulfed her. He gave it a minute. And another. Excusing himself, he made his way through the vacation-buzzed tourists and billiard tables, more high-tops, until he reached the bathrooms.

Waiting outside the door labeled *Mermaids*, he debated if she was alone in there. Nope. Not going to be the guy that barges in looking for his invalid wife. He felt creepy enough, waiting outside the women's bathroom in a darkened hallway, tipsy tourists filing in and out.

She'd been so easygoing about this whole thing, hadn't even railed with one of her furious tirades. When she'd released his hand and retreated so serenely, he knew something was up. Right before he gave up and stormed in anyway, she came out. "Zane," she gasped as she looked up and saw him waiting.

"You okay?" he asked.

She nodded. "Yeah. This whole thing is so weird."

A trio of women weaved between them. Once they passed, he said, "Know what you mean."

Straightening her dress, she sighed, "It seemed so easy, to declare it invalid. No, it wouldn't have happened if we were in our right minds, but still, I had a great time otherwise." A guy passed through them and into the *Sailor's* room. Once he'd disappeared, she said, "The timing is awful, to be going through this right now, when you're trying to figure out what you want, and I've got so much going on."

When their server came down the hallway, trying to decide to go between them or around, a pair of women with full bladders behind her, he could have backed up again, but his brain was so haywire these days, he grabbed Freya and pulled her out of the way, right into his arms. Her breasts, pelvis... everything pasted against him to make room for the crowd. All the blood flooding south in a rush of throbbing heat, he clutched her hips and held on for dear life.

She melted into him, her eyes swimming with every reason this wasn't as easy as they'd both been banking on. As he moved to release her, another pair of women came down the hall. Freya plastered herself against him again. Damn, she smelled so good; she'd hit the shops while he got a haircut, and she smelled like lavender and sage, fresh and earthy and of everything home should be.

Biting the corner of her lip, her gaze dropped to his lips. Breath coming fast, heat radiating from every point of contact, he leaned in.

Movement at the end of the hall shattered what shouldn't have been a moment to begin with. Pippa held out his phone, an apologetic smile on her face. "Sorry to interrupt. Zane, your phone's been blowing up. Your dad's calling."

Shit. He released Freya and she brushed past Pippa, her hand grazing her cousin's shoulder on the way by. Pippa looked devastated to have interrupted, her brow scrunched with sincere apology. Asher had described her as sensitive, but Zane suspected she took every emotion in the room personally.

"Thanks," he said. He played the voicemails as he walked back to the table. Stomach churning, pulse pounding in his skull, he slumped back into his seat. He looked at Freya, "My parents will be here in two weeks."

Hand linked with his as they eased back to the table, she nodded, "Okay. Whatever you need."

He dropped onto his stool and added, "And they want to stay at my place for the weekend."

"Why?"

"Fuck if I know. Apparently everywhere in Foothills is booked for the rest of the summer, and they wanted to be close so we can go hiking and all that touchy-feely bullshit. Not a good time to decide to be parents of the year."

"Ugh," she groaned. "We'll make it work."

He turned to the rest of the table, "My parents are crazy. I may have told them I got married to get them off my back, which may actually have been what precipitated the drunk idea in the first place, and, well, shit, they're coming for a visit. Mind pretending that we didn't get trashed and elope and are looking to have this annulled? But that we actually know each other?"

Asher laughed out loud, nearly crying in his enjoyment. "What's your story?"

Eyebrow raised in a plotting nod, a little spooky like she was accustomed to scheming, Freya locked eyes with Zane, "Naturally, I'd go visit Asher regularly, and you came home with him a number of times. It was love at first sight. We wrote to each other while I travelled, and while you were deployed, you'd sneak messages to me. Of course, we regularly engaged in phone sex and sending naked pictures. Now and again we'd meet up in some far corner of the world and make love until dawn."

"Naturally," he nodded, suppressing the groan as he listened to her sultry voice describing what would have been an ideal relationship, particularly the globally-separated erotica where there would be no pressure to be home in time for dinner or offense that he hadn't called on time, even when he'd been entrenched in a mission.

"Then the day you got out, you said the word and I came home, as I'd been planning. I met you halfway and we tied the knot in Tahoe."

Sophie smiled. "Sounds incredibly romantic. And suits you both."

Sitting back, Grady sipped his beer, the corners of his mouth turned down. Pippa nudged him, "Don't be such a downer."

He shrugged, "Going to be risky, pretending to be married. You might not get that annulment if you get caught. Marriages are rarely declared invalid anyway, so it won't take much to have it denied. I mean, a divorce would be more straightforward since you have no shared assets."

A pit forming in his gut, Zane shook his head, "I can't go through another divorce. Even a clean cut one."

"Just keep a low profile." Grady took a long pull on his beer, then stared at the glass for a minute. "This isn't nearly as good as the beer Asher brought over."

"That's half the reason I make my own."

"What's the other half?" Grady asked.

"Gives me something to think about. Takes focus and patience. And it's never monotonous. Doesn't always turn out the way I intend. Sometimes it's predictably acceptable. Other times, I go to all that work and it tastes like feet. Or, maybe a recipe gone wrong turns out to be fantastic."

"Did you know we don't have any craft breweries in Foothills? Nearest is in North Bend. With the number of tourists we have here in Foothills alone? Not to mention the folks passing through on their way to the trails and national parks? Craft brewing is huge in Washington. There's a market."

"Really?" Zane's chest clenched around that odd pang again. A hope that had the power to crush him if gave in to it.

Nodding, Grady snagged a slider from the tray. "Really. Just saying. I mean, it's mostly selfish; I like good beer."

As the pang sank into his gut, it wrenched and folded over on itself. Cool idea, but probably more than he could manage.

Asher kicked his foot. "Dude," he scowled. "You were always the first guy out of the plane when the clock was ticking. Always pulled more than your own weight, even when the rest of us wanted to give up." His amber eyes flooded, and he added softly, "And the one that ran into the rubble to get to Jack and the other guys that had fallen."

Clenching his jaw, he muttered. "Yeah."

"Yeah," Asher leaned his elbows on the table, hands in his hair. "Things are a hell of a lot scarier in the civilian world. Less black and white, not life or death but risky all the same. I've still got your back."

Fingers still laced with his under the table, Freya gave a gentle squeeze, her warmth keeping his blood pumping when it threatened to stop.

Pippa smiled, "You always brought my brother back home. Anything you need, I'm there."

Grady took a long gulp, then added, "You've already got a hell of a team to get it off the ground, if that's what you decide. An accountant, an artist, legal advice, and, well, if you're open, I'd love to be involved."

Lincoln grinned, "And a cop if you get your ass in trouble. A teacher if you need a scolding now and again." Pippa jammed her elbow into his side. Grunting at the impact, he added, "But seriously, Pippa can plan anything. Terrifying for all involved, but it will get done and be done right."

Feeling that pang surface from the pit of his stomach, Zane swallowed before it slammed into his throat and forced his eyes to water. He nodded, jaw clenched tight, words completely inadequate.

14

Dirty Laundry

"Flowers and ruffles, pink and skimpy, or black and sleek?" Freya stared blankly at the swimsuits she'd laid out on her bed.

Sophie rubbed her chin in exaggerated contemplation. "Although the flowers are fun, a bit too tropical. The pink skimpy is damn sexy, but not family friendly. The black accents your eyes nicely and is low risk for wardrobe malfunction, yet is still hot."

"You may be onto something." She stuffed the black suit into her bag and added a cotton sundress from her closet. Not that she was worried about what to wear, but, well, she needed to look good. Something about ending a marriage that dragged her self-esteem in a downward dump.

As Sophie strolled out to grab her own swim stuff, Freya pulled her hair back into a messy bun, slipping her feet into her nearly-disintegrated flip-flops and headed for the front door. She called out as she opened the door, "Meet you outside."

From the main bedroom, Sophie hollered back, "I'll be out in five."

Turning too late as she dashed outside, she slammed into a brick wall. Crashing smack-dab into Zane, he grunted on impact, catching her against him and steadying them both. "Hi," he murmured.

"Hi," she whispered as her eyes met his, more out of breath from the gleam in his expression than the collision. Clearing her throat, she stepped back and politely nodded. "Ready?"

His head tilted as he uttered a simple, "Yeah. Sophie riding with us?"

She nodded again, fearing she'd reached full bobblehead. It was either that or lace her arms back around his middle and steal a taste of those pouty lips. Not many guys had such suckable lips that said everything his words, or lack thereof, didn't. "Asher's already there helping Denise with the hors d'oeuvres."

"Damn, he's really working on this responsible thing, huh?"

Standing awkwardly with a precise eighteen inches separating them, she nodded again, "As the party is for you, she said he had to help since she doesn't know your favorite foods."

"You too. I believe she called it a *Welcome Home* party for both of us."

"Yes, but I have been to their house many times already this summer because of Pippa's wedding. They've got a great place for entertaining. The pool is huge; I suspect they built it in an effort to keep Asher out of trouble. But the patio has plenty of seating and the barbeque is massive enough to feed an army."

"I hate crowds."

"You know everyone that will be there. Just my parents, Asher's of course, you and me, Asher and Sophie, and Pippa and Lincoln."

"Guess that's not so bad." He paused, his jaw ticking madly—a tell that she had already learned meant that he was holding back his words until he figured out how to say something potentially controversial without offending anyone. "Do your folks know?"

"I didn't tell them."

"Bad enough there will be a crowd, but the in-laws?" He faked a whole-body shiver, the corner of his mouth quirked up in ornery enjoyment of his own joke.

She burst out laughing at the awkwardness of the gesture. Unable to resist, she closed the distance between them and nuzzled into his neck. Inhaling as many Zane-molecules as possible, she savored. "How bad were your in-laws before?"

Without pause, his arms wrapped fully around her. "Actually, they weren't that bad. Better than my parents anyway. My parents thought she was perfect, like as a couple, we were to be their perfect clones. But Blaire's parents would flat-out call her on her nagging, or if she complained about money or dragged me out to some party that she knew I'd hate."

"Not just a PTSD thing then, you've never liked crowds?"

"Hell no. As you saw, it's a lot worse now. Not just a dislike, but genuine meltdown." He pressed his lips to her temple. "As nothing seems to scare you, I'm hiding behind you."

She snorted against his neck, but didn't say it out loud. *He* scared her. More than anything. Vince had never admitted to weakness. Giovanni had never stood and embraced for no good reason. Randy had been a youthful playmate. Zane was built to shatter what was left of her heart.

The door creaked open behind her. Clearing his throat and stepping back, Zane dug the keys out of his pocket. "Let's go."

T he long driveway to the Sutherland's place was en-closed in a fairytale grove of maples. Zane had kept both hands firm on the steering wheel nearly the entire drive, since Freya's skirt had slid up her thigh – not quite to the point of showing all the goods, but one glance at the curve of her inner thigh, exquisitely remembering how he'd traced his tongue along that contour, straight to the honeyed silk of her... breathing in and out, his knuckles turned white as he clenched the wheel.

Imagination on the verge of exploding, he tried to keep his eyes locked on the road. *Maybe an oatmeal stout with a coffee edge...* Never polite to arrive at your best friend's parents' house with a raging hard-on. Even worse to admit it was because he'd been fantasizing about the erotic weekend he'd spent with his soon-to-be annulled wife who happened to also be their niece.

There were already a few of cars in the driveway. Eamon and Tammy were just getting out of their car, carrying a red-flowered bowl that looked to contain a potato or pasta salad. Seeing Zane's truck arrive, they turned and waited before going in. His heart thundered in his chest, wondering if they knew, and if they did, what the hell was he going to say?

Although, on the plus side, nothing calmed a massive boner like in-law scrutiny.

Parking next to their car, he held back while Freya hopped out to chat, Sophie joining her. He grabbed the box of beers he'd brought and took his time walking to the front of the truck.

Eamon moved to greet him. "I hear you've got quite the home brewing set-up."

Zane nodded, gesturing to the opened box.

A warm smile, damn disarming, Eamon accepted the subtle offer. Remembering he'd forgotten to take his ring off, Zane checked his grip to make sure the eye-catching piece of jewelry was hidden.

If he'd seen it, Eamon didn't let on. Instead, he popped the cap off and took a long swig. "Damn, that is good," he held the bottle back and admired.

"Thanks. I've always got more than I'll drink and try to pass them off, so I can have Freya bring more over next time."

"Great." Eamon gestured toward the gate to the back patio where Freya, Sophie, and Tammy were disappearing. "I hope my family wasn't too overwhelming for you. We're a big bunch, and that was a rowdy crowd."

He snorted, holding back on the eye-roll. "Both of my parents are only children, so it was... different." Biting his tongue, he held back before he said anything potentially more offensive than he'd already implied.

Eamon threw his head back and let out a chortle. "Got that right. Different. We're a unique group, that's for sure. I am really sorry about the toxic drinks and laced cupcakes. Lulu's parents are so furious, they're making them write formal apologies to all the guests and return the gifts. I can't remember the last time I got stoned. And the combination? It's lucky Tammy and I made it back to the hotel room. I don't remember much after dinner."

Zane let out a long sigh of relief that their secret might be safe.

Until Eamon laughed, "I mean, can you imagine what trouble we all might have gotten into? I've got the wildest pictures on my phone."

Blood draining from his face, Zane cleared his throat and backed away, "Yeah, I can imagine. I, uh..." he trailed off, on an urgent mission to deliver the beer to Paul at the outdoor kitchen. He set the box on the ground, slipped the ring off, and jammed it into his pocket in one smooth motion.

Paul immediately grabbed one from the box and helped Zane load up the minifridge. "Thanks for bringing the beer. As soon as Asher mentioned how talented you were, I hinted you ought to bring some."

Denise pranced out the door and threw her arms around him, clearing her throat, "Hinted? Honey, I believe *begged* is the word." She flipped her salt and pepper braid out of the way and looked up at Zane, "I'm so glad you came. Asher said to give you space, so we did. But now that you're all settled in, please say you'll come over often? If you want to use the pool but aren't in the mood for company, just text us and come on over so we know to give you some privacy. That's what Asher and Sophie do. We don't get enough use out of it on our own, so really, I'm not kidding."

Hugging her right back, he felt the familiar affection that had grown with each of their visits to San Diego. Asher was damn lucky. Clenching in his chest, that growing pang tugged at him. "I'd like that. Thanks again for making that apartment so great and inviting me over today. Looks like a hell of a setup." He checked out the patio, its clusters of conversation-arranged furniture, an outdoor sofa set under a huge gazebo, Pippa and Lincoln snuggled up in one of the overstuffed chairs.

"You've kept our boy out of enough trouble over the years, and aside from all that, we like you. We are truly glad you're here."

Paul nodded, "Good to have you."

Sashaying over, her breezy tank skimming above the edge of her skirt, Freya grabbed a glass and poured some ice water from the fancy dispenser filled with lemon slices and cucumber. She leaned against the counter and smiled knowingly, lacing her arm around Denise's other side.

Shifting, Denise squeezed them both and then stood comfortably with her arm around her niece. What was it about Freya, that, okay, shit, hokey as it sounded, but she was so damn huggable? She exuded this warmth and easy affection that settled those around her. Zane stepped back and grabbed a beer for himself, enjoying watching Freya interact amongst those she'd known her whole life.

"And you," Denise smiled. "Home at last. How are things going? Have you found a space to work that makes you feel productive? Selling globally going okay from our small corner of the world?"

Freya crossed one foot in front of the other as she stood linked with her aunt, the casual gesture showing how close they were. "It's tough. I haven't been as productive as I'd like. I need a studio."

"None of the bedrooms work at the house?"

"Maybe the dining room. But I doubt Asher's going to make it the full six months before moving in, and, although I know I'd be welcome, I do want to use the next few months to find a space to make my own; someplace I can knock out walls if I have to, as good lighting can make a piece."

"I understand that. You just let us know if there's anything we can do to help."

Tammy came out of the house, joining at Freya's other side. "You liked the light in your old bedroom; you can always move back home, or even use it as a temporary studio."

Freya's smile remained genuine, but Zane could see the nine-one-one emergency flashing behind those brilliant blues. He nodded to Freya, "You were going to give me a tour?"

She leaped to his side. "Of course." Linking elbows with him, she strolled toward the pool and cascading hot tub. "Thanks."

"They're supportive of you. But, well, I know I like to have my feet steady beneath me before I'm open to help."

"Me too," she leaned in, then immediately righted her posture at the familiarity of the gesture. Waving her arm over the water in front of them, she commented, "So. This is the pool."

Grinning, he brushed his thumb over hers, then pulled away. "Yup. Lovely."

Standing a few feet away, her body moved smoothly, openly, as if they were still joined. "Think my parents know more than they're letting on?"

"Your dad mentioned 'wild' pictures on his phone. Honestly, I ran away before I could find out what he meant. I immediately envisioned pictures from our wedding and wanted to ask to see, then I realized, shit, what if he meant he and your mom were up to something I *don't* want to see?"

She threw her head back and laughed, "Good call. They've never exactly been closed off about sex, but I think my dad would have a stroke if he discovered naked pictures of he or my mom on his phone."

Continuing their tour, he followed Freya over to the seating area where Lincoln, Pippa, and Sophie had already settled. He heard a splash as Asher came sprinting out of the house and dove into the pool.

Pippa had set out flutes on the lip of the propane fireplace and had a champagne bottle nestled in a silvery bucket filled with ice. "Hey guys, we're toasting," she grinned.

At his side, Freya shivered like she'd teased him about earlier. "No thank you. I'm all champagned out these days, and I'll bet Zane would agree."

Pippa rose to her feet and pulled the bottle from the ice. "We have twenty more bottles leftover from our wedding that we need to use up. Please have a few sips at least. Besides," she winked and whispered, "we never got to toast your wedding."

Flashing her cousin a death glare, Freya whispered, "Shush. You're lucky I told you."

Pippa grinned mischievously, "No matter. I will be supportive of whatever you decide, but I can tell you right now, you're not getting an annulment."

Zane clenched his jaw and moved to her side, forming a quiet wall of resistance.

Rolling her eyes, Freya's flip-flopped foot tapped furiously, "Please, Pip, this is hard enough."

Instantly, Pippa showed her sweet side and held the champagne bottle to one side, wrapping her other around Freya's upper back, speaking softly. "I'm sorry. I love you and want you to be happy. And you look happy with Zane. He's twice the man any of the others ever were. But if he's not the one, or you're not ready, I've got your back."

Zane bit his cheek and stared at the ground as Pippa stepped back. He wasn't sure if she'd meant for him to hear all that, but something told him that had been her intent. As if he weren't miserable enough already.

Twisting the wire safety off the champagne bottle, Pippa grimaced as she muttered, "You don't even have to drink any of this, but at least pretend." Rocking the top, Pippa struggled to uncork the heavy bottle.

Zane reached to help, having opened enough when hiding in the kitchen at his parents' parties. "May I?"

"No, I got it," she grumbled, putting more muscle into it.

Having seen it coming a mile away, the pop didn't scare him, nor the cork whizzing passed his ear as he ducked out of the way. But the spray of foamy bubbles soaking him head-to-toe was shocking and unpleasant.

Closing his eyes, he wiped off the sticky sweet liquid from his face. As soon as he could see again, he looked down to see he was utterly drenched. At his side, Freya was scowling and equally soaked, her top and skirt pasted to her skin. She licked the champagne off her lips and adopted one of those I'm-pissed-but-won't-admit-it-because-I-love-you smiles to mask her irritation. She blinked and looked up at the sky.

Pippa laughed out loud, covering her mouth to hide her obvious amusement. "I'm so sorry," she said over and over. "Really. I'm so, so sorry."

Shaking more of the bubbly off his hand, Zane shook his head and managed a smile, "That's okay. Really. I've got my swim stuff in the car anyway."

Denise came dashing over. "Oh my. Pippa, honey, really? Could you not soak our guests?"

Rolling her eyes, Pippa laughed again, her grin almost sheepish. "I do feel bad. Someone else can open the next bottle."

"Why don't you guys get your swim stuff on and I'll get those clothes washed for you so they're ready before you leave," Denise offered, her sincerity more convincing than Pippa's laughing remorse.

Freya finally found a smile, "Thanks. We'll need to head in to get changed anyway, so I'll toss our things in the wash." She motioned for Zane to follow, reaching out to take his hand, realizing her mistake and withdrawing just as fast.

Leaving wet footprints on the driveway as they stepped off the patio, Zane ran ahead to the truck, calling to Freya, "I got it." Keeping both of their bags outstretched to avoid any further champagne-contamination, Zane met Freya at the house.

On the front step, she slipped off her flip-flops and scooted her feet along the doormat. "Have I mentioned how much I hate champagne?"

Catching up to her, he slipped off his shoes, leaving them to dry in the sun. "Me too. I'd like to see if there was anything left in the bottle or if it's all on us."

She grinned and opened the front door. "At least we didn't have to drink it."

The house was open and airy, yet warm and inviting. Like a postcard, the massive windows overlooked the valley beyond. Instead of going up the stairs to the open loft-style bedrooms, Freya led the way past the kitchen, past the bathroom and opened the next door.

Not much more than a closet, the laundry room was just shy of feeling cluttered. The washer and dryer were covered with folded towels and linens on the right, and a wall of shelves filled with cleaning supplies, coats, and other odds and ends covered most of the wall on the left. Dimly lit, the edges of the room were cloaked in shadow, the only light an uncovered bulb overhead.

Freya reached around him and shut the door behind him. As he held out her clothing bag, she peeled her sopping top over her head, then efficiently scooted her skirt over her hips.

Mouth dropping open, his breath whooshed out as if he'd been punched in the gut. Wet and built and covered only by the skimpiest damn bra that barely supported her breasts, a wisp of lace panties covering the rest of the goods, she stepped close to him. A whisper away, she didn't quite touch him, the space between them tantalizing with possibility.

She murmured as she reached around him, "Excuse me." A squeal of hinges shattered the flimsy hope that she'd been coming onto him, and she tossed her clothes in the top-load washer.

Too late, he was already rock hard. Hell, since Freya had come into his life, he'd been a blink away from a full erection at pretty much all moments of the day. No ignoring it at night.

As she moved, she brushed against him... right against his groin.

Closing his eyes, he groaned, trying fruitlessly to tame things before she noticed. Not that she wouldn't notice the rigid tenting action, even in the dim light.

Biting her lip, she traced her hands along the edge of his waistline. "Okay, you win. I wasn't exactly subtle."

Inhaling sharply as her hands grazed the skin of his abs, he murmured, "I'll go take a cold shower."

She continued her exploration before tugging his shirt over his head, tracing her fingertips down every hard-earned muscle on her way down to his shorts. Sliding his cargos, his briefs over his hips, she trailed those long, clever fingers over his shaft.

"Fuck, you're killing me," he gasped. Before he embarrassed himself right into her hands, he gripped her hips and spun her, pressing her up against the washing machine.

She gasped at the cool metal against her skin.

Taking advantage of her open mouth, he kissed her urgently, plundered, hungry for her lush lips, her savory taste he hadn't stopped dreaming about since that first kiss on her bedroom floor. Her fingertips dug into his shoulder blades as she kissed him back with equal fervor, the soft roundness of her breasts, the skin of her abdomen pressing against him. Every muscle in his body tensed as he tried to hold back, but he was completely lost. Painfully hard, he relinquished and pulled her against him; she pressed back, writhing and murmuring her equal need.

The world around them nonexistent, he shifted, nipping at her ear, her neck, grazing his tongue along her collarbone and to the narrow recess between her breasts. Hands encircling her, he flicked off her bra and took a breast deep into his mouth. She gasped, her soft moans suppressed under a frantic whisper. Sweet and damp from the champagne, her skin prickled as he wrapped his hands around each breast. Sucking and laving, he nearly came at the feel of her, at the sound of the response she couldn't silence.

Dropping to his knees, he slid her panties down and clutched her hips, flattening his tongue against her clit before either had room to doubt. Wet and ready, her breath came fast. He flicked his tongue against her, then savored a long, slow lick as she melted against his mouth. Leaning into him, she tightened her fingers in his hair, urging him on.

Increasing the pace as the shudder in her voice accelerated, he pulsed and vibrated. He groaned against her soft curls as she grew slicker, sweeter, her body temperature raising to feverish in response.

One weekend together, hell, one night really, and he felt her, anticipated each need, knowing she was nearing her peak. Not giving an inch, he intensified his movements, wet against wet; he nearly came as her soprano moans became an aria.

As her body slackened, relaxing into him, he slowed his pace and brought her down gently. His heart thundered in his chest as the urgency, the thrill, tapered to a yearning.

Lowering, he sat on his heels before her, biting his lip as he savored one last taste of her, and looked up to see her response.

15

Need a Hand?

Flipping and flopping of shoes against the hardwood floor outside the laundry room tapped closer. Still hazy from epic orgasm, it took Freya a moment to identify the sound.

Silencing a squeal, she moved and stood in front of the door, blocking in case anyone tried to come in. Shit, what if they'd been caught? Thirty seconds ago, she couldn't hear anything beyond her pulse in her ears, her irrepressible sighs as Zane sent her across the brilliant sky, grounding her with his rumbling moans that echoed hers, his strong hands bracing her hips.

As he rose to his feet, lower lip still teasing between his teeth, he grinned. Holding her finger up in front of her mouth, she nodded outside in case he hadn't heard. Nodding, he acknowledged the sound and casually slipped the rest of the way out of his shorts, tossing them in the washer.

Breathless, she nearly came again watching him. Damn, that man was built. In every possible way.

The flopping feet halted, followed by the creak of the bathroom door. The sound heightened over the tile floor of the bathroom, no more than a layer of sheetrock between them. Relaxing against the door, she tried to slow her pulse.

Instead of pulling on his swim shorts, Zane set them on top of the dryer and closed the narrow distance between them, his bare skin an inch from hers. It took about every bit of restraint she was capable of to not plaster herself against him, her breasts heavy as she craved more of his touch. As much as her brain understood where that would lead, again, her nipples tightened and pulled her toward him. Dammit, her body knew pheromones, and didn't give a shit about annulments.

Whispering in her ear, his breath against her skin reminding her of how clever that mouth was, he said, "Was that closer to handholding or consummating?"

A silent chuckle escaped her lips, their eyes meeting in the dim room, both sporting devious grins. "I have no idea what you're talking about. I happened to have bumped into you while doing my laundry."

The sink through the wall turned on, their unwelcome neighbor washing their hands. Stepping back, he grabbed her bag and handed it to her before finally pulling on his swim shorts. Freya slipped on the black bikini.

The bathroom door swung open and closed again, a few quick flip-flops, then a soft knock at the door stopped Freya's heart entirely. Pippa's voice echoed through the door, "Freya?"

"Yes?" she managed to answer, her voice crackling as the panic started to ease that it wasn't either of her parents or her aunt or uncle.

"If you're hungry, we're dishing up. Is Zane upstairs? I'll go let him know."

"I, uh, I've about got the washer figured out. I'll tell him."

"I forgot they bought a new machine. Need a hand in there?"

"Nope. I've got all the hands I need," she stifled a chuckle as very, very capable hands traced down her sternum, then scooped under her swimsuit top and grasped her breasts in his palms, simultaneously tweaking her taut nipples until she lost her voice. She flashed him a glare; not easy to appear convincing as she leaned into his grip, her breath caught in her throat as she was already primed to react to his touch and halfway to another orgasm.

"Okay. Well, again, I'm really sorry about the champagne. I've got an extra change of clothes if yours aren't done in time."

More footsteps walked toward them as Pippa continued her painfully long conversation, Zane driving her out of her mind as he massaged.

Asher's voice echoed through the door, "Zane? Quit ruining your annulment with my cousin and get your ass out here. Dinner's ready."

Slipping his hands out of her top, Zane placed a lingering kiss on the upper curve of her breast as he checked that she was tucked back in properly, then swung the door open. "Cockblock," he muttered at Asher as he headed out.

As they walked away, Asher corrected, "Wingman."

While Pippa stood shellshocked in the hall, Freya dumped in the laundry soap and turned on the washing machine. Finally, she bit her lip to hide her smile and acknowledged Pippa. "Not a word," she raised her eyebrows.

"Of course not," Pippa shrugged dramatically. "Come on. How many times did you cover for me when I'd sneak out to Lincoln's?"

Freya's head tipped back as laughter bubbled up from her throat. "Once. Your graduation night when you finally gave Lincoln your virginity." She turned and pulled her sundress from her bag.

"That's it? Sophie's right. I should have gotten into more trouble."

"Or not. Look where it's gotten me? Three broken engagements and a drunk wedding I'm going to blow the annulment for because every time I'm with the man, we end up fooling around. You couldn't handle breaking the rules, and I can't resist quality pheromones."

"Maybe this time they're right."

"Doesn't matter. Do you know the last time I painted anything?"

Pippa's eyebrows dropped. They halted before going out the front door. "I'm sorry."

"It's okay. I have artist's block. Zane is a distraction I don't need."

"You've only been home a few weeks. It's probably more the stress of the move than Zane. Be patient, it'll come back."

"You sound like me."

"See? I'm not a hopeless case." Pippa grinned and waved Freya ahead. "You're right. Sometimes you should go with the flow."

Dinner was relaxed; burgers in the shade, the sun glinting off the pool, not a sound but the easy conversation of her favorite people on the planet. Swallowing her last bite of burger, she walked to the garbage bag that hung over the edge of the fence.

Tammy followed close behind and dashed to catch up while Freya held the trash bag open. "Thanks," she smiled. "You look relaxed."

"I guess I am. It's really good to be home," she curled her toes on the rough concrete, eyeing the pool and counting the minutes until she could climb in.

Halting before they rejoined the others, Tammy twiddled her thumbs awkwardly.

"What's up, Mom?" Freya nodded to Tammy's restless hands and crossed her arms.

"There's a rumor floating around. About you. And Zane."

Oh shit. Freya's pulse thundered in her ears as she accepted that at least some of the hundreds of people had probably witnessed her stupidity. "Okay."

"You know your Aunt Clara. She says that after leaving the party, you two headed across the street and had a romantic dinner, then wandered into the wedding chapel across from the hotel and came out laughing and smiling and kissing and... married."

Freya kicked her foot against the patio. Grimacing as a sharp pebble jabbed into her skin, she hissed, "Aunt Clara is a busybody. That doesn't sound like a coincidence, it sounds like spying."

"Well, yes, that's why I unfriended her on Facebook. But tell me..." Tammy stared into Freya, the maternal-worried-frown extracting the tears she poorly attempted to blink away. "Wait. I'm sorry. I shouldn't have brought it up here. Can I come visit you Wednesday? Better yet, let me take you out to breakfast."

Keeping her lips pursed tight, she nodded.

Clearing her throat, Tammy said, "Wasn't Lulu's gown awful? I could see her butt crack."

A tickle of laughter released Freya's throat. "It was terrible. What was she thinking, wearing a red thong with a white dress?"

"Oh, and you'll love this. After you left, Aunt Del came over and asked where your special friend had gone. Kept saying how she'd hoped to rope him in for a dance so she could pinch that butt."

The tickle turned into a riotous chortle. "She implied as much when she met him. Was she always so inappropriate?"

"To an extent. I talked to Gloria, and she said it's worse since her divorce; she's been trying to start an affair with some hot young thing. Gloria has tried to reign her in, letting her know she could, and should, get in serious trouble for that sort of behavior."

"I can't even tell Zane; he'd be so horrified."

Tammy bit her lips together, then whispered, "I like him. And I think he likes you a lot."

"Thought we weren't talking about it."

"Sorry. Sorry. We'll talk Wednesday."

"Thanks." Freya tugged her dress over her head and set it on the back of a chair, then slipped into the pool. Warm as the Mediterranean, she put her head under so only her own thoughts could get to her.

After crossing the length of the pool, she turned to see Pippa chuck a ball to her with a half-assed *heads up*. Fortunately, she had terrible aim and the ball didn't even make it halfway to Freya. Her quiet swim rapidly morphed into a rambunctious game of water basketball. Once her fingers were entirely pruned, her muscles heavy from the workout, she climbed the ladder and wrapped herself in a plush towel, still warm from the setting sun.

She dried off her feet on the doormat again and walked through the house to the laundry room. Denise had moved their clothes along while they goofed off in the pool like a bunch of rowdy kids, all overdue for the release after the last few months. Between Pippa and Lincoln's wedding, everyone moving, new jobs... eloping... it had been a hell of a time for all of them.

Closing the door, she slipped off her swimsuit and pulled on her luxuriously warm panties fresh from the dryer. Her bra was hung neatly from a hook, so she tucked it in the bag with her wet swim stuff. Just as toasty from the sun, her dress brushed over her bare breasts, sensitized as she relived her earlier venture into the laundry room.

This time they'd been smart. Zane waited outside while she got changed. After watching him swim like he'd been born to the water, her imagination was running wild enough. Water basketball hadn't been much safer, as man-to-man defense was so much more fun when the man was so damn sexy, and she could tug him by the waistband to get around him, whisper naked ideas in his ear to distract him... but torture of the worst sort when all she wanted to do was strip off her top and... shaking her head, she tried to focus on the laundry.

She folded Zane's shorts and t-shirt, neatly tucking them in his bag. Checking the dryer to make sure she hadn't missed anything, her hand brushed over something metal, a soft scraping sound as it spun on the metal wall of the dryer. Grabbing it, she realized Zane's ring must have been in his pocket.

Sliding it onto her thumb, she walked out with their things. Zane was already on the way in and froze when he saw her. The corner of his mouth quirked up, and he resumed his progress toward her, his plush towel wrapped around his waist. Standing inches apart, his voice hoarse, he asked, "You about ready?"

She nodded. "Yeah. Sophie riding home with Asher?"

"Yeah. They're staying at your place tonight."

"K. I'll meet you at the truck?" She handed him his clean clothes.

He nodded and dug his keys from his bag, handing them to her. "Go ahead. I'll be just a minute."

L ying wide awake in bed, Zane gave up on sleep. At least it hadn't been nightmares, as he couldn't even get to sleep to begin with. He'd calculated adjustments to favorite beer recipes, considered the possibility of opening his own brewhouse, maybe even have some food on the menu but small scale. When that didn't work, he resorted to reciting architectural principles to bore himself to sleep, but that pissed him off, remembering his parents would be arriving soon and would do their utmost to get him interested in architecture again.

He lumbered to the bathroom and took a long shower, but the soap Freya had bought him reminded him of how good she always smelled. Earthy, spicy, refreshing, as complex as she was. When even the glass of hot milk he'd resorted to didn't work, he gave up.

He'd already spent all damn day and the night before reliving his stolen moment with Freya. What had he been thinking, doing what he'd done with her in the laundry room in the middle of a family party? And, fuck, she'd been so damn hot, tasted so damn good, her response so genuine. Yeah, they weren't supposed to be fooling around, but the moment had been so natural, like their weekend before the damn wedding.

No doubt about it, they couldn't see each other anymore. At least not until the annulment hearing was over and they were free to be free again.

Maybe he'd walk over there, sneak in, and if she was awake, he'd make sure she was okay with everything that had happened; she'd been so quiet on the drive home. He given her space, but it was killing him.

And if she was asleep? Even better. It wasn't cohabitating if he stole a few hours snuggle. And she'd have to sleep over when his parents got there anyway.

He opened the closet to grab his shoes, only to find they'd landed on Jack, a muddy shoeprint tarnishing his stainless-steel case in his isolated corner.

Fucking shit, Jack. Lowering to his knees, he tried to brush away the crusted dirt, a few fine scratches already etched into the side.

You couldn't have waited two more days? Staring at the lifeless box, he was roped into the mental trap he'd been avoiding. Two fucking days, that's it. Maybe he could have...

Nope. Not doing it. It was past time.

Rising to his feet, he stalked back to the bedroom. He picked up the phone and put it back down again. Asher didn't deserve his night ruined by Zane waking him to demand they set a time to scatter Jack.

He couldn't have said why he did it, but hell, he did. Before he could second guess himself, he hit send. Answering before the first ring even finished, Freya's bleary voice soothed the ache in his chest, "Zane? Are you okay?"

"Yeah," he exhaled.

"Okay. Good." She paused, waiting for him to speak.

His mouth opened to say something, anything, but no sound came out. Burning in his chest, a million notions refused to emerge as anything coherent. "Sorry I woke you."

"I'll come over."

"No. That's okay. Just... talk to me."

"Okay. Um, I painted all day. It felt amazing."

"That's great. I know you hadn't been feeling it lately." His breath came easier, lighter as he shifted his focus.

"I hadn't, but something clicked. It felt... better than ever."

"Can I see it? Tomorrow?"

"Anytime."

"I'd say right now. I couldn't sleep and was on my way over, but... anyway. Tomorrow?"

"Absolutely." He could hear her smile on the other end, coated with those nerves he knew she couldn't hide when it came to sharing her work. So damn confident in all things, but so vulnerable when she shared something so personal.

"I set up an Instagram account."

"I'm sorry. You hate social media."

"I really, really do. But I really love being home again, so it's a necessary evil."

"What are you going to post?"

"I have no idea. I think I'll follow a few interesting people first, you know, get a feel for things first."

"I let Jack die," he blurted out, the words having been waiting until he wasn't holding them back.

"What? No you didn't. You were there when he died. They couldn't revive him."

"Before that. I knew something was up. But we left him."

"You couldn't have known what would happen."

"Logically, I know you're right. By some miracle, he made it out of there. But he never got over it. Never walked again. So damn many surgeries. I should have been there with him. I was trying to hurry my ass out of the Navy and get out of the shitshow it had become without Asher and Jack... and I watched him slip away. Too many pain pills. Then harder stuff when he couldn't make the pain go away."

"He was a lucky guy."

What?

"To have you worry about him. To regret that you couldn't save him. I know you left the Navy to take care of him. He knew you were coming for him."

"I wasn't fast enough."

"He would have held on if he could. He waited for you and Asher in the end. He didn't die alone."

Rubbing a hand over his face Zane let the image of Jack lying motionless in the hospital bed, so many tubes and wires. His ears still rang with the flatline alarm.

"What would he say, if he saw you in this holding pattern, refusing to move on? It's not that you don't have a dream, it's that you won't let yourself."

He chuckled under his breath, a burning behind his eyes at the absurdity, "Jack didn't like to word things pretty. He'd tell me to shit or get off the pot."

Her smile resonated in her voice, "He's lucky to have friends that will be sure he's remembered. Tell me something crazy about him."

Dropping back on the bed, his throat threatened to close at the barrage of memories flooding in. "He was afraid of heights."

"Seriously? He was a Navy SEAL."

"I know, right? He'd get to the door of the plane, and he'd grip the sides and whisper so the other guys couldn't hear, 'I can't. Just push me out before I start bawling like a baby.'"

"Did you?"

"Fuck yeah. Kept his trap shut the entire fall, but the second we hit the water, he was the first to the surface so he could dunk me the moment I came up for air and promise to kick my ass if we survived the op."

"And when you got home?"

"By then he was thankful. Until Asher and I took him on a surprise trip to the Grand Canyon."

"You guys had some good times."

"Yeah, yeah we did."

"Sounds like a good friend. Would he blame you?"

Shit. "Of course not. It's the job. Always a risk."

"I wish I'd known about you while you were in. I was already worrying about Asher; I could have worried about you too."

"And sent me care packages? His parents would send me the best stuff. Fancy chocolate and magazines with sports updates and Paul even snuck in a Playboy when Asher hinted that we were going stir-crazy overseas."

"Maybe I would have sent you some naked pics."

Laughter bubbled up and loosened the damn frog in his throat. "Tell me exactly in detail how you would have posed for those."

She laughed out loud; he closed his eyes and pictured those rosy lips turned up in whole-hearted amusement.

"Phone sex isn't cohabitating or consummating." He grinned, shifting the pillow under his head to get comfy. "Although, video-chatting would be way better, then you can show me exactly what you'd be wearing, or not, for my dirty pics."

"As much as I would love to accommodate you, especially after our laundry room adventure, I'm going to pass tonight."

"Tomorrow then?"

"We'll see. Goodnight, Zane."

"'Night, Freya. Thanks."

"Anytime. Seriously."

Closing his eyes, he indulged in the what-ifs.

16

FUBARed

F uck. Nothing was going the way it was supposed to. Having no plan had seemed brilliant. What better way to let the last few years fade?

Zane stared into the closet at his muddy black running shoes, teetering against Jack again. Biting his cheek, he forced air in and out before the fucking waterworks started. Not that he was some macho ass that refused to cry. Hell, if anyone deserved to have someone down on their knees, screaming at the sky and furiously crying rageful tears of life's-not-fucking-fair, it was Jack.

Freya had talked him down last night, but he couldn't call her every time he opened the damn closet. The run had burned off a lot of it. About a mile in, he'd felt the blissful sensation of an empty mind, cool air flowing in and out of his lungs, muscles burning with the lactic acid of escapism.

Then he'd seen the empty garage spot that Freya would eventually be filling with a car; a bleak reminder that she was in a tough place in life. Teetering on the edge of success and failure, her lifelong dreams at risk of shattering on impact, she didn't deserve to be dragged down by a needy ex-SEAL that didn't even have a dream. He didn't have anything to fill that void she needed filling, and he loved that she would kick his ass for implying she didn't have all her shit together.

The headache hit as he'd dashed up the stairs, each footfall echoing off the hills in the distance and pinging right back into his pulsating skull. After slamming the front door, egging on his headache, he'd mindlessly kicked his shoes into the closet. Crashing into the tin can, he'd nearly spilled the ashes across the floor... *ashes*. Fuck that. Ground up carcass that was too damn stubborn to burn.

Searing hot brine coated his eyes as he shifted his shoes to the side. Staring down at the latest set of muddy footprints to tarnish the can, he growled, "Come on, man. Asher was the goof-off playboy. I was the quiet, socially awkward one. You were the heart of us. The guy that knew when to laugh, when to grit his teeth and dig in harder, and when to go with the flow."

He dropped to his knees, the impact vibrating into his hips, his ribs, his pounding head. "Asher blames himself for us leaving you guys. Not his fault; he followed his gut and it was the right thing to do. Your stubborn ass said we should go check it out, that you'd keep all those family men safe while we risked our expendable asses."

Boiling down his sweat-encrusted cheek, the tear trailed down and sloshed onto the floor. "Dumbshit. You knew. Maybe not consciously, but you knew staying was a fucking death sentence, and you pushed us to get the hell out of there. Too damn stubborn to die that day, you let me drag your ass back to the LZ. Fuck, man. If *you* couldn't keep it together, couldn't tolerate the pain, living with the quiet of life on the outside, how do you expect me to?"

His throat raw, vision useless from the damn watery coating, he wiped the shit that drained from his nose and rose to his feet. He picked up his phone and texted Asher, *Pick a spot; we're scattering next time you're home.*

A few minutes later, his phone buzzed. *K.*

Turning to hit the shower, he caught sight of the time. Stupidly, recklessly, he drifted to the window. As he'd hoped, or dreaded, Freya strolled barefoot across the lawn, yoga mat tucked under one arm. She unrolled the mat and gazed out at the endless vista, feet anchored to the ground while the wind tossed her hair around in a turbulent mass. From afar, he breathed with her, letting his brain calm enough to go about his day.

He stalked to the shower and let the hot water rush over his skin. Sandalwood and tangy grapefruit with bits of oatmeal formed a refreshing foam as he scrubbed the morning away. The corner of his mouth quirked up at the oddity; while he'd been at the barber, Freya had, apparently, not only found an irresistible lotion of black tea and honey that he'd licked off her the other night in an indulgence that shouldn't have happened, but she'd picked up a bar of soap that "made her imagine him naked."

Hell, even if they could make this work, she was so far out of his league it wasn't funny. Sure, they'd both traveled the world. He'd inhaled the top of the sky in numbing freefall, felt the pressure of the bottom of the sea threaten to crush his skull, broken his heart rescuing the darkest parts of humanity... while she'd reveled in the light, from painting and sketching from hills upon hills of grapevines, to smiling children where smiles were priceless, and even to one of his favorite goofy sketches of her own feet.

Full-on smile taking over his face as he resolved to ask her for the self-portrait foot sketch for the lonely spot on the bathroom wall, he tipped his head back and rinsed the suds from his body. Hand trailing down, goosebumps forming in his wake, he let himself enjoy one of the solo aspects of married life before it was gone. Closing his eyes, he relived the heat, the exquisite pull of her mouth on his cock. Not a trace of shyness, she'd shown him just how sheltered of a life he'd led before meeting her. How much he'd craved her without knowing what had been missing.

After drying off and pulling on an ancient pair of cargo shorts and a black t-shirt, Zane slipped on a pair of sneakers. No way was he sitting inside today. Too much time in his head already.

What, he'd been up for two hours, and had already pushed his body beyond anything he'd done in months, cried his fucking eyes out, debated the safest way to end his mistake of a marriage, then jerked off at the very thought of the woman that he really, really shouldn't have in his life. Maybe he should go back to the Navy. At least then he knew… well, he knew what to do when he got up in the morning, what his day would look like, and would be so wrecked from exhaustion that he'd sleep through the night.

As his feet hit the gravel at the base of the steps, he saw Freya wandering across the field, her cheeks flushed from her favorite way to welcome the day. She glanced his direction and offered a soft smile that tugged at that stupid pang again, a pathetic hope that her heart was doing the same fricking pitter patter that his was.

Pushing past the burning in the hollow cavern of his chest, he nodded toward his truck and said, "Need a ride into town this morning? I can wait."

She shook her head as she continued toward the main house. "No, thanks though."

Firing up the engine, the sound of its powerful rumble vibrated into his veins. Easing down the driveway, he halted at the main road. Staring down the empty road to the left, he ignored the lazy drive that beckoned to him; his brain couldn't handle anymore quiet. To the right, he could just make out the sign announcing Foothills was only a mile ahead.

Tires crunching over the gravel, he took the right. A couple that had to be pushing a hundred was already out for a walk, decked out with their sun hats, Keens, and what looked to be a picnic in their backpacks, probably headed for the River-side Trail for a well-deserved scenic breakfast. As he passed a driveway on the left, a guy in a suit behind the wheel of a BMW gave him a neighborly wave, then pulled onto the road behind him as he headed to work.

Nearing town, the driveways became closer together, and eventually there were a few smaller neighborhoods with settled houses on large lots. Across from the downtown park, Zane parked on the side of the street; not enough folks out yet to necessitate parallel parking the beast of a rig. Puffing his cheeks out, he exhaled through pursed lips.

Strolling along, he passed Sutherland's Hardware, not daring to go in, as he had gotten the distinct impression that Paul would rope him into some temp work in an effort to woo him into the role he wished Asher had taken. Nope. Not living someone else's dream, even for a man he respected. Smoky scents wafted out of a hole-in-the-wall restaurant, Halseth's Smokehouse and Pub, but the sign said they didn't open until eleven. Too bad; something smelled good.

Larissa's Diner was bursting at the seams with people from all walks of life. A vivacious southern woman was hollering to someone inside as she propped the door open to let in the morning air. His stomach growled, reminding him he'd been too tied up to eat anything this morning.

"You must be Asher's friend. Come on in," she waved him in before he had a chance to say no.

"Am I that obvious?"

"Honey, I know everyone in town, and I can spot a tourist a mile off. Plus, you've got that look he does. Eyes that have seen too much, a heavy burden on that heart."

Was she a therapist or a psychic or diner owner? He suspected a little of all three. "You're not wrong. You know Asher pretty well?" He followed her to a seat at the bar, sliding onto a shiny chrome stool with a blue vinyl cushion.

"Known that kid since he was in diapers." She strolled around the bar and grabbed a pot of coffee, flipping his cup over and filling it to the brim. "What can I get you for breakfast?"

Rather than opening the menu, he glanced around at the crowded restaurant. "That hash looks great."

"It's the best. Avocado gruyere or sausage cheddar?"

"Avocado."

She scooted away and disappeared into the kitchen. A familiar voice stood out from the crowd behind him. Turning, he saw the neighbor.

Turning, she caught sight of him and granted him a smile as warm as a toasty fire on a snowy day. "Zane, right?"

He nodded, not having a damn clue what to say that wouldn't come across as the misogynistic crap that Freya accused him of that day. "Yeah."

"Thanks again for that pie. I've been meaning to return the favor with some cookies or something. You like chocolate chip?"

"My favorite."

"I'll bring some by sometime."

He couldn't help it; he studied her face, noting the yellow at the edge of her jaw that told of a healing bruise. As she turned away, he added softly, "Sienna?"

"Yeah?" Her expression fell heavy as she took in the gravity of his look. Damn, he was obvious; he needed to tuck a few positive life experiences under his belt. "I know what you're going to say. I'm okay."

"Please, Freya and I are a few hundred yards away. Don't hesitate."

She squeezed her lips together and looked around. "Thank you. Really. But I don't need any heroes in my life."

He nodded in acceptance and turned around to find Larissa delivering his hash. Rescuing him from even more unsettled thoughts while he ate, Larissa stopped by and chatted between customers, filling him in with local gossip, plus a few stories of Asher rabble-rousing in his younger days.

After Larissa ran his card and gave him a friendly wave as he strolled out, he looked up and down the street. He could barely see Grady and Lincoln's practice a few blocks down, Sophie's across the way, but he wasn't sure he was in the mood for company. Across the road, the park was a little too cheerful. And he wasn't ready to sit and feed the birds like the old guy with a gnarled cane, seated serenely on the bench under a massive dogwood tree.

So, he walked north. Didn't make it far when a green and blue sign in front of a cedar and steel building blocked his path. Turning, he looked at a large, empty patio, in through the expansive glass windows at a two-story-plus industrial-meets-northwest style vacant building. Flip-flopping in his chest, his heart beat deafeningly.

He pulled out his phone and dialed the number on the sign. A polished charm answered immediately.

Finding his voice, Zane cleared the frog from his throat and asked. "What can you tell me about the building for sale across from the park on Main in Foothills?"

"Glad you asked. The property went on the market this morning. A couple from Denver had it built for their daughter to open a café and gift shop, but, apparently, she had other plans and moved to DC to become an environmental lobbyist. Or that's the story anyway. You interested?"

"Thinking about it," he admitted.

"Are you working with a realtor yet?"

"No. I'm really not even in the market, just brewing some ideas."

"How about this. I've got a buddy, decent guy, that's right down the street from the property and can show you around, and, if you decide to make an offer, if you want, he can represent you."

"Sounds fine."

After ending the call, Zane's phone buzzed in his pocket no more than sixty seconds later and he had an appointment. In twenty minutes. There goes the time to think it over.

Instead of feeding the birds, he leaned against the fence and did some quick research on the basic specs he'd need; space, plumbing, electrical. As much as he had no desire to follow in his parents' footsteps, his degree was suddenly coming in handy.

Brain swimming with millions of details, more seeming to add on each time he found a new piece of info, he sealed his eyes shut to still the mental vertigo. Dammit. He swiped up his dialer and hit send.

"Hey, Zane," Grady answered. "Please tell me you're behaving yourselves."

He rolled his eyes and let out a weak laugh. "Mostly. Actually, I'm not calling as a client, but... What do you know about running a craft brewery?"

"I don't know squat about beer. But I know enough about business."

"So, no pressure or anything. But Asher mentioned you're bored and need a project."

"Hey, Asher's just pissy because the bathroom's a mess and I've been refusing to clean it until he realizes there's nothing wrong with the toilet, the black grime is the result of no one cleaning it for an extended period of time."

Crossing his feet as he relaxed against the fence, he laughed, "Don't tell him about toilet brushes or bleach tablets."

Grady laughed out loud mirthlessly, "That's brilliant. Seriously though, I'm not exactly bored, but my job satisfaction is low, and I need something interesting to do."

"I fucking hate talking to people. I'm decent with numbers and projections and all that bullshit, but I'd rather make good beer and maybe even design a menu and, hell, even use that stupid-ass architecture degree for something and make a place people can come to drink the beer, have some food while they do, and maybe hang out and relax."

"Sounds like you've been thinking this through."

"I've been letting the idea bounce around since you brought it up at Ahab's."

"I can talk to people. And run numbers, projections, market, network. Interested in taking on a business partner?"

"Thought you'd never ask."

"Or you could get me drunk. But no backing out after I've signed the dotted line."

"Hey, I fully blame Freya's cousin for getting me trashed. And I have no intention of backing out."

"On the marriage or the partnership?"

"Fuck. I'm not looking for a damn therapist."

"And I have no interest in being your therapist, but I'll be happy to give you shit when you need to get your head out of your ass."

"That I can handle. So I'm looking at the place on Main. Owners backed out."

"The new construction? That place is nice. Great location, appealing design."

"I've got a realtor that will be here in a few minutes."

"I've got a client coming soon, but I'm right down the street from you. Want to swing by my office after, and we can nail down some details?"

"Sounds good."

As they disconnected, a guy in cuffed skinny jeans with ankle boots and a button-up shirt dashed across the street toward him. "Zane?"

He extended his hand and shook, "Yep."

"Mark Sutherland."

He stilled, "Any relation to Asher?"

Cracking a grin, the guy nodded, "My cousin. You know him?" Damn, how many cousins did Asher have? He didn't dare ask if he was on the same side as Freya; he already couldn't keep track of the side of the family he'd met. Nor did he want to explain just how well he knew her.

"Yeah. He's the one that dragged my ass to this absurdly scenic place."

"Are you a SEAL, too?"

He nodded. "Was."

"That's great, man. Thanks for serving our country."

He shrugged. What was with people in this town? They were all so nice, and, well, didn't sound like political asses when they said it.

"You must know Asher pretty well then."

The corners of his mouth quirked up, his head tilting as he thought about the answer to that one. Not many others could say that about either Asher or him.

"You'll have to ask him about my bachelor party sometime," Mark winked.

"He does feel bad about that, somewhere deep down," he laughed, the headache he'd been brewing all morning finally starting to ease.

Mark laughed out loud, shaking his head with an exhaling smile. "So he claims. Anyway, let's head in." He followed Mark as he unlocked and swung open the large French-style doors that led into the cavernous building.

Most of the building had high ceilings with huge beams that would give about any architect wet dreams. The place screamed with possibility.

"What sort of business are you thinking of opening up?"

"Craft brewery."

"Good spot for it. Locations like this don't come up very often around here, so you'll want to move fast."

"I've done a little research. I'll want to bring in a contractor who's done other breweries, see what they think."

"I can get you some names; Uncle Paul can give you a bluntly honest reference on any of the locals."

"That'd be great."

They toured the structure; Zane took notes on the technical aspects. The place was about perfect. Mark was right, he needed to move fast.

As promised, Tammy's truck rumbled down the dusty drive precisely at eight Wednesday morning. Hair still wet and extra curly from the shower, muscles limber from her morning routine that took way longer than normal in a futile attempt to clear her mind of Zane, Freya slipped on a hooded sweatshirt and strolled outside in her bare feet.

Holding up a plain white paper bag, Tammy grinned. When she reached easy chatting distance, she asked, "Coffee? Thought we'd be able to visit more openly if we stayed in."

Freya waved her in.

Tammy set the bag on the island, her feet locking in place as she saw Freya's set-up in the dining area. The floor and table were covered in paint-stained drop cloths, her brushes were clean on a tray on the table, paints lined up in rainbow order, easels stacked in the corner except the largest with her latest still drying. Heart fluttering with an insecurity she despised when it came to her work, Freya bit down on her cheek and set the coffee to brew, keeping her eyes on her mother as she awaited the expected judgment.

Not that Tammy judged, but everyone did. Rarely was their honest opinion verbalized in front of her, but their body language said it all.

"Wow. This isn't like anything I've seen of yours." Tammy's movements were slow, inching closer to the canvas.

That's a nice word for, *I hate it*. Clenching her jaw, Freya tried to force back the heat welling behind her eyes. Insecurity was natural but stupid. "I know."

Tammy stepped to the side, scrutinizing from a new angle. "It's incredible." Eyes locked on the painting, Tammy's voice grew bolder. "The way you captured each muscle, the anguish in his posture; I can feel the grief of a war hero without even needing to see his face or uniform or any specifics, I can tell."

And the burning started to blur her vision. She blinked away the moisture, trying to see last night's insomniac binge work through someone else's eyes. A figure, a man in exercise shorts sprinting down a mountain path. His body was tense, his pace rapid. A storm festered in the background, even the trees in the distance succumbed to its power, but the runner's grief outmatched the ferocity of the weather.

She'd tossed and turned before Zane's late-night call. After they'd hung up, she couldn't have slept if her life depended on it. She hadn't been able to shake the vision, the emotions he'd stirred.

Tammy turned back and wrapped her arms around Freya, tugging her close until Freya hugged her mom. "You're a gifted artist," she said softly as Freya slumped into her. "Your landscapes, your flowers and your grapevines are breathtaking. This... this is raw emotion I've never seen you project into your work."

Ignoring her coffee, the savory pastries rapidly cooling in the bag, Tammy walked around to see the other drying. The one she'd told Zane about and... well, part of her felt guilty he didn't get to see it first. Tammy immediately smiled. "Tell me about this one," she said.

Freya stepped closer. "That was..." Nope, not telling her mother that had been inspired by their stolen moment in the laundry room.

"I love it. It's like your other landscapes, except bolder, like the..." Tammy blushed, then continued, "Okay, I'm not good at this stuff, and saying it out loud makes me blush, but you know me. It's like the sun is making love to the mountains. If that makes any sense? Not in a dirty way, I mean, there's nothing overtly sexual about it, it's more of a feeling. Like there's a passion to it, and it's not just serenity."

"It does make sense. If it helps, I was absolutely thinking about sex and all the good feelings that go with it."

Her mother blushed and dove into the bag and pulled out a croissant.

She continued, "I hadn't realized the intimacy between the setting sun and the mountains before, but it struck me as the brush stroked the canvas."

"Intimacy, that's it. Anyway, I like it."

"The auction went well." Freya lifted Tammy's coffee from the machine, delivering it to the island before retrieving her own.

Tammy eased onto a stool and took a bite of her breakfast. "The big one in Rome?"

Freya nodded. Her breath leached from her chest as she told her mother about the fat paycheck on the way, the bidding battle that had ensued, still lightheaded at the shock of it.

"That's fantastic. I'm so proud of you."

As much as she wanted to jump and cheer, her legs were floppy as unset jam. "They want me to send five more pieces now, with the hope of forming a long-term relationship if those sell well."

"I can't believe how things are coming together. You've worked so hard for this."

"It's so much pressure. The gallery in Florence is great, but there are so many and I'm one more tourist-pleaser. The galleries in London and New York are great, but they're so big, I'll be lucky if my paintings don't collect dust. But this... this gallery is one of the most renowned and selective. But I don't have five more like it. I have a few that I'm pleased with that I could send, but they're not of the same caliber."

Tammy looked back to the runner again. "I know these aren't what they're expecting, but send them anyway. Show them your range."

"They're expecting crowd-pleaser landscapes."

"What's the deadline?"

"Two months for all five, but they're hoping I'll send one now to hold my place." Freya grabbed her coffee from the brewer and dropped onto her stool. She grabbed a croissant from the bag and ripped into it. "I've been home a month. I've painted two things, neither of which are even remotely like what I have done before. I have a website, a newsletter, a group of friends I adore... and a husband I don't get to keep."

Tammy set down her cinnamon roll. "So it's true."

Pinching her lips together, Freya managed a nod.

"You two seem really good together. Are you sure you don't get to keep him?"

She shook her head. "In the last month, I've completed a handful of charcoals, one I gave as a gift to an undeserving cousin, two are of Zane—I couldn't help it—and one of my foot. Seriously." Her toes wiggled beneath her. "I gave him my best landscape as a gift, which I meant and I'm not taking back; he needed the serenity of that painting in his life. I have a few decent pieces in the closet of one of the spare bedrooms. And these two." She nodded behind her.

"And?"

"And? The only things I have produced worth mentioning are inspired by my inebriated mistake of a husband. I can't get him out of my head."

Tammy sipped her coffee, pondering over the steam of it, then set it down again. She took a measured bite of cinnamon roll, chewed twice as long as she needed, then swallowed. "I know you don't want to hear it, but that's called falling in—"

"Nope. Don't say it," Freya cut her off, jumping to her feet and crumpling the breakfast packaging into a tiny ball. "That's called blinding lust that kills your useful creativity, then when you think you've finally found a good rhythm, you discover he's not who you thought he was. While he was all sweet and sexy and insatiable at first, when the urgency of falling in lust fades, where you thought there was love, there's nothing but a few meaningless words passed with someone who doesn't like your famous lasagna after all, he no longer finds your smile so irresistible, and wonders why you folded his underwear but didn't match up his socks."

Tammy sighed heavily, holding back the lecture Freya would refuse to hear anyway. "When is the divorce final?"

"Annulment," she sneered, slamming the cabinet door after chucking the bag.

"When is the annulment final?"

"Two weeks."

"Send the runner painting. Let them see your range. If they hate it, then they don't deserve you and I'll fly with you to find other galleries. Then no pressure the next two weeks. Build your website, your brand. Nurture your soul. Hang out with your friends. Get through this, however it works out."

17

Cohabitating

"**O**nce the annulment goes through, are we going to have to keep up this awkward, choose Freya *or* Zane? I like hanging out with you both and don't like choosing one over the other." Asher griped as he drove at a snail's pace over the loose chip-sealed road, the scent of tar pervading the cab, glancing at Zane with an exaggerated glower.

Rubbing his hand over the scruff of his jaw, Zane sighed, "Hey, this is tough enough. I like hanging out with her too. More than I should. Look what happened last time we were together? Come on, your parents' laundry room in the middle of a party?"

"I'm impressed. I think that's the one room in the house I haven't had a quickie in." Slowing from ten to two miles an hour, Asher pulled off down an overgrown driveway and parked in front of a metal gate. He hopped out and pushed the thing open, dove back in to roll through, then hopped out again to shut it behind them.

Grass and opportunistic shrubs brushed along the bottom of the truck's chassis as they bumped along the ancient logging road. "Exactly. When she's around, I make stupid-ass decisions. Like getting married."

"And when the marriage is over?"

"If something happens after, at least it won't ruin our chances at dissolving the marriage without a big-ass paper trail that puts a stamp on my forehead as a guy that can't get his shit together."

"What about her?"

Zane shrugged. Shit. Freya didn't deserve all this. A few memories leaked in every so often. Last night, in a painful effort to get some damn sleep, trying not to think about today, he'd played some mind games and tapped his memory until he could come up with some flashes from that night.

It *had* been his idea. She'd downed the biggest cheeseburger on the menu. He'd consumed about a gallon of ice water. A smiling couple had danced in with a group of friends, declaring they were ordering the lava cake for their reception, the chapel next door having been freaking awesome.

He'd paid for dinner and they'd strolled outside together. A flashy sign declared no waiting required for your dream wedding. She'd wrapped her arms around him and kissed his brains out until the earth spun, its axis irreversibly offset.

Let's get married, He'd slurred.

Now? She'd asked.

Hell yeah. Sober me would run like hell, so drunk me is taking a stand.

She'd laughed from deep under her diaphragm, *Sober me has been engaged three times. I think slashed me should take over.*

"Zane?" Asher interrupted his blinding flashback.

"Yeah. Sorry." The engine revved with enthusiasm; the tires didn't argue as they passed through a muddy dip in the road. "I'll be doing her a damn favor. She made it clear, she doesn't have the capacity for guys like me."

They pulled to a stop. A winding grove hinted at a creek ahead. Asher shook his head but didn't say anything. Zane unlocked his feet from bracing the tin can and grabbed Jack as he hopped out of the truck. He shifted a backpack over his shoulder, bottles clanking inside.

Without a word between them, they crossed over a log spanning the crystal-clear stream, then up the overgrown switchbacks for a few hours. They'd traded off the heavy load now and again; Jack should have come with some sort of shoulder strap or something. He weighed a fricking ton and was awkward to carry.

But had been a hell of a lot heavier and scary as fuck when Zane had packed him through the firefight to the LZ, Jack's head bobbing as he went in and out of consciousness, his legs lifeless.

They reached a flat with a scattering of boulders, then the best damn view he'd ever seen as he stepped to the edge, looking miles across the rugged Cascades. Asher set Jack on a boulder at their side while Zane pulled out a trio of beers. He popped off the caps. They stood and raised their glasses.

After a long, hollow breath, Asher said, "To a hell of a friend."

Zane nodded, "The best." Nothing more to say, Zane took a swig while Asher did the same, then set his beer at his feet. He levered the cap off the urn and held it out. "I'm pretty sure this is illegal."

Asher shrugged, "Yeah, you're probably right. I don't think Jack would mind."

Leaning as far out as he could, Zane tipped the urn over and let the wind pick up the ashes, sending fine particles across the cliffside, carried away with the breeze. Asher popped open the beer and poured Jack's over the ledge for him. Pulling back his arm, Zane slung the metal urn into the valley.

Silently, they stood and sipped, taking in the moment. Eventually, they sat down on the boulders overlooking the view. The draining sadness he expected didn't come. No drenching tears ending in hiccups. Instead? A lightness brushed over his shoulders, a weight lifted as Jack drifted into the sky.

Jack would have preferred just hanging out, feeling normal anyway. He'd have ragged on them for not bringing snacks or more beers.

Shit, when Zane explained why, even for such a somber occasion, he wasn't getting trashed? Jack would have kicked his ass for being such a dumbass, letting himself get tied up in knots over what to do about Freya. That he should get over himself and admit he was a sap.

Letting all the air out of his lungs, Zane stared out at nothing, then blurted out, "I love her."

Asher's lips tugged up. He squinted and looked out over the mountaintops beyond. "I know."

"She doesn't want to be married."

"Doesn't she? For a woman that's been engaged three times, sounds like she's interested in forever."

"But not with me."

"Why not you?"

"Fuck if I know. Something about 'pheromones and muscles and broodiness.'"

"What does that mean?" Asher shook his head, clearly as puzzled at his cousin's statement as Zane had been.

"Pretty sure it means she wants someone steady and cheerful, without the fricking accidental make-outs."

"That's stupid."

"Is it? Who sounds like a safer happily ever after bet? Steady job, doesn't interrupt your work, and is a halfway decent communicator? Or, how about the guy that rents the apartment over the garage because he has no place else to go, gets a panic attack every time he gets swallowed by a crowd, seems to think fooling around in someone else's laundry room during a family party is acceptable, and has little more than his ability to brew a decent beer on his resume?"

"Don't forget, is a total badass and can solve about any global conflict."

"Let's not forget that," he scoffed. "I actually think those are points *not* in my favor. Goes against the steady and cheerful aspects."

Asher downed the rest of his beer and hopped off the boulder. "I know my cousin; she's been one of my best friends since we were in diapers. She's got a hell of a heart that she's learned not to trust, thanks to those assholes that took more than they gave. You truly love her? Prove it to her."

"She'll run away scared, and she sure as hell won't want to socialize anywhere near me and we're back to the Freya *or* Zane issue again."

"She might. Or, as I've been telling her all along, she'll see that you're not Randy or Vince or Giovanni. That you'll always have her back. You've always had mine, and we're not even lovers."

"Dude. This is getting weird."

"Come on, you don't think I'm pretty enough?"

Zane rolled his eyes, chugging the last of his beer that he'd forgotten about before stuffing the empty bottles in the backpack. Heading down the slope, he tried to let it sink in. Asher was so fucking happy these days, brighter than Zane had ever seen, and not just because he was a civilian. Asher was the last guy to have talked like such a romantic sap, before meeting Sophie. He might actually know what he was talking about.

But Freya had been burned before. Zane couldn't guarantee following through on any promises he wished he could make. The annulment hearing was in eleven days. After that, they could see where things led. Without pressure, simply two people that liked each other.

They'd made it almost two weeks. No kissing. No groping. Not even handholding.

This wasn't so hard.

Okay, so they'd hardly even been in the same room with each other. But her imagination, conscious and not, planned the many, many activities they could try out after this stupid annulment went through.

Groaning, Freya slammed the couch pillow against her face. It was even worse for the hour or two each day she'd gone to Zane's to work on his computer. Not that he hung around; a few polite words exchanged, awkward shifting on his feet as he came up with some excuse to avoid her.

Well, that's what it felt like anyway. But sharing the same air, even for a few minutes, being able to catch a hint of the fresh grapefruit and sandalwood soap she'd bought him, made her want to tear his clothes off... utter torture. Worse, seeing that he was as miserable as she was? It was a crappy situation.

Sophie dropped onto the recliner opposite and shifted the lever until her feet were elevated. "Maybe Pippa's right."

Moving the pillow, not caring that her hair had succumb to the static electricity of dry summer air and a fuzzy pillow, she muttered, "Hey, she's my neurotic dreamer. You're my realist. Don't mess with my flow."

"Sorry. When do his parents get in?"

Freya nodded to the front door where her suitcase waited. "Three hours. They'd better be worth it."

"They won't be. But if Zane needs this to feel some sort of acceptance, or to let them know he's happy without them..."

"Shit, I didn't even think of that." Freya sprawled her limbs in a floppy star position as she sunk deeper into the sofa. "I have no filter. What if I embarrass him?"

"Go with your gut. Something tells me he needs someone to support him and only him, the consequences be damned. And you're good at that."

"You're not wrong." She sighed and sucked her cheeks between her teeth. For this to be believable, she needed to get over there soon and get settled like she actually lived there.

Sophie sat quietly while Freya scowled at the tip of her nose. The sound of Zane's truck rumbling down the drive added another level to her torture. He'd probably be cool as a cat right now, at least, on the surface.

With a noisy inhalation filled with meaning, Sophie nodded to the kitchen that Freya had converted into a mini studio. "On the bright side, you finished all five pieces quicker than they would have expected. Did they get the first one yet?"

She turned her head and looked at the blank canvas, the workspace painfully empty now that she'd sent off everything she had, plus a few odds and ends to some of the other galleries she'd built a relationship with. Her stomach churned with acid-soaked gravel grinding in her belly. It was always nerve-wracking, putting herself out there. This time... she was upending the style she'd built her brand on. "It should arrive tomorrow, the rest in about a week. I will have exceeded the deadline by a long shot, so I can always work my ass off at creating and sending off more of my traditional style they requested." If they wanted anything more from her after seeing the edgier style she hadn't even known herself capable of. Driven by the thrill of something new radiating from her brush, she'd powered through and couldn't wait to make more.

"Those pieces were incredible. If they don't want them, there are hundreds of others that will."

Dragging her ass off the couch, she shrugged. "I'll know soon enough."

Taking her water glass to the kitchen, she drained the last of it and set it in the sink with the lunch dishes. Freya ad-

justed the waist of her jeans, ensured her top was feminine, somewhere between sweet and edgy, and worked her
tongue over her teeth to ensure no lunch greens remained.
Okay. No problem.

Why was she so nervous? It wasn't like they were her
real in-laws. Or, well, they were real... just not permanent.
Ouch, that was almost worse.

She swung her backpack and heaved her suitcase and
glared at the door, wishing she could hide under the covers
like she had when she was a little girl and tried to skip
school. Not that the strategy had ever worked.

From her burrow on the recliner, Sophie laughed, "I
thought they were only here for a few days. Why did you
pack your entire wardrobe?"

"Toiletries, personal items, and a variety of outfits with
layers, in part because I need to make it look like I live
there, and because I don't know if we'll be taking them for
a drive to the city or hiking or sit around all day. I know
nothing about these people, except that they don't deserve
Zane for a son."

"Makes sense. I'm lucky; my future in-laws had pretty
much adopted me before I even met Asher. And as much
as Paul drives Asher nuts, he loves him to bits."

"You do have good future in-laws. Are you letting him
propose yet?"

"Nah. I'm thinking of beating him to the punch just to be
ornery."

Inhaling every molecule of oxygen that would squeeze
into her lungs, she rested her hand on the doorknob. "Wish
me luck?"

"You don't need it. But good luck anyway."

Turning the knob and swinging the door open, Freya
dashed out the door and slammed into the brick wall she had
almost considered anticipating this time. Hands steadying her
shoulders, sweeping down her arms, Zane chuckled in his

gruff timbre that vibrated deep into her as effectively as the little toy she kept in her bedside table.

"Sorry," she murmured, the smile inevitable as she looked up and met his gaze for the first time in weeks. Were his eyes always so rich? Biting her cheek, she grinned even bigger. "You know what? I used to be considered graceful. Aware of my surroundings. Yet whenever you're around, I rush and knock into things and feel like a complete moron."

"I hear that a lot."

"Smartass."

He snatched her suitcase in one hand and laced his fingers with hers in the other. Weeks ago, the simple gesture had rocked her resolve. Now... it anchored her to the here and now, yet set her flying into the clouds like one of those expensive dragon kites she'd never been able to master.

Annulment. Freedom. No man to affect her productivity or change her plans or... Shit. This sucked.

At the stairs, he waved her on ahead. His groan was audible as he walked a few steps behind. "What?" she asked.

"Has anyone ever told you that you should be an ass model?"

"Huh. Nope. Little weird."

"Just saying. If you could see it the way I do? You'd paint nothing but that ass."

"I have no response to that," she laughed as she walked into the apartment.

"The rest of you is good too. Hell, your rack could be on the cover of Playboy."

"Not so much," she rolled her eyes.

"Again, just saying. I'm fond of them. They've gotten me into a whole lot of trouble."

"It's been a long two weeks, hasn't it?"

He tugged his short hair in his fist. "Apparently. Okay. I'm moving on. We're not officially cohabitating, we're merely covering for a lie I told before the marriage issue. Nor will we have sex or anything resembling what married people do."

"Except meet the in-laws."

"Except that." He grinned and set her suitcase on his bed. "Oh shit, I almost forgot." He opened his bedside drawer and pulled out her ring. He stepped close and held the ring up for inspection.

Taking a deep breath, he took her hand and exhaled slowly, his eyes heavy on the thin piece of expensive metal. Prickles danced over her skin as he slid the ring over her finger, only the slightest resistance at the knuckle before settling in like it belonged.

"This is really pretty," she sighed.

"I, uh... I picked it out." His cheeks flushed pink.

"You remember?"

He nodded. "Bits and pieces have popped back in. You insisted we pick out each other's rings. Some sort of test."

Biting her lip, she resisted the flutter that beat in her chest. Randy had picked out a sweet ring for her, a gold band with a fleck of a solitary diamond, but boring. Vince hadn't exactly bothered with anything fancy; they were broke art students at the time anyway, so he'd folded an IOU into an origami-style ring. Clever, but it hadn't even lasted as long as their pitifully short engagement. Giovanni had a lovely ring passed down through his family, but it was so extravagant it felt heavy on her finger, and he'd delivered so many warnings that she better not lose it, that it never felt like hers.

"Oh," she startled, digging into her pocket. "I have yours, too." When he held out his open hand, she set it gingerly in his palm. It suited him.

Clearing his throat, unloading the weight of the untimely moment, Zane opened the top drawer of his dresser and gestured to the closet. "Make yourself at home," he shrugged. "Really, I can't thank you enough for doing this."

She wanted to scoff that they probably didn't deserve all the effort, but swallowed her judgment. Who knows, maybe they weren't the jerks she'd made them out to be. Just a few comments from Zane now and again, and she had the distinct feeling they were heartless pricks. But if it helped Zane to find what he was looking for, she was all in. "You can pay me back later."

"Yeah?" he tugged his lower lip between his teeth in a wicked grin and stepped toward her... then backed up again. Yep, this was going to be a long couple of days. "Anyway, I'll, uh, go put away the groceries."

18

Saved by the Bell

They managed to behave themselves for a solid two hours until his parents arrived. His jaw had been ticking like mad as he stared at the words swimming around on the page. Giving up, he tossed the book onto the middle cushion their bare feet shared.

Setting her sketch onto the chaise next to her, Freya nudged his foot, a snarky grin on her face.

"What?" He nodded.

"You."

He feigned a scowl.

"You could have told them to stay in a hotel."

"I know."

"But you were pleased they were showing an interest."

"Thanks Freud, but, yeah, I suppose you're probably right."

She scooched across the couch and scooped his arm up until he wrapped it around her and pulled her against him, then rested her head on his chest. Worry already lightening, the easy connection was both stirring and painful as she filled the hollow in his chest. "You have siblings, right? Do they get along with your parents?"

"We don't not get along. They're decent parents, when they pay attention. Honestly, they're overbearing as shit and self-absorbed, so any of their attention is usually uninvited. I think we all prefer flying under the radar."

"You're not close with your siblings?"

"I think we'd like to be closer, but my sister's always on the go with the Air Force, and my brother never stops to take a break. And, well, you know me, I'm not one to call just to chat."

"You chat with me."

"That's different."

"Because I'm your wife?" She leaned up and grinned.

Reaching around, he pinched her middle and tickled until she squealed out of his grip. "Drunk or not, you said yes, and now you're stuck with me for the next five days."

Swinging her leg over, she straddled her knees around him and bit her lip, grinning and scowling and shaking her head at him. "I can't help but say '*yes*' to you."

Adjusting his posture, he tried to resist. He really did. But with those perfectly rounded breasts right in front of his face, well, he was fresh out of the willpower to fight it. Teasing at the hem of her top, her skin like silk, he trailed his fingertips up her sides and around her ribs.

Resting her hands on his jaw, thumbs teasing over his stubbled cheeks, she leaned in and pressed her mouth to the corner of his lower lip. Nipping, she pleaded entrance.

With a hungry growl, he swept his tongue over hers, exploring the furnace that blazed as their mouths met. Rising higher, he slipped under her bra and cupped her breasts with his hands, thumbs pinching over the instantly tightening buds.

Tipping her head back, she gasped, leaning into his grip.

Massaging, squeezing gently, heat blazed through him, his cock painfully hardening. Slipping up her top, he shifted the bra out of his way and continued his caress, pressing an open-mouthed kiss to her chest, the curve of her breast. As she panted and hummed at his touch, he took her into his mouth and suckled.

Crying out, she trailed her hands down his abdomen, rocking against his cock that was aching, straining for release. With her clever fingers, she slid his zipper down torturously slow. The second he was free, she didn't give him an inch, her hands gripping and driving him out of his damn mind. Halfway to heaven, he thrusted into her hands.

And the fucking doorbell.

Leaning back on the couch, he let out a mirthless groan before buttoning back up, his cock aching from lack of release. "Typical."

Breathless, she laughed as she pulled her bra back over the girls and adjusted her top, "Saved by the bell, I think you mean. I was about two seconds from, well, you can pretty much guess."

"Fuck, me too. A little too effective of a distraction," he added.

Shaking her head, Freya rose to her feet and extended her hand, hoisting him off the couch. She opened her mouth to speak, but shook her head again. Straightening his shirt, smoothing his hair, leaving him a little rumpled like he knew she preferred, she moved to his side and laced her fingers with his.

Clinging to her quiet support, he moved to the door and twisted the knob, bracing for the inevitable.

"Zane, honey, we're so glad to see you." His mother blasted into the room with the force of a damn nuke. Her arms wrapped around him and ripped him from Freya.

His father followed close behind, extending his hand and shaking Freya's vigorously. Pasting on a chipper smile, Freya said, "It's great to finally meet you."

Releasing her son, Susan Harris turned to Freya and offered a half-assed shoulder-pat hug. Freya complied. Craig Harris hugged his son as vigorously as Susan had.

Neither of his parents came close to matching his or Freya's heights. Zane had always wondered where he came from, as Craig's eyes were a murky brown and his mother's were a stony gray. Where Zane's hair was a rebellious brown, Craig's was white blond and, well, no one knew Susan's actual hair color, as she'd donned multicolored highlights since before he was born. Craig sported a slight tummy, but was otherwise stalky trim, while Susan was rail thin.

Like so many discontented youth, Zane had always wondered if he had been adopted. He still silently clung to at least the idea of artificial insemination with egg and sperm donors, but he'd seen photographs of pretty much the entire pregnancy. Including his slimy red body screeching as his parents smiled for the camera with their new baby.

"Zane, honey, I can't believe how long it's been. Wow," Susan stepped back and admired her son.

Lacing his fingers with Freya, he pasted on a relaxed smile while chewing his cheek raw. "Yep," he forced through gritted teeth and a tight smile.

Craig nodded buoyantly. "Wow is right. Since we saw you last Christmas, you've been busy. Out of the Navy and married, and you moved to this delightful town."

Under his breath, Zane couldn't help but mutter, "Christmas before last."

Susan looked up, her scowl lines deep between her eyebrows as she considered. "Has it really been so long? Wasn't that a wonderful holiday. All three of our children, home at last."

The unmistakable metallic taste of blood flooded his mouth as Zane bit down harder into his cheek. They didn't deserve to be reminded that his brother hadn't been there.

Squeezing his hand to let him know she was on it, Freya smiled, "How was the drive? I hear you can see the glow from the Eastern Washington wildfires on the horizon?"

Craig scooped up their bags and strolled inside, grinning his typical dopey grin, "That was something. We've never seen anything like it."

Nodding, Freya's hand stayed locked with his, her smile equally forced. Anyone from the area, or with half a brain, really, had been following the devastation. She smiled and responded, "*Something*, yes. Your flight was uneventful?"

Susan sauntered into the kitchen and stared into the refrigerator.

Releasing Freya's hand and giving in to the inevitable, Zane followed and rested his hand on the fridge door. "I should have picked up some wine. Sorry, I wasn't thinking about it. Would you like water or beer?"

His mother pondered, her famous pensive face not diminishing the perfection of her eyebrows. "Is the beer local? I would love something original."

"It's original alright," he muttered.

Craig set their suitcases next to the bed-height air mattress Zane had picked up in anticipation of their arrival. "I'd love one, too. Thanks."

Susan took her beer and wandered around the apartment, nosy and curious. Good thing Freya had merged her stuff with his. She even checked the medicine cabinet, smiling and commenting on what a cozy home they'd made. As expected, she asked, "This apartment is lovely. Do you know the neighbors that own the house?"

Releasing all the air from his lungs, Zane gulped the first half of his beer and dropped onto the couch. "Yeah. Remember, Asher and his girlfriend are buying the place, so we're staying here while we find something more permanent?"

Susan nodded knowingly before lowering to the opposite end of the couch, "Oh yes, of course. I remember now. Will you be designing your own place? Or, well, I guess it's been a while. If you need some creative input, we'll be happy to help."

Cheek worn away to little more than hamburger, Zane tried to chew on his tongue instead. *Maybe he'd try some Irish moss for the next batch, with some Northwest hops.*

Freya glanced out the window, then back again, "We're not quite there yet. Foothills has some great properties, but we'll wait for something perfect to open up and go from there."

Craig nodded, "Of course. You can't create the design before you know the location."

U tter darkness. Blackness. Where mysteries began. And where Freya's imagination took over. Crisp night air cooled the overheated bedroom while dark clouds shifted to conceal the moon.

Scooted until she was about to fall off the side of the bed, she knew Zane was at the opposite edge. He smelled so damn good, that hint of cedar and sex that spun her in a confused tornado. His breath was forced and steady, equally unsettled.

"Zane?" she asked.

"Yeah?"

"You awake?"

He chuckled under his breath. "I am now. The creaking wheels in your brain woke me up."

"Want to have sex?" Her massive grin scrunched up her nose so far, she squinted.

He groaned, counting so quietly she almost couldn't tell, slower than the bathroom clock on the other side of the wall.

"I mean, we're already cohabitating."

Five more counts. "We're already going to be damn lucky to get that annulment. The only thing we have going for us is that we haven't consummated it."

"I was kidding anyway."

"No you weren't." She could hear the lilt in his voice, the subtle smile as he teased her.

"How do you know?"

"It's like the handholding. You don't like being told you can't do something."

"I can follow rules."

"Can? Yes. Easily and with grace? No."

"Smartass."

He chuckled again. "Hey, I've got twelve years of following orders under my belt."

"I'm not sure I've ever cared for rules." She glared up at the growing light on the ceiling as the clouds broke to reveal the moon.

"I can see that." The sheets shifted and rustled as Zane rolled to face her. Like a submarine in rough seas, Zane's hand crossed the divide between them. He intertwined his fingers with hers.

A lead weight on her chest, Freya forced each breath in and out. The subtle connection, so natural, insignificant by all accounts, was exactly who he was. He wouldn't break the rules, but would bend them for her. And she really, really shouldn't let him. "Your parents are nice."

"Yeah, they are that."

"You're right though, they don't see you at all."

"Nope." His thumb grazed along hers, circling over each groove.

"I don't think it's personal. They seem quite content with their own interests."

Zane didn't respond, but took a protracted deep breath; she could just make out his tightening posture in the dim light.

"Have you thought about what to do tomorrow?"

"I haven't exactly done anything touristy around here. What do you think?"

"There's always Mount Rainier. Or the wildlife park to see bison and elk. Downtown Seattle, the waterfront, aquarium, the underground, shopping."

He audibly winced, "Not downtown. Where normal people like you and I will want to do the typical touristy things, they'll turn it into an architectural tour."

"No wonder that's what you studied in school."

"I'm a glutton for punishment?"

"No. It's what you grew up with. Probably how your brain works."

"I guess. Sometimes it comes in handy. Like the damn building that blew up around Jack and the other guys; one wrong move and the whole thing could have come down. And Sophie and Asher already showed their contractor some of my ideas. I have to confess, I'm looking forward to nailing down the details of the brewhouse."

"Did it go through already?"

"Almost. Mostly formalities now, but I'm leaving that to Grady."

"Brewing takes a lot of design."

"Without having to present my idea to dozens of people ready to rearrange every fine detail and criticize every nuance, then when something's half an inch off, it all falls on the architect." He shifted their joined hands up but didn't let go. Or move closer. Sadly. "But with beer? They can drink it or not, no skin off my back. Think it'll be fun to design the menu, too. Mostly snacks and stuff to munch while folks can hang out all night. Relaxed, no pressure environment. Maybe distribute to local places first."

Freya felt her grin widening, a flutter in her chest as he spoke. "I'd say you're moving forward on a pretty great dream."

He chuckled softly. "Yeah, you may be right."

The flutter morphed into a gnawing ache as she realized his dreams didn't include her. Relief. Nausea. A gripping pain as she craved inclusion. But wasn't this what she wanted? Independence? Individuality? Non-codependence?

Randy had big dreams. A house and a career and living the picture perfect, white picket fence life. Freya had even quit her birth control a few weeks before the wedding, ready to get started on his dream. Midway through that awful bridal shower that had turned so distasteful, her poor mother and Aunt Denise trying to bring it back to the realm of tolerably appropriate, Freya snuck outside and curled up in a blanket on the grassy slope as darkness enfolded around the Sutherland's property.

Paul had just picked up Asher from the airport. When Asher saw her sitting outside, he came out and plopped down at her side. *"Big day tomorrow."*

"Yep."

"Did you get your tickets to Italy for the honeymoon?"

"No." She wiggled her toes in the sharp cut grass. *"We're going to Hawaii instead."*

"Hawaii's nice." Long pause. *"What about after?"*

"There's a house for rent a few blocks from Main."

"Good studio space in it?"

"No." Cackling resonated from the house. *"I, uh, Uncle Paul hired me, and I'll be taking some online classes to finish my degree, so I won't have much time to paint anyway."*

Freya closed her eyes and refused to keep reliving it. Nor to picture the tiny studio she'd lived in with Vince, how he'd taken over the space near the window because he needed more natural light to complete his nudes. Or how Giovanni had been too busy to fly home with her for Pippa's wedding; the impetus for the break-up.

19

Paradise... or Something Like It

Paradise was exactly as the name implied. Wildflowers dotted the slopes, trails zagged across the hillside, and the clouds below created the illusion they were atop a mythical island in the sky. On one side of the massive parking lot, a modern visitor center stood ready to teach. Opposite and at the foot of the slope, the century-old lodge paid tribute to the early days of alpine tourism. Zane parked the truck in the crowded lot. Dozens of hiking boots, quick-dry bucket hats, and fleece jackets were already heading up the hill toward the paved trails.

His parents piled out and were off, aimed straight for the lodge. Closing his door, Zane strolled to the front of the truck and took Freya's outstretched hand. "You were right. This is the spot to bring out-of-town guests."

She shrugged, a smug-ass grin on her face, dimple in full-force. "I used to come up here alone when I first got my driver's license. Most kids would sneak off to parties or something, but I'd sneak off to secret places to paint. Not that I didn't sneak out for all those other reasons too." They started walking in the direction of his parents. "One perfect morning,

I saw a marmot off the trail and sat and sketched the little guy for an hour before we were interrupted, then he dove back into his burrow."

"We'll have to come up here some morning before the crowds." His parents had spent half the damn morning on the phone for work, so it was near lunch by the time they arrived. Not much changed. He didn't rush to join them.

Inside the lodge, he found his mother staring up at the old growth timber beams, his father checking out the fireplace big enough to stand in. They were nudging each other and remarking on the caliber of the job, impressive for so long ago. At least they got along well with each other. Actually, he rather suspected they had merged their conscious minds when they got married. Had they ever dissented on anything? It couldn't be healthy.

Freya's stomach rumbled so loudly, it nearly matched her giggle that erupted at the sound. "Think we can have lunch before going for a hike?"

Taking a long inhale, he caught a whiff of something savory. Didn't care what, he was starving. His mother had offered to fix breakfast, and the tasteless biscuits and lumpy gravy had left him feeling hollower than before they'd eaten. Damn, he did not miss his mother's cooking. At least she hadn't attempted pancakes; hers were famously pasty and tasteless and left an inexplicable gurgle in the intestines for days after.

He gave the host their name, and had about ten minutes to kill before their table was ready. Freya snuck off to the bathroom while he wandered the gift shop. There was a collection of cobalt blue, handmade ceramic pitchers, bowls, and mugs by a local artist. He picked out two mugs that were just the right size for Freya's fancy instant espresso. Maybe he'd pick up a real espresso machine one of these days and see what she thought. By the checkout, he grabbed a hokey magnet of a pair of adorable marmots poking their heads out of a hollow log for Freya.

When the host called his name, he waved to his parents to join. Freya was strolling back from the bathrooms, looking so damn sexy, she took his breath away, which seemed to happen about every time he looked at her. Wrapped in her towel after showering this morning, her dark hair almost wicked, the curls were sharp and decisive. In her jeans as she sipped her coffee on the couch this morning, her bare feet tucked underneath her, the dark blue nail polish teasing at her sense of adventure.

And now. With her black leggings that ended inches above her ankles, her sleek black trailrunners, topped off with the pale pink quick-dry tank top he knew was under her light-weight wool sweater. She was a constant surprise. Sometimes she strolled across the lawn in her bare feet, wearing nothing but a drapey sun dress and her hair wild, no trace of make-up, telling of the artist she was. Other times, like at the wedding, she was a fricking siren straight out of a magazine. Or like now, she was utter practicality, but always sexy as fuck.

She grinned at his dumbfounded ogle as his parents followed the host, a wanton spark in her infinite blues as she winked at him. With a sheepish grin, he tilted his head and shrugged, then picked up the pace to catch up.

His parents took a damn hour to peruse the menu, and it wasn't that complicated. They compared whether to try the burger made from local grass-fed beef or the shepherd's pie, reading the details to each other. Beyond hungry, his vision blurred as he stared out the window.

Freya's stomach rumbled at his side. She pasted on a winning smile, "Why don't you each order one of them, then you can split and share?"

Susan chuckled softly and put down her menu. "That's what Blaire is always suggesting."

Shit. Here we go. He figured remarrying would neatly dodge this bit. No wonder his brother didn't even fly home for Christmas anymore. "Mom," he warned.

"I'm sorry, I know I shouldn't bring up your ex-wife, but we see her every day. It would be like you trying to tell a story without it including Archer."

"Asher," he muttered.

The server rescued them for a solid sixty seconds and got to deal with his parents' arguing who would order which, before the server offered to have them plated in two separate halves.

"So, Freya," Susan began. "What do you do for a living?" Yep, she hadn't listened to the answer when she had complimented the painting over his dining table.

"I'm an artist." Her tone wasn't even sarcastic, as she'd been asked the same question a handful of times already.

"Oh," she nodded, her cheeks were pulled so cheerfully tight, her facelift was showing. "I took quite a few art classes in school. It's so important to be able to accurately sketch your designs. That's probably part of why Zane never took to design."

Zane answered before Freya could, "Her work is sold in galleries all over the world. Remember, the painting in my apartment?"

"Right, of course. That painting is delightful. I guess I didn't realize you were serious that art was her occupation and not her hobby." Long silence. His father refolded his napkin, draping it over his lap at a slightly different angle.

After a painfully awkward pause, their food arrived, and the excuse for continued silence was well timed. Smoked duck over a spring mix, plus a side of chowder; he was thrilled they shut up long enough for him to enjoy his meal. By the time he'd downed everything on his plate and ate the last of Freya's fish, his father had finished a quarter of his half-burger.

Swallowing a bite, his mother asked, "Zane, are you planning to go back to school?"

Brow scrunched in utter confusion, he shook his head. "No…"

"Oh. Okay. I wondered. I mean, I would imagine that you are too rusty to go straight back into architecture, and there's probably not much demand for such specialized expertise in Foothills, but you could work remotely."

"I don't want to be an architect now, any more than I did fourteen years ago."

His father set down his burger and dabbed the cloth napkin on the corner of his mouth. "Then why did you study architecture? I mean, I know you joined the Navy for time to reflect and to save some money, but we always assumed you would return to the field."

Leaning back in his chair, Zane folded his arms over his chest and chewed his cheek to keep his mouth shut. His gaze shifted out the window, watching the tourists hike up the paved trail.

Again the enthusiastic duo that had encouraged him to study architecture to begin with, his mother took her turn. "If Foothills is where you want to settle, then you'll make it work. I mean, you already have the degree, plus we would be happy to help you get started. You could commute or even start your own business. We would be happy to hire you on as a remote designer and fly you out to the sites when needed."

He could hear Freya's teeth grinding at his side. She sat up in her chair, her back straightening as she inhaled to deliver a volcanic defense. He rested his hand over her thigh, letting her know it wasn't worth the fight. For now, she bit her lip and stayed quiet.

The rest of lunch dwindled to awkward silence. No one felt like much of a hike after. They roamed the visitor center, but at their own pace.

Far from Foothills, Zane had no qualms about public hand-holding with Freya. Despite the awful morning and even worse lunch, she was a breath of fresh air. He'd wanted to skip the science lesson and wait outside, maybe sit on a shady park bench and make out for a bit. Nope, Freya had dragged him through the exhibits.

Right about the time he caught sight of his parents standing by the window in a pathetic attempt to find cellphone service, Freya jumped on the seismometer and whooped at her power, that dimple in her cheek flashing her delight. Dragging him over, she raised her eyebrows and bit her lip in gleeful challenge. Rolling his eyes, grinning like an idiot, he leaped into the air and slammed down onto the meter, making the biggest line of the day.

Flashing her a wink, he laced his arm around her waist and pulled her close. Sliding his hand into her hair, he cradled her against him as he softly pressed his lips to hers. Fluidly, without pause, she kissed him back. When they ended the kiss, she nuzzled against his neck and inhaled. Arms wrapped around her, he buried his face in her wild hair, breathing her in.

On the drive back, winding down the narrow fishhook turns, Zane counted the hours until his parents left. Three nights hadn't sounded so bad, but his head might explode if he had to attempt polite conversation with them much longer.

The bustling on Main Street was particularly peppy today. Zane plotted how he might avoid talking for the rest of the visit. Maybe they could watch a movie or something that didn't require speaking.

Freya could chill when the situation called for it, like no other. But she also seethed like no one else he'd met. Bottling up whatever she held on the tip of her tongue seemed to be festering into the air. She nodded to an empty stretch ahead, "Let's hop out."

Without argument, he parallel parked, then turned to see what the hell had prompted the impromptu stop. He tilted his head in subtle question.

She quietly cleared her throat, "When do you get the keys?"

"Seriously? No," he winced.

"Trust me?"

He exhaled slowly, hating where this was going. "I got them yesterday morning."

She scowled, whispering, "Seriously? I didn't think the loan had been finalized yet."

His father leaned in, visibly eavesdropping where there was no need in the cramped space. This was a conversation he'd planned to have with her *after* they'd left. His stomach lurched as he accepted how much he was about to share with his parents. And their inevitable "constructive criticism."

"I didn't end up needing such a big loan." He'd been miserable, not being able to talk to Freya sooner about all this. To not drag her over to show her the building, his plans. But that was more serious than handholding, than quickies in the laundry room... than consummating. Fuck, that pang clenched and screamed and told him to stop being a fucking idiot. But Freya didn't need another selfish asshole in her life, determined to force her to live *his* dream, when hers was so big and beautiful and fragile.

"What? How?"

"Grady."

"He did?" Her smile grew wide, her eyes downright sparkly blue like the fricking Mediterranean on an August afternoon.

"Yeah," he chuckled as he accepted the strange turns his life was taking. "In part to piss off his mother, and, apparently, because he hates his job. And I hate the damn schmoozing end of things, the nuances of running a business, so he's no longer my attorney. We're full partners."

She reached across and squeezed his hand, grinning from ear to ear and showing off that dimple.

His mother's head leaned in and knocked into his fathers, but they managed to stay quiet. The effort seemed to be killing them, their eager faces clenched tight with phony smiles.

"Come on," he nodded for her to hop out. He turned to face his parents, "Since we're here, I'll show you what I'm up to."

Before they could respond, he took advantage of the lull in traffic and climbed out of the truck, meeting Freya at the sidewalk and accepting her extended hand. His chest tightened then released, the building—his building, standing proudly before them. A smile tugged at the corner of his mouth, the thrill of possibility less terrifying than it had been a few short weeks ago.

Shattering his moment, his parents came up from behind. "Well?" his mother asked in her bright tone.

"This is it," he shrugged. "Black Op Brewing Company."

His father scowled, his dull green eyes squinting against the bright sun. "Oh. The building has good structure."

Zane could see it. A welcoming gate and fencing he planned install so they could serve drinks outside. Outdoor tables with built-in fireplaces, plus propane standing heaters in the cooler months, navy blue umbrellas in the summer. Globe string lights overhead. He'd paint the trim the same navy blue and white, but finish the cedar siding to age naturally.

Inside, he could envision the copper tabletops over dark-stained plank floors that would only improve with wear. He could practically smell the oaky hops. As his parents wandered, he asked Freya, "Hey, do you know Scott and Brenda Halseth?"

Hand still linked with his, a sweet smile didn't leave her lips, her gaze taking in every inch of the place. "Of course. Halseth's Smokehouse and Pub is one of my favorites. Have you been?"

He nodded. "I grabbed lunch there the other day. Scott heard about my business plan and we chatted for a bit. He wants to carry Black Op beers on tap, and in exchange, I'll use some of their smoked goods in some of the recipes and maybe even sell some. Apparently, he has started carrying Cascade Bakery's desserts, she's using some of their meats and cheeses in her savory quiches and other baked goods, and he's wondering if I want to join in their system. Promoting each other symbiotically rather than competing."

"Of course Scott would think of that. Good family. You'd like them. His son plays for the San Francisco Fire."

"Seriously? Finn Halseth is from Foothills?"

She grinned. "Maybe you'll be lucky enough to get an autograph. Anyway, yes, the Halseths and Perrys are great people. Teaming up with them is a surefire way for this place to hit the ground running."

Ignoring his parents and their banter as they inspected every beam and pillar in the place, he showed Freya the rest. Like the walls and floors, the stairs were unfinished and the walls nothing more than a shell upstairs.

Releasing his hand, she floated across the area he had envisioned for offices. Spinning in the diffuse light, she spread her arms wide. "The lighting in here is perfect. Some shiplap on that wall, a subdued sky blue on the others, and *these windows*."

Hovering halfway to the ceiling, she looked like a fairy in her element. Fucking contagious. He crossed the distance between them and slipped his arm around her waist.

Leaning in, he rode her thrill, her fairy dust coating them together as their lips met fluidly. Familiar, irresistible, he felt the zing prickle over his skin, his pulse kick up in a steady rhythm to match hers. His hand splayed over her low back as hers laced around the back of his neck, fingers teasing in his short hair.

Footsteps behind him shattered what was a pretty epic moment, each footfall crushing the words he wished he'd said when he had the chance.

Pulling away, he let go and walked to the window. Overlooking the park, he watched a trio of kids playing tag, young lovers gazing into each other's eyes on their picnic blanket, elderly sisters strolling arm-in-arm down the gravel path, and the old man feeding the birds.

"This building is lovely," his mom began hopefully. He couldn't turn his back, knowing exactly the expression she wore. It wasn't flattering to either of them. He should have kept on driving instead of sharing this with them.

His father added, "I'll look forward to seeing your mockups for the final designs."

No fucking way.

And his mom's turn. "This room is nice, but impractical for what you need. You should knock out these walls and create a formal meeting space for rent."

And his dad. "I suppose you'll be brewing onsite. No one will want to see those ugly tanks, so I can help with a façade to hide them."

He muttered under his breath, "No thanks." He'd envisioned letting folks see the industrial look of it, feeling like they were part of the process.

"Zane, honey. This is a lovely project for you. We just want to help."

Turning, he glared, "Why?"

His father's cheek raised with shock, "Why? We're your parents. We love you."

Whatever pang, whatever new rhythm his pulse had been settling into, was masked by searing hot blood boiling under his skin. "Sure." He gritted his teeth, refusing to say more.

Striding past, he checked his pace and walked out of the unfinished room.

Freya's voice was laced with an edge he hadn't heard, cutting through the hollow building. "Why did you come?"

Uppity as fuck, his mother huffed, "To see *our* son. To meet the wife that we'd never even heard of."

"Right. Of course. Because you'd hate for him to make the wrong choice. To decide what he wants for himself."

"That's not–" His father tried to interrupt.

Freya was a hurricane that wouldn't be stopped. "No. That *is* what's happened. How many times was he out on a mission, and you didn't even know your son was risking his life? For his country? For innocents that couldn't defend themselves? For his friends? Because it was the right thing to do. Because he wanted to challenge himself. Because that was his dream."

Zane leaned against the doorframe, arms crossed as he watched his furious wife. She was a sight to be seen, livid on fire on his behalf. Did she really think all that? Aching, filling with a hope he hadn't known, he let the corners of his mouth quirk up as she said all the words he'd swallowed for too damn long.

"And where were *you* when he lost his best friend? When he decided to leave the Navy because he had lost himself? And when he's finally found something he enjoys and wants to make a career out of it, found a hometown he wants to settle in... and a wife that thinks his dreams are beautiful?" She crossed her arms over her chest, smoke billowing from the top of her head.

His parents fell silent, but not for long enough. His mom found her voice, hissing, "Who do you think you are–"

"*I* am his wife. In the short time I've known him, I *know* that he's so much more than you give him credit for. If you paid attention for half a damn minute, you'd see the promise of this place. The beauty of something new."

Blood beyond boiling, reaching volcanic levels as Freya defended him, his parents clearly not getting the point, Zane's fists clenched at his sides, molars ground to nothing, he opened his mouth to speak. To stand up for his wife that stood up for him.

His mother gulped a bubble of air, "Well, I... I think I need some fresh air." She turned and nearly ran into Zane.

He let out the breath he'd been holding. "Freya's right. This is what *I* want. I..." *Just get it over with*. He couldn't unclench his teeth, his raw cheek wedged between his molars the only thing warding off a broken jaw. "I'm sorry I've always been such a disappointment for you. Blaire didn't get it any more than either of you. I won't bother describing the last twelve years of my life to you. But I've known so much loss, yet lived to the limits. And now? I've got this incredible wife that will fight for my dreams, and I hope to hell she'll let me fight for hers."

Craig let out a heavy exhale. "I've got to say, it was tough, watching you push yourself, saying you wanted to be a damn Navy SEAL. What were we supposed to do? Let you risk your life on a dream that probably wouldn't come true? When you agreed to give the architecture program a try, then married a woman whose ideals aligned so perfectly with those we'd taught you?"

Shaking her head, Susan crossed to Craig and leaned into him. "It's hard to watch your son risk everything when you don't understand why. It was easier to be patient and hope you'd come back one day."

Continuing where she left off, Craig nodded. "And now you've married some artist you never mentioned, suddenly want to start some brewery, and live in this remote town? I guess we don't know how to respond."

Zane backed out of the doorway, catching Freya's eye. "Let's go."

20

Walk in the Park

Dinner was... well, awkward would be putting it lightly. Freya had worked at Zane's side in the kitchen, tossing together the salad base while he shredded and heated the chicken, garlic, and almonds. Nothing fancy, as he was too crabby to bake the salmon he'd planned. Craig had complimented the beer over dinner, the food, and he and Susan were both pleasantly surprised by the understated gourmet meal.

After watching a generic movie in a darkened living room until it was late enough to call it a night without looking rude, Freya dragged Zane to bed. He hadn't said much. Nobody had said much. Nothing like the verbose Marks family meals.

Sliding into the cool sheets, the crisp moon illuminating the room, Freya reached across and smoothed the thick line between Zane's eyebrows.

Taking her wrist, he kissed the base of her palm. "Thank you."

"For what?"

"Everything."

"I understand why you don't talk about your family much. That must have been hard to grow up with, not feeling supported."

"Know what?" his voice was laced with gravel like he was suffering from back-to-back red-eye jetlag. "I don't really want to talk about them right now either."

His arm laced around her middle and pulled her closer. Pasting her body against his, entwining their legs, she didn't argue.

Warm and pliant, his lips contrasted the hardness of his body, still tense from the day. Savoring, he tasted and explored. Like their first kiss, zings of thrill fired through her veins. Slow and easy, he trailed his thumb over her jaw and cradled her against him.

A soft sigh passed her lips. Heat licked through her, her breasts aching for him to touch her, kiss her again. Needing more, she pressed her hips against his and rocked against him.

"Uh-uh," he murmured. "Only a few more days."

A chuckle bubbled up from her throat. "We must be the first people in history waiting until we're not married to have sex."

Still kissing her, he grinned. "One weekend wasn't enough for me. But a lifetime is more than we planned. So just a few more days, and then, I say we make up for the last few weeks."

She pulled his tongue into her mouth and tugged before releasing him. "Think you could explain your plan to celebrate our annulment in precise detail? It might hold me over."

One last kiss and he drew back to the edge of the bed. "This could take all night."

"I'm not going anywhere." Freya lay facing him, letting the strap of her top fall off her shoulder.

Inhaling sharply, he groaned. "First, I'm going to..."

Closing her eyes, Freya listened to him talk for longer and with more detail than he had since she'd met him. His descriptions were explicit, his voice hungry as he described exactly what he had in mind, and the laundry room romp was nothing by comparison as he sent her soaring with nothing more than his words.

After a sleepless night, Freya awoke entangled in Zane. Sitting up, she caught him watching her with a sleepy smile, his eyes still unfocused and heavy, sleepy as he'd kept her up all night.

Consequences be damned, she leaned in and stole a languorous kiss. Skin warm and smooth against hers, he slipped on top and grazed his lips along the curve of her neck. In a trail of pure ecstasy, he circled her breast with his hands, his mouth, sucking until she cried out.

Whispering a teasing, "*Shhh*," he lowered and pressed his mouth to her core. Laving, he gave her a taste of what he'd teased at last night. Her breath came faster, heat blazing over her skin, she came again and again.

Propping up to his elbows, he kissed her thigh and grinned. "So," he croaked, "Breakfast?"

She scowled. "We'd better hurry before your mother tries to cook again."

He bolted upright, "Fuck, I forgot they were here. Let's grab a quick shower and then I'll fry up some sausage to go with your scrambled eggs?"

"Is that code?"

"Ha. No."

"At least say you meant to shower together?"

"It's going to involve more than handholding."

"It's a date."

During their not-short shower, Freya was convinced she might spontaneously combust. How much more could she take? There had been handholding. Among other... things. She'd demonstrated some of what she had planned for their post-annulment celebration. Showering and non-penetrative intercourse wasn't consummating. Probably. She definitely wasn't calling Grady to ask for details on the semantics.

After a quiet breakfast, with actually not unpleasant small talk about the area, the weather, and even a few stories of Zane as a child, they agreed a local hike would be perfect. Freya scooped in her last bite of eggs and rose to clear her plate. "Riverside Trail is a lazy walk along the river. My grandparents and I used to walk along the main road and hop on the trail at the bridge."

Susan smiled with an extra buoyancy, "Of course. That sounds wonderful. We'll get ready to go."

Zane rose from the table and cleared the remaining plates, even though his father still hadn't finished. "Know what? It's a really gentle hike. You're perfect in what you're wearing. Grab some shoes and we can get going so we beat the weekend crowds."

"Oh, of course." Susan smoothed her khaki shorts and scuttled into the bathroom.

Craig looked to be working at jumping on board but hadn't quite gotten there yet, but Susan maintained the overly accommodating attitude. He fumbled his phone in his hands. "I'll uh, just fire off a text to... I'll let work know we'll be unavailable for the day."

Quickly tossing on her sneakers, Freya zipped into the kitchen to at least get the breakfast pan soaking and dishes rinsed. She barely had time to wipe down the countertops when Zane's parents were pulling their shoes on and heading to the door. Impressive.

She tossed the rag next to the sink and followed them out the door. A few steps behind, Zane's phone buzzed in his pocket. He checked the screen and held up his hand, "It's Grady. I'll catch up."

Snagging a quick kiss as he put the phone to his ear, Zane flashed her a sizzling wink before answering. Bouncing down the steps like gravity wasn't a thing, Freya joined Susan and Craig as they waited at the base of the stairs, studying the main house.

Pointing to the awning, Susan nodded knowingly, "Excellent color choices, and I can see where the shutters have been updated."

Craig considered, then added, "Sharper of an angled roof for a craftsman than is typical. Must be handy if there's a heavy snow."

Braving the topic, keeping her voice light, Freya said, "My grandfather was quite particular about that. He wanted to build a home that would stand for generations."

"That's right, your grandparents owned this," Craig nodded. Freya resisted snorting. Maybe they should have their memories checked. Or their attention span.

Tires crunched the gravel in the distance, an engine growling at too high of a speed for a low gear. Instinct sent adrenaline coursing deep under Freya's skin, setting her gut rumbling in protest at the sound. No one friendly drove up that fast.

"Go," she motioned for her in-laws to head up the stairs.

"What? Um, okay," the slow-pokes began to meander up the steps.

Too late. Stranded at the base of the steps, Freya turned as the truck came into view.

No longer shiny, chunks of dried mud dropped off the wheel wells as the truck slammed on the brakes, sending loose gravel splaying in all directions. Arms crossed, Freya stood tall.

Toby flung open the driver's side door and stomped out. "Where is he?" Eyes bloodshot, greasy hair plastered flat to his scalp, he growled and scanned the property.

"What?" Not good. Freya could smell the liquor through the dust that hung in the air.

"That cheating husband of yours."

"I don't know what you're talking about." She forced her voice steady, hating the underlying waver.

"You ought to be as pissed as I am. He's been fucking my wife behind both our backs."

Toby stormed closer, his arms stiff at his sides, a snarl on his teeth.

Freya stood her ground, her pulse thundering, breath coming fast as panic set in. If Zane came out now? She held her ground, dreading what he had planned for Zane.

As Toby neared, he reached to shove her out of the way. "Don't protect that two-timing piece of shit."

Creaking on its hinges, the apartment door swung open. *Dammit, Zane*. Freya anchored her feet, whipping her head toward the open door. "Don't you fucking touch her," Zane roared.

Sneering, Toby growled, "'Bout time you show your face. Although, tit for tat, Freya here can come on with me and I'll show her the good time you showed my wife."

Rather than the shove she'd been anticipating, Toby grabbed her arm and yanked her against him.

"Don't touch me," she tried to rip free, but his grip was iron. Trying to swing her body to throw her hip into him and drop using some strategies she'd learned in self-defense class, she froze when he reached behind his back with his free hand.

Spitting in his face, she bought more time before he could take aim.

"Bitch," Toby let the spit stream down his face as he drew the gun.

From the corner of her vision, she saw Zane's parents still frozen on the steps. Bypassing the statues they'd become, Zane leaped over the rail and landed on the gravel, his feet moving before he even hit the ground, taking off at a furious sprint toward them.

As Zane closed in, Toby swung the gun and aimed directly at Zane.

Stopping on a dime, Zane raised his arms and Zane froze in place. "She has nothing to do with it. Let her go."

"But she does. I heard about you sweet talking Sienna while she was at work, thinking word wouldn't get back to me. Bitch didn't even deny it. So, Freya and I are going for a little drive so I can show her what being fucked by a real man looks like."

"In your dreams," she roared. Straining at his grip, she tried to get him to look away, to lower the gun, something, but he didn't move his eyes or the gun from Zane.

Never taking an eye off of Zane, Toby tugged at Freya, dragging her toward his truck. Her arm throbbed from his tight hold.

"Don't think you're going to be able to get her into the truck without losing your grip on that gun," Zane nodded, his expression remarkably calm.

"You're right," he sneered. "Get in the truck or he's dead." Her gut hollowed as she realized she was out of options. Didn't matter if she could get away, his finger was already twitching over the trigger. One wrong move, and Zane was dead.

At the open driver's side door, Freya stepped onto the side runner.

A sputtering engine rattled down the driveway.

Toby blinked and hissed, "Move it." His eyes darted as he was tempted to look down the driveway, but he caught his waver and lengthened his arm, then took a testing squeeze at the trigger.

Dashing down the steps, Craig hollered and ran for his son. Susan stood and held her hands over her face. Zane held up his hand to still his dad and whispered something Freya couldn't hear. Craig froze.

Zane stood stone still, his arms relaxed at his sides. If it weren't for the tension in his jaw, Freya would have thought he wasn't even fazed.

Sienna's ancient sedan flew down the driveway, the chassis rocking, gravel flying as she came to an abrupt stop. "Toby, let her go," she cried as she slammed out of the car. Her left eye was sealed shut from swelling, shiny with dark purple. She held an arm braced around her ribs, wincing with each movement as she hobbled closer.

Toby glanced to Sienna.

Freya sprinted full out into the carport and dove to the ground next to Zane's truck. From her post, she pulled out her phone and called 911.

Taking advantage of the interruption, Zane was on the move as she was.

Closing the distance in a flash, Zane didn't hesitate.

Toby turned back and realized his aim had shifted.

Movements swift and calculated, Zane knocked Toby's wrist with one hand, ejecting the gun with his other.

Disarmed, Toby swung with a brick-like fist.

Dodging the blow by no more than a whisper, Zane twisted his arm around Toby's and tugged him closer while his other hand balled into a fist. Throwing a solid punch, he cracked Toby's nose, the crunch audible from Freya's hiding spot.

Recoiling as he held his broken nose, Toby threw rapid, wild punches at Zane.

Juking, Zane dodged another hit and nailed him with an uppercut in the beer belly. Solid steel underneath, Toby doubled over but didn't fall.

Toby shook it off and barreled into Zane's middle.

Holding steady like the rock he was, Zane didn't even falter. Driving his elbow into the guy's back, Toby squealed and dropped to the ground.

Struggling to stand, Toby called out, "Sienna, get your ass home."

Rising to his hands and knees, his limbs shuddered beneath him. He looked up at Zane and sneered. Blood-stained saliva dripped down his chin and landing in the dust, sharp gravel digging into his palms and knees. Struggling to get to his feet, his limbs shook beneath him. "Sienna. Get in the truck. Let's go," he muttered.

She shook her head, not daring to come closer. "Not today."

Zane stood with his hands on his hips. "Cops are on the way. I suggest you stay on the ground."

"Fuck you," he muttered and grabbed the open truck door to pull himself to his feet.

Grabbing Toby's arm and twisting it behind his back, Zane asked again, "Not kidding." Wrenching his shoulder nearly out of its socket, Zane growled, "I said down."

Squealing as his shoulder bent beyond what should be possible, just shy of shattering, Toby dropped to his knees.

Shaking his head, Zane sighed. "I didn't sleep with your wife you fucking moron. I was trying to offer to kick your ass before you killed her with your stupidity."

Not giving an inch, Zane pinned him to the ground, his foot unmoving from Toby's shoulder. Plastered to the ground, Toby grumbled.

Freya rose from behind the truck and took in the scene.

Sienna cried out, repeating, "I'm so sorry, I'm so sorry." She flipped her head back and forth, her gaze landing on Toby, her feet locked in place across the drive.

Craig and Susan stood shellshocked, unsure whether to run out or stay put.

Freya rubbed some life back into her arm after tucking her phone back into her pocket and came out from behind Zane's truck. "Cops should be here..." she heard the sirens in the distance, exhaling a heavy sigh of relief. "Any second."

Toby writhed, but whimpered and quit when he realized he was only making it worse. Zane wasn't giving him an inch.

Shaking her head, she crossed to Zane. Still unmoving, Zane granted Freya a sly grin.

Leaving him to stand guard over his prisoner, she turned to check on Sienna. Craig and Susan were now at the foot of the stairs together, arm in arm and watching their son's every movement, both a little red-eyed.

Freya stopped a few feet from Sienna. "Are you okay?"

"I'm fine. What about you?" Sienna winced as she took a deep breath and motioned to Freya's arm, the hand-shaped bruise already starting to shine.

"I'm okay." She wanted to wrap her arms around the overly calm woman and tell her it was okay to stomp and scream and maybe even kick her lousy husband.

"Do you have someplace you can go?"

She nodded. "Yeah. I have a few friends that have been offering."

"Good. If you need anything, don't be a stranger."

Despite the bruised eye that was rapidly spreading to her entire cheek, Sienna smiled and nodded.

A cluster of police cars filed in. The officers took in the scene as they stepped out of their cars.

Zane nodded from his post, "All clear."

Chief Larson came straight to Sienna. "Are you okay?" he asked while the other officers ran toward Zane and Toby.

She nodded. "I'm fine."

More lights flashed down the driveway. Jonah rested his hands on his hips, "I'm glad. I'll let the paramedics check you out. Then, would you mind chatting with me about what happened?"

"Yes. I know I should have listened sooner, I just..."

"Don't worry about it. It's over now. Right?"

She nodded, "I'm done."

He gave Sienna a polite nod, then to Freya, "I'd heard you were back in town. This is your grandpa's old place, right?"

"Yeah, I'm staying in the apartment over the garage." Why did she say that? She was living in the house, for the moment.

He nodded to Zane, "Friend of yours?"

She smiled, "Yes. Zane is a SEAL buddy of Asher's."

He grinned. "These guys are handy to have around." Trotting toward Zane, Jonah threw out his hand to introduce himself now that Zane's hands were free, Toby in cuffs and being escorted to one of the police cars. Zane was so calm, so at ease despite everything that had happened. She was nauseous from the adrenaline letting down, but Zane looked like this was an easy stroll in the park.

The ambulance pulled in and Sienna said to Freya, "Thanks again. Really. Your husband, he's a good guy. Those are hard to find."

"I know. Look, you take care of yourself, okay?"

"I will. Please, come on over to Larissa's sometime for some pie. My treat this time." She crossed the driveway, her spine straight and her head held high, despite her hand gripping her ribs and the hitch in every step as she approached the paramedics that were already heading her way.

One of the police officers was talking with Susan and Craig, Jonah still chatted with Zane, and the others were already stuffing Toby into the squad car, one paramedic strolling over to check on him. Freya stuffed her hands in her pockets, her focus homing in on Zane. He was warming up, a full smile on his face when she reached his side.

As she neared, he stepped close and wrapped his arm around her, tucking her against him. "No, uh, thanks though. Asher already tried to convince me to join you guys. Not interested."

Jonah laughed with him, "Worth a shot."

Freya melted into Zane's side as her adrenaline plummeted. Her legs about crumpled beneath her. This may be routine for him, but the fear of losing him was entirely new to her.

He planted a kiss on her temple, then nodded to Jonah, "Are we good here? I mean, you can swing by anytime if you need anything, but we were just heading out for a walk."

Gaze notably falling at the bling on each of their left ring fingers, Jonah nodded to Freya, the corner of his mouth teasing up. "You know, my mother is about the biggest gossip in town and does Zumba with Tammy. I can't believe I didn't know you'd gotten married."

She shoved her left hand into her pocket. "Well, I mean..."

Zane cleared his throat, but didn't say anything.

"It's a really long story," she bit her lip as it wavered between laughing and crying.

"Well, congratulations either way. You guys can head on your way and I'll swing by or give you a call sometime in the next few days."

Zane linked hands with Freya and they walked over to his stunned parents. As soon as they saw him approaching, Susan and Craig leaped over and wrapped their arms around them both, passing back and forth with emotional hugs and tears. Fingers laced together, Zane didn't let go of Freya.

Susan released Zane long enough to let Craig have a turn, then hugged him again before wiping a juicy tear from her cheek. "I guess I..."

Craig nodded, standing back and taking in the scene, the blood on the gravel, the tow truck coming down the driveway for the truck, the police cars clearing out. "That was something else. I... you..."

Zane stepped out of their grip and nodding to the driveway. "Let's go for that walk."

Susan shook her head, "But Zane, you, and that..."

He shrugged. "Yeah. That. We could go back inside and hash and rehash and I could explain that's the sort of shit I did the last twelve years of my life, but honestly? I'd rather get some fresh air."

Turning, Zane looked at Freya with a heavy hopefulness. "Sound okay? Feel up to a walk with me?" His shirt was rumpled from the fight, his hair spiked rebelliously, an adoring glimmer in his look that said everything she wished he'd say.

She nodded. "Anytime." Heart breaking a little more as he chipped away at her armor, she rose to press her lips to his. Breathless, she leaned her forehead against his.

She wanted to say everything that should be said, to ignore the fear that caged her heart, but she couldn't do that to him. A romantic, he would agree. And then six months from now? When the thrill of the pheromones faded?

The marriage would be over in two days. How in the hell was she going to stand in front of a judge and say she didn't love him, she didn't want to stay married to him, and that she regretted the drunken mistake?

Zane deserved the freedom to decide who and when and how much. Not be stuck in a drunken mistake.

21

That Look

Zane trailed his hand along the angle of her jaw, stealing one last kiss. He didn't give a damn that his parents were watching, not having a clue what was going on between them. That there were a dozen first responders beginning to clear out, a violent bastard of a man he'd just kicked the shit out of, and a tough but injured woman that had a long journey ahead of her... all with the potential to ruin a perfect sunny morning in which he held the woman he loved in his arms.

Could he really stand in front of a judge and declare this marriage was a mistake? His mouth opened to say the words that needed to be said, but as usual, his timing fucking sucked.

Freya's phone buzzed in a cheerful jingle. Chest still heaving from the kiss or the adrenaline or... all of it, she pulled her phone from her pocket. Her brow scrunched at the number. She held her finger up and wandered up the stairs, answering, "Hello?"

His parents turned and started to speak to him. He shook his head, placing his finger over his lips let them know it wasn't the time. Feet light on the steps, he followed Freya. Something about the paintings she'd sent, something urgent. Shit, had something been ruined in transit?

A breath-holding grin grew on her expression, about to burst with something. After another few minutes of nodding and accepting and clarifying, she hung up. "Um," she began. "That was the gallery in Rome."

He crossed to her. "What happened? Everything okay?"

She bit her lips, the smile too massive to be contained. "They loved the paintings I sent. They had intended to add whatever I sent to their routine stock, but they are running a show highlighting warriors, and they're hoping I can come to mingle as a featured artist... But it's tomorrow."

"That's incredible. Really. Shit, Freya, that's so amazing." He pulled out his phone to check flights. While he searched, aching with the strangest sensation of pride he had no idea he could feel for someone, he said, "I'll find the next flight out while you pack."

"They booked me a flight already." She glanced at her phone, her breath rushing out through pursed lips. "I'm sorry, I–"

He tugged her close and plastered his lips to hers.

His parents slowly filed in the door, as puzzled as they'd been for most of the morning.

Freya grabbed her suitcase and started loading up, frazzled and frantic and vibrant.

"Need a ride to the airport?" he asked, eager to do something helpful, standing with his arms crossed and leaned against the door jamb, feeling completely useless.

She shook her head. "Apparently, they hired a car for me. It should be here any minute." Leaving her suitcase on the bed, she rushed toward the door. "I need to invade Sophie's closet," she grinned on her way out the door.

Within twenty minutes, he was loading the trunk of the fancy-ass sedan that came for her. Thrilled, bouncing and glowing, she plastered him with a fierce kiss that set his hair on fire, then dove into the car and took off.

Breath rushing from his lungs as she left, the adrenaline of the last few hours crashed and left his head pounding and stomach in knots. Fucking shit. She... this was exactly the moment she deserved. The moment she'd been waiting for. Not simply an auction that went well. Not just a few sales. But a feature, to be invited and flown out.

The dust from the unmarked black sedan had yet to settle when a postal car came puttering down the drive. As he stood at the base of the stairs, a uniformed delivery woman dashed up the stairs and handed him a priority envelope. "Have a nice afternoon," she smiled, ignoring the distant look on his face.

Mindlessly, he opened the package as he strolled into the apartment. His parents were still uncharacteristically quiet, thank fuck. They made themselves at home in the kitchen, pouring a trio of beers, as if their son hadn't lost the love of his life to her career. Which was so incredible for her, why the hell would he not support this, unlike the other assholes she'd committed to? With all this attention, no way she would want to come home. She shouldn't; the limelight was there, and she was going to be fucking amazing in it.

Glossy bright photographs spilled from the package and onto his bed as he hid to avoid his parents while he got a grip on what the hell was going on. Shuffling the loose photographs together, that stupid fucking pang gripped every organ in his trunk and nearly suffocated him. Burning behind his eyes, flooding his sinuses, he felt memory after memory wash over him. Still a blur, but that feeling, that wholehearted affection... a gust of fresh air rushed in the window, a bizarre inkling of hope he'd hesitated to consider filling him.

On top of the stack, an eight-by-ten captured that look. The look he knew so well and craved more than the mountain air around him. In her stunning blue dress, her hair loose around her shoulders, his ring on her hand that rested on his chest, Freya gazed at him. And he looked back at her, unmasked joy in his grin, his arms holding her close.

No judge would see that photograph and think them anything but a couple decidedly entering marriage with clear heads and forever intent.

He flipped through a few more. Damn, they had an incredible photographer. Or they had been so fricking happy, it would have been impossible to miss. In another, he stood behind Freya, his arms wrapped around her middle, they both were laughing about something, moving synchronously in the candid shot.

A few more, all fricking amazing. And then the shocker. The ceremony. Her parents standing witness, beaming and, well, as tipsy as they were. Did they not remember either?

He snapped a pic and texted it to his in-laws.

A half a second later, his phone rang. Closing the bedroom door, he answered Eamon's call in private.

"The pictures finally arrived?"

What? Zane's sigh was heavy, his heart still totally unsure how to beat, his head spinning from the effort. "Yeah. You knew?"

"I wasn't sure where you two were at with all this. Honestly, it's a huge blur for Tammy and me, but the pictures on my phone brought things back clear enough."

"Why didn't you say anything?"

"We wanted you two to decide what you wanted without any input from us. Freya's had enough pressure in her relationships; we certainly have pushed where we shouldn't have and it was time to step back and trust. Has Freya seen them? We were hoping she'd get to see those before the court date." A soft chuckle, "We've tried to not indicate our preference, but we have been hopeful."

"She's on her way to a huge event in Rome."

"Is that what's going on? Tammy's on the phone with her now and hasn't gotten to read her text from you. Um... she's now jumping up and down and giggling."

"The gallery in Rome called about the new paintings. They want to highlight her work, and apparently one will be a perfect keystone piece for the show."

Eamon sighed into the receiver, "She must be a wreck. She gets so nervous when her work is on display, when she might have to deal with criticism face to face."

"Think she could use some support? I... I'm trying to figure out how to be what she needs."

A moment later, he heard two voices muttering and arguing on the other end of the line. Finally, Tammy's voice blasted into his ear, "Zane? How are you?"

"Um, I'm fine."

"Tell me exactly what Freya said when she left."

"The last thing she said was that she needed to raid Sophie's closet."

A chuckle on the other side. "Huh. Well. The annulment hearing is on Wednesday?"

Fuck. It was. He'd forgotten in all the commotion. Freya would flip if they missed it. Three broken engagements and a divorce? No way could he do that to her. "I can go alone."

"No. You're going to Rome."

"What?"

Whispering on the other end, *Hurry up, Eamon. No, I don't care how much it costs. First class. He paid for the wedding... yes, dip into the wedding fund.* "Your flight leaves in..." More whispering. "Four hours."

"My flight?"

His mother-in-law's frank disappointment battered against his eardrum. "Don't be an idiot. Do you love her?"

"Yes."

"You know how terrible her last relationships have been?"

"Yeah." He rubbed a hand over his face. This is what Asher had been ready to kick his ass about. "I'm not one of those guys. I will do whatever she needs."

"I would love to be the one there to support her again, but it's not me she needs right now. It's *you*. Eamon is sending you your flight information as we speak. Can you get to SeaTac okay?"

"Of course. But—"

"You need to prove her wrong. I've tried telling her that no relationship is perfect. That you need to make compromises for each other, but you also need to build each other up. Be honest with me, Zane. Do you?"

"What? Build each other up?"

"Yes."

"Fuck yeah. I mean, sorry, yes, I hope so. She... she's... everything."

"Then get on the plane. Go tell her. Everything."

Shit. Holy shit. His pulse was downright thready. He hung up and stared blankly ahead, feeling more terrified than when he had a gun trained on his head this morning.

When he came back inside, his mother held out a beer for him. "This is rather tasty. I mean, a little bitter for my liking. But I thought, after the morning we've had, Saturday lunch beer sounded perfect."

He shook his head. "I've got to go. You guys can stay tonight and head out in the morning as you planned."

"Oh. But we came to see you."

A derisive laugh pushed out from his throat. "Of course. You've graced me with your presence and think I should rearrange my life for you. No. I need to be with my wife." He took a slow breath, then added under his breath, "I just need to convince her to keep me around."

His mother's eyebrows raise, her unwavering polite smile twitching. "Oh."

He didn't have time for this bullshit. Dashing to the bedroom, he packed his garment bag and his backpack.

Standing in the doorway behind him, his mother said, "I'm sorry."

Without glancing her way, he asked, "For what?"

"We missed you. It was easy when you wanted to be an architect like us. When you were with Blaire, and she was like a daughter to us. When you turned your back on all that to join the Navy, the SEALs of all things, and risked your life day in and day out, well, we let you down. It was scary and we couldn't handle it. But we should have."

He brushed past her and stuffed his toothbrush and supplies into his bag. "Yeah, you should have," he uttered, not bothering to put any effort into the admonishment.

"And now you've moved across the country, are becoming a beer maker, of all things, and married some moody artist. I guess we've missed so much, that we don't know you."

He shoved past her again and grabbed his bags. "Not sure you ever did."

Craig cleared his throat and pushed his shoulders back. "You're right. I would never have dreamed my son would be capable of what he did this morning."

Fuck. Not this again. His stomach churned as he readied himself for another lecture about who and what he was supposed to be.

His dad continued, "You were right. You're not an architect. Not the partner Blaire wanted. Nor are you the agreeable son we'd hoped for." Eyes softening, his gray eyebrows pulling together, Craig sighed. "You're so much more. If some monster had come threatening your mother or one of you kids? I... I couldn't have done what you did. And you didn't even break a sweat or look worried or scared. Steady. I guess we had no idea you were built for... that."

Zane snorted. *What the hell do you say to that?*

His mother inched closer, hesitant, then finally wrapped her arms around him. "We're so proud of you," she whispered, her voice broken.

Burning acid welled behind his eyes. Picked a shitty time to decide to be attentive parents. "I have a flight to catch."

Susan pulled away and nodded, wiping the gooey tears from her eyes. "We'll lock up on our way out tomorrow. Let us know if you need anything."

"Sure," he muttered, hoisting his backpack over his shoulder.

Craig put his arms around Susan and nodded. "Maybe on your way back through, you could stop and visit us. We'd like to get to know you better."

Zane halted with his hand on the door. Knowing he needed to say it, he turned and said, "Maybe next time. It's going to take more than recognizing that I can handle a hostage situation, or drinking my beer and complimenting it."

"What will it take?"

He let out a heavy exhale, adjusting his backpack tighter. "You can start by asking me what *I* want. By letting it sink in that I'm not you. I fucking hate boardrooms and presentations and schmoozing to impress people that I don't care about, and I have no interest in designing shit for other people to judge and tweak. I joined the Navy because I wanted to. I'm starting a damn brewing company because I like it. And I'm flying to Rome to tell the woman I love that she's incredible, to stand by in case she needs back up and make her know that I always will."

"Okay." She glanced to the photographs of the wedding. "She's a lovely woman."

"She is. I've got a flight to catch."

D ozens of flutes of prosecco swished in the hands of the dazzling patrons, each bubble reflecting the glowing pendant lights and created a starlit ambience. Blinding heat from the summer sun had yet to fade, the crisp air conditioner struggling to keep up. Freya twisted her ring on her finger, her hair tickling her upper back as she held her head high and watched the crowd.

In the center of the gallery's entrance was a sculpture of a warrior woman with a babe on her breast and a sword drawn in challenge. A grainy, muted color photograph of a modern soldier down on one knee, a reflective tear on his cheek took up much of the entry. Some of the pieces were bereft with dark emotion, others were achingly uplifting, depicting the recovery period, the why of war, and the heart of the soldiers.

Persephone, the gallery owner, sauntered toward her with a pair of crystal flutes, a magical flick of each swing of her hips in the mile-high heels. Freya had wondered about her when they'd first met, as she appeared so vain, but Freya quickly learned she adored daring fashion like she treasured passionate art. "Freya, darling, I am so happy you agreed to come on such short notice."

Exchanging cheek kisses, she accepted the offered prosecco and let the bubbles loosen her voice. "Are you kidding? It was such a risk, sending you that painting. You were expecting my traditional serenity, but I sent you my soldier."

"That's what I love about you and what makes your work so beautiful. And why I will continue to always have a Freya Marks piece in my gallery. Every piece you have brought me is pure love." Dark hair slicked back in a high ponytail, Persephone nodded deeper into the gallery. "May I introduce you to some of my favorite patrons?"

"You know I am a nervous wreck around potential critics, but as this is my favorite gallery and I am honored to be here, by all means." Some were hailed as mysterious, broody artists. In her early days, Freya had thought them self-absorbed.

As her stomach threatened to wretch out the prosecco that battled with the gallon of espresso she'd attempted to battle the jetlag with, she yet again acknowledged her premature judgment in others. She'd much rather be home with Zane, curled up and reading and sketching on the couch together. Not self-absorbed, but terrified of revealing such a critical piece of her.

As they reached the favored patrons, she slowed her pace, hoping to hear a secret opinion as they openly discussed her painting. Even though she knew that painting like her own body, the freckles on her cheeks, the feel of the cold Foothills breeze ruffling the fine hairs on her arms, the permanent curl where she parked her hair behind her ears when she forgot not to, she knew the painting more. Each brush stroke was passed from her soul through the paint, the subject's emotion, the curve of his jaw, the precise angle where deltoid met tricep, and the grief that drove his punishing run.

In his Versace tuxedo and her Dolce and Gabbana gown, the patrons held warm smiles as they examined her work. "Can you feel it?" the woman asked her husband.

"The burn in his muscles from the run?"

"Yes, that, but I can almost taste the salty sweat of his skin, and almost see the tremble in his muscles from the exertion. And that mountain behind him? We need to find out where that is."

Persephone rested her hand on the woman's shoulder, "Jacqueline?"

The woman turned, lit up and embraced Persephone. "What a wonderful show you've put on this evening. I have ensured the charities highlighted tonight will receive an equal match on your donations."

Freya held back, pinching her lips together and keeping her heels locked as the absurdity of the conversation made her feel that much more out of place. Yes, this was technically her world, but it *really* wasn't. Which was why she'd moved back home. Her worlds were so different, and she knew where her heart lived.

As soon as Persephone made the introductions, Freya was tossed in cheek-kiss after cheek-kiss, dozens complimenting her work, the edginess of this new piece, inquiring when she would be sending more, could they commission a piece... Inhaling slow and steady, she kept her pulse at a tolerable level, her knees only occasionally threatening to give out, but her stomach remained too tightly clenched to even consider trying one of the prosciutto-wrapped mozzarellas.

Persephone remained at her side, at one point whispering, "You're doing great. In another hour, you can head back to your hotel and relax. I've arranged for your room to be stocked with wine, antipasto, plus some dark chocolate and raspberries. Please say you'll stay a few nights?"

She felt a pang in her chest that set her heartbeat on edge. About to refuse the offer, she took another small sip of prosecco and looked to the door, craving the serenity of home. Of curling up with Zane under the stars.

Of not leaving Zane to go to court alone to invalidate their marriage.

Shattering the fear, victorious thrill pumped through her veins, weakening her knees in the best way possible as the best damn vision of her existence strolled in the door. Larger than life, flipping gorgeous, she laid eyes on the Norse god, superhero, Italian model, Navy SEAL... sweet, sincere man that bit his tongue to avoid the argument, but wouldn't hesitate to risk his life to save another.

Where he'd worn simple slacks and a button-up to the wedding, tonight he wore a slick tuxedo that hugged his broad shoulders. His gait powerful, controlled like a wolf in the night, he stood illuminated in the bold light.

At her side, Persephone swallowed loudly, "Oh my. Is that your soldier?"

Breath still caught in her throat, Freya nodded.

"Well. I'll leave you to it," she gave Freya's shoulder a squeeze and left her alone.

Unable to move as her body had turned into a timeless statue, she waited. Striding across the gallery floor, he stopped just out of reach. His head tilted to the side, and a shy smile tugged at his lips.

She exhaled carefully, hoping sound came out when she spoke, "You came."

"Of course."

"But your parents?"

"You're more important."

"You hate to fly."

"I do."

"And you hate crowds."

"I do, but I'll make an exception when they're here to talk about how amazing you are."

"How did you get in?"

He winked, "I look an awful lot like the guy in the painting by tonight's featured artist."

"What about our annulment?"

Had she said something about a superhero before? Thundering in her chest, tiny lightning blasts healed the lingering fractures in her heart as he knelt down on one knee. "I got the pictures back. It was a gorgeous wedding. Your parents were there."

"What? Those jerks, they didn't say a thing," she laughed, throwing her head back as she felt a giddiness take over that had nothing to do with the prosecco.

He grinned, "They didn't want us to feel pressured. Freya, I don't care what it took for us to get married, because I'm so glad we did. I would never have dared trying it again. I was so terrified of marrying someone that didn't believe in me, of not believing in myself. But you... you want me to be me. And I want you to be you. I love you so damn much. Please, please stay married to me."

"Get up here," she pulled on his hands and dragged him to his feet. Standing inches away, she breathed him in, his homey scent, warmed like a soothing aromatherapy in the spotlights and summer evening. Searching his eyes, falling into the forest of them, she let the lava pump through her veins and bring a thrill she'd never known. "I love you."

"That's a *yes*?"

"Hell yes."

He leaned in and brushed his lips over hers, placing a soft kiss on her lower lip, gliding his tongue along the crease of her lips before she gripped the back of his neck and poured all of her into him, accepting everything in return. Breathless, he pulled away enough to look her in the eyes, alert and steady.

Cheers erupted from the gallery. Toasts and words of wisdom and love echoed around them.

Glancing around at the crowd, Freya found Persephone beaming at her, a subtle nod said the night had gone brilliantly, and she mouthed a *thank you*, which Freya returned before lacing her fingers with Zane's and leading him back to the hotel.

Epilogue

Sure as shit, Pippa was a ridiculously effective planner. Frightening, quite frankly. But the brewery looked incredible.

Exactly as he'd imagined, the outdoor tables held small fireplaces and heaters to combat the chill of the November evening. Forming weatherproof roofs overhead, connected glass and timber beamed gazebos kept the rain off them, and left the dining area welcome no matter the weather. The outdoor furniture and gazebos were a weird-as-fuck gift from his parents, but it showed their support in a way their self-absorbed dialogue couldn't.

Asher and Grady sat joking at one of the smaller round tables, leaning back and ragging on each other with some inside joke. Pippa looked quite the hostess at the invitation-only opening, dressed in a flowered dress, ensuring the guests were happy. Of course, he knew everyone here, but Pippa insisted on perfection for the beta night. Sophie and Lincoln were touring inside, sipping from sampler glasses with the Black Op Brewing Company logo emblazoned on the side. Asher's parents were exploring inside with Tammy and Eamon.

Over the door, the Black Op Brewing Company sign matched the glasses. Edgy and bold to match the logo, it was designed by a top graphic designer in Phoenix that Grady's brother knew.

Dressed in the sexiest damn blue dress that matched her eyes, topped off with her Italian heels and a leather jacket, Freya's hips swayed with each step as she joined him. "Sorry I'm late," she apologized breathlessly as she crossed through the iron gate and linked her hand with his.

"How did it go?" he asked.

She grinned, "Great. My online presence is paying off. The gallery in Seattle has asked me to be one of their permanent featured artists and added a link to my website."

One of the servers, Miles, greeted them both with a sampler glass of the blackberry brew he'd decided to be one of his first featured. Miles grinned, "Wow, Zane. This place is awesome. Half of Foothills has already called to see if you accept reservations or sell growlers and kegs. I'm betting the other half are trying to get through."

He accepted the sampler glass and shook Miles' hand. "Fantastic. You letting anyone know if they want something we don't have, we'll work on it? I like experimenting with new recipes."

"Absolutely."

Freya watched with a sappy grin on her face. "Thanks, Miles," she nodded. Once he walked outside with another round of samplers for everyone else, Freya whispered, "I dated his brother in high school."

"Seth?"

She squeezed his hand, "You're too cute. Nope. But we're not going to dwell on the many times Freya Harris has thought herself in love."

"Harris? I thought you were keeping your name."

"Professionally, yes. Personally? In a few years, when we have a house and are bored with sex all day, maybe we should have some kids, and I want them to have the same last name as their parents. But I'm hoping you like Marks for a middle name?"

That pang was no longer a pang, but a steady beat in his heart that filled his veins with safety and security... and a thrill that everything was going to be okay. After stealing a savoring kiss, he pulled back. "Hell yeah I'll take your name, too. Come on, I have a surprise for you."

"As if all this isn't impressive enough?" She followed him upstairs. She'd seen all of this before, but he hadn't let her see the offices until the finishing touches were nailed down.

The hollow he knew would never fully heal knocked about in his brain like a ping pong ball as he passed the photographs that lined the stairs. Jack with a comically panicked expression as he tried a glass from Zane's first attempt. Another of the three of them in the plaid and pastel Jack had picked out for them to try out golf; it hadn't gone well, especially when they wrecked the golf cart, but they'd had a hell of a lot of fun. Another of the three of them just coming back from the worst sort of op; exhausted and aching and heartbroken. A few more of the whole team, in their gear and relaxing on the beach waiting for their ride home. The collection supported the name of the business of course, but also included a sign with information on how to support wounded veterans.

Without a word, Freya studied each photograph with him, her expression matching the tone of each, her heart broken for him. How the hell had he gotten so lucky?

He dragged her up the stairs, past the central workspace. They stopped in Grady's office; he bit his cheek as he grinned at the romance novel he'd left on the desk for his new partner as a little thank you gift. About a spoiled attorney falling for completely the wrong woman. It had been easier to find than he thought, apparently, some people enjoyed sexy books about spoiled rich guys too.

Freya checked out his office, promising to fulfill a few fantasies he hadn't even come up with yet, behind and on top of that desk. Then he pulled her back into the room she'd fallen in love with. Shiplap wall and tranquil blue walls, consistent lighting, and an easel in the center of the room to demonstrate.

She strolled to the middle and spun in a circle. "For me?"

"Is it okay? I mean, you can work wherever you want..."

"But it's your building. This is the nicest space in the building. Don't you want the better office?"

He crossed his arms over his chest and a flash of red heated his cheeks. "You kidding? Maybe I'm a little codependent, but I love the idea of getting to work next to each other. But if you want your own space, no problem, we'll find or build a studio wherever you want. As long as you keep doing what you love."

"It's perfect." She strode toward him and tugged him close by the waistband of his jeans. "Really. You astonish me at every turn. You see *me*."

Wrapping his arms around her waist, he leaned his forehead against hers. "Ditto. Whatever you need."

"You. I need you." She kissed him and smiled against his mouth.

The End

Carrie Thorne is the author of kick-ass romance novels, specializing in white-hot chemistry, healthy relationships, and a mix of action and dreamily falling in love. Whether it's a sinuous flow down a lazy river or evil bad dudes hot on heels, Carrie's stories will draw you in and ruin your sleep. Happily ever afters are for everyone, and kindness is everything.

She's also an introvert who loves people, travel, fitness, video games, food, and is a true Pacific Northwesterner who lives for rain and outdoors and trees and mountains and ocean, and... she's a total dork. At home, she's lucky to have two creative and confident kids, a witty veteran husband she fell at-first-sight for, and a tiny pup snuggled at her side. In addition to writing romance, Carrie has been a nurse practitioner, a Martian and Earthling geologist, a banker, and she is usually elbow-deep in a DIY project in which she bit off more than she could chew.

Where is she now? Depends on the weather. Cozied up by the fire with a steaming mug of black coffee, or stretched out on the hammock with a frothy IPA in the shade of her forest. Either way, she's working on the next great love story to conquer your TBR list.

www.CarrieThorne.com